"YOU ARE NOT TO WEAR THAT GOWN AGAIN," HE BEGAN.

"Who is to prevent me from doing so?" Sophie asked sweetly.

"It is indecent," he muttered, running his hand through his hair to totally destroy what remained of the carefully achieved windswept his valet had created.

"Jonathan, hear me out," Sophie pleaded, taking several steps in his direction. "Madame Clotilde has created nice gowns for me and I fully intend to wear them. Cease your fussing. You remind me of my nanny!"

"Nanny! By heaven!" Jonathan crossed to confront Sophie and stare down into her face, framed by golden curls and possessing the most beautiful blue eyes ever seen. "I doubt this is like your nanny," he murmured. Then he kissed Sophie with all his expertise

An Uncommon Bequest

by

Emily Hendrickson

A SIGNET BOOK

SIGNET
Published by the Penguin Group
Penguin Putnam Inc., 375 Hudson Street,
New York, New York 10014, U.S.A.
Penguin Books Ltd, 27 Wrights Lane,
London W8 5TZ, England
Penguin Books Australia Ltd, Ringwood,
Victoria, Australia
Penguin Books Canada Ltd, 10 Alcorn Avenue,
Toronto, Ontario, Canada M4V 3B2
Penguin Books (N.Z.) Ltd, 182-190 Wairau Road,
Auckland 10, New Zealand

Penguin Books Ltd, Registered Offices:
Harmondsworth, Middlesex, England

First published by Signet, an imprint of Dutton Signet,
a member of Penguin Putnam Inc.

First Printing, February, 1998
10 9 8 7 6 5 4 3 2 1

With thanks to all eccentric relatives
decorating our family trees.

Chapter One

A green finch warbled in a bush near the little Cotswold inn. Its glorious song filled the air, adding to a sense of well-being that had been slow to return to Sophie Garnett. Life of late had taken a great number of twists and turns, all unexpected. She was just now finding her feet and was secretly pleased at how well she had coped with the misfortune dealt her by her family.

Fate had unpleasantly surprised her with a cruel joke. Instead of swanning up to London for her expected come-out, Sophie found herself without a farthing and totally dependent on the mercy of others. Destitute! Thanks to Papa's untimely death before he could recoup his fortune following a disastrous investment, this particular branch of the Garnett family was without means, except for a sum that had been set aside for Lawrence.

Her older brother had been able to purchase a good spot in the navy, where he happily sailed the seas.

Her wisp of a mother had moved into the tiny home belonging to her widowed sister, Emma. There had been no room for Sophie—unless she was willing to occupy a small space in the attic that looked to be boiling in summer and frigid come winter.

Bless old school friends who stand by one in time of need. Lady Anne Margrave, now the beloved wife of Sir Cecil Radcliffe, had recommended Sophie to a lady in want of a companion. It wasn't one of those sit-and-read-improving-books or winding-yarn sort of jobs. Lady Mary Croscombe simply wanted a traveling companion.

Sophie had rapidly grown fond of the lively spinster who had such great curiosity about everything in her path. Wherever they traveled, Lady Mary delved into the history of the area with an enthusiasm that proved infectious. This morning they were to visit the Broadway Tower to enjoy the supposedly splendid view of the surrounding countryside on a pleasant summer day. Sophie had donned a simple white muslin from better days with a pretty pink spencer Lady Mary had insisted upon giving her. Sophie tucked a stray blond curl that wanted to spring free back under her neat little cottage bonnet. Trimmed with a small cluster of pink silk roses and tied under her chin with a simple pink bow, it seemed to be most appropriate wear for a companion.

Her inspection of the sheep grazing in the meadow across the road from the inn was disturbed by the entry of a maid holding a letter. "Post for you, miss."

"Thank you," Sophie said with absent courtesy while she puzzled over the missive now in her hand. It looked ominously like the one bearing the news of her father's failed investment.

"Ready to go, my dear?" Lady Mary cheerfully inquired as she entered the little sitting room they shared. She carried a sensible umbrella in hand, not one of those silly parasols that offered precious little shade for tender skin. Her lavender walking dress was the latest fashion, albeit a trifle conservative in style, quite suitable for a wealthy lady who had elected to remain unwed.

"A letter came for me, forwarded from home. How lucky we decided to remain here for another week."

"Well, best to open it and find out what it says. No point in simply staring at the outside, is there?" Lady Mary said in her bracing manner.

Sophie shook off her feeling of unease and slit the seal with an impatient finger. Unfolding the stiff parchment, she hastily scanned the contents, gasped, then read it again far more slowly.

"Are you going to keep me in suspense after that gasp, dear child?" Lady Mary asked with a trace of impatience.

Shaking her head as though to clear out a fog, Sophie replied, "I do not understand. I am summoned to appear at Lowell Hall for the reading of my Uncle Philip's will."

"And where is Lowell Hall, if I may ask?"

" 'Tis located not far from Cheltenham—just north a few miles," Sophie said, meeting her employer's gaze with troubled eyes, then looking again at the letter as if to verify that the contents were indeed true.

"And Uncle Philip—he was perhaps a well-fixed bachelor? One with a fondness for you?"

"I always enjoyed the annual visits to Lowell Hall. He married but had no children and his wife died ages ago." Sophie thought back to those halcyon summer days spent with other cousins while roaming the gardens and fields on Uncle Philip's vast estate. With an unconscious sigh for things lost, she added, "He does have an heir—a distant cousin of mine, Jonathan Garnett—who is now Viscount Lowell."

Another sigh followed this remark, this time with Sophie well aware of the past and its secrets. "The estate is south of here, not far off the main road."

"Well, that is no problem, then. You shall go at once. After all, Cheltenham is no more than fifteen miles from here, more or less." She gave Sophie a shrewd look, then added, "I should like to go with you if I may. I've a fancy to see that area better."

Sophie gave the older woman a grateful look. Bless her heart, Lady Mary was not only a curious person, she had developed a rather protective attitude toward Sophie. It made Sophie wish to do everything in her power to please the adventuresome spinster. Again tucking the rebellious blond curl back under her bonnet and giving a little nod, she fixed determined blue eyes, first on the letter, then on her employer. "Very well. I would be pleased for your company. Whilst I doubt I inherit much from Uncle Philip, I would value a wise head for counsel should I have need of one."

"I fancy the Broadway Tower will be there for some years to come. I can see it in another trip. Come, let us pack our things and make arrangements to travel south to . . . Lowell Hall, did you say?" Lady Mary gave Sophie an inquiring look.

"Indeed, ma'am. I shall order up your traveling coach at once," Sophie said promptly, referring to her employer's luxurious mode of travel.

"Do so. Wickens shall pack my things in a trice. I trust it will not take you long?" She paused to study the still-bemused Sophie.

At this prompting, Sophie bestirred herself and smiled as she moved toward the door leading to the stairs. "Indeed, it will not take me long at all. I shall be packed long before your coach can be drawn up before the inn."

"Good," Lady Mary said with a decided snap, then disappeared into her room, issuing orders to her maid like a general about to embark on a battle.

It was a simple matter to order Lady Mary's coach, for the inn possessed an excellent stable, one which the coachman had declared first-rate. Sophie scanned the bill offered by the proprietor and after seeing no improper charges, settled with him on behalf of Lady Mary. He was sorry to lose so good a patron, but smiled when Sophie informed him that Lady Mary had been so pleased with the area and his inn that she planned a future visit.

Reflecting that she would enjoy a return to this area as well, Sophie went to her room and carefully packed her few belongings. What a change for the pampered daughter of Sir William Garnett to be stowing her own garments, tending to their care and improvement. It was a blessing that she was an excellent seamstress, for she had needed that skill more than once in repairing and altering her gowns, not to mention mending stockings that seemed to acquire holes with shocking speed. While Lady Mary was not niggardly in her pay, Sophie hoarded every pence she could against a time when Lady Mary would no longer require her services.

It was shortly after noon and a pleasant repast—Lady Mary refused to travel without a meal first—that they left the quiet little inn.

"A woman of my size," her ladyship declared as the coach headed south at a leisurely pace, "must eat to sustain her body and energy."

"Yes, ma'am." Sophie eyed the tall woman seated across from her on the comfortably cushioned seat. Large she might be, but she had an excellent figure and carried herself well. Her red hair streaked with gray was always neatly arranged in a modish style. Her clothing was of the finest quality and the latest fashion.

Sophie had merely nibbled at the food presented to them, her mind far away. How many of her cousins would be present? And how would she cope with facing Jonathan again? Her tall, handsome cousin—never mind how far removed— would of course be present at the reading of the will. He stood to inherit the bulk of the estate as well as the entailed property. Would he recall her past folly? Surely his memory would be required for more important matters than girlish nonsense. Or would his dark eyes mock her with remembered foolishness?

"What curious thoughts you must be having. I declare, I have never seen you blush in such an delightful manner," Lady Mary remarked in a considering way.

"Nonsense," Sophie replied without heat, giving voice to her thoughts. "It was merely nonsense. How silly girls can be at times."

"Let me see . . . you expect to see your cousins at the reading—or at least one of them, the heir. Is there perhaps an interest of the heart involved?" Lady Mary firmly believed that roundaboutation was to be avoided.

Giving the lady an alarmed look, Sophie turned away to stare out of the window at the passing scenery, yet saw nothing of the rolling green hills dotted with oxeye daisies and cattle. "No, just silly girlish nonsense," she said at last.

"I see," Lady Mary said with the manner of one who didn't see in the least.

Five miles down the road the ladies paused for a restoring cup of tea at Winchcombe. Sophie welcomed the delay. Her fears at seeing Jonathan again had grown with each passing mile. She would have been quite happy to have escaped from attendance at the reading of the will.

"You enjoyed spending time with your cousins in years past?" Lady Mary inquired casually while keeping a sharp eye trained on Sophie over their modest tea.

"Oh, yes, indeed," Sophie replied warmly. "They were some of my happiest days while growing up. Or most of them were pleasant," she amended, thinking of the last time she had seen Jonathan. "The last visit did not go well."

"What happened that time?" Lady Mary softly probed, looking quite intrigued with this side of her quiet companion.

"As I said, nonsense." Sophie had never mentioned the matter to anyone, feeling the utter fool for her silliness. Then looking into Lady Mary's kind face, so full of sympathy, and suddenly wishing for a comforting talk, Sophie plunged into an explanation. "That last summer I went we played games as usual; only this time we were more grown up and some of the girls wanted to do something more venturesome."

"And what drastic thing happened between you and your cousin Jonathan?" the older woman asked, wise in the ways of young girls in spite of her spinster state.

"Jonathan was required to kiss me as forfeit in a game. He proved to be, er, very good at that sort of thing." Sophie blushed again at the memory of the feelings that had raced through her sensitive self as Jonathan kissed her. "Silly twit that I was, I tumbled headlong into an infatuation with the dratted man." She paused to reflect, then added, "He might have been young in years but he was never really as boyish as my other male cousins were. His dark eyes always saw too much. I suspect he was born with that air about him that attracts every female in sight. He was extremely masculine, even then."

"A veritable Adonis, I gather. I look forward to meeting the gentleman," Lady Mary murmured.

"I can only hope that he didn't notice my passion for him. No one has ever teased me about it so I suspect I may have successfully concealed my feelings. But I felt such a fool when a short time later I learned of his entanglement with a very lovely and sophisticated woman in London. I was but sixteen—a rather immature sixteen, at that!"

Sophie shared a look of amusement with Lady Mary and felt better for telling her foolish little history. Somehow, giving voice to the incident brought it into perspective. Surely she could laugh it off now, even if her cousin did recall the event—something she very much doubted.

"And you had melted at his kiss?"

Sophie gave Lady Mary a shocked look. How could this spinster know the turmoil that had swept through the young

Sophie at the touch of Jonathan's lips on hers? He had studied her face, bestowing a most unfathomable look. Then, with exquisite slowness, he had claimed her lips in a scorching kiss. Sophie had never been the same since. She had unconsciously measured every man she met against her handsome cousin. There had been a few stolen kisses, but they had been a mere brushing of lips. No one had matched Jonathan, more's the pity.

"I did mention that I was a silly girl, did I not? Sophie gave the older woman a rueful look.

"Have you changed a great deal since you last saw Viscount Lowell?" Lady Mary inquired as they strolled to the coach and the continuation of their journey.

"It will be difficult to think of him with the title. And yes, I suppose that I have altered in the past four years. I filled out, acquired a bosom, and grew up, for one thing. And I suppose I have attained a modicum of common sense, not to mention a smidgen of polish.

"You did not see him in London for you had no come-out, did you?" Lady Mary observed in a most matter-of-fact way as she settled on the cushioned coach seat.

"No." Sophie examined her neatly gloved hands after she also settled in place. One glove now had a barely perceptible darn in it, something Sir William's daughter ought not to have. But then, no one had ever promised that life would be fair. She was lucky to have a position with a most agreeable lady.

"And he has not seen you since the visit with the infamous kiss?" Lady Mary persisted.

"That is quite true," Sophie said, giving Lady Mary a puzzled look.

"Well! I believe it may prove to be most interesting when the Viscount Lowell gets a look at his little cousin who is no longer an immature girl of sixteen. Rather"—and Lady Mary examined Sophie with an appraising gaze—"he will find a vision of heavenly loveliness, an incomparable from that halo of feathery blond curls to those delft blue eyes and sweet rosebud mouth right down to dainty slippered feet below a pair of remarkably neat ankles. We must find you some perfume to suit you—honeysuckle, perhaps," she concluded in what had to be an aside.

Flustered at the extravagant praise, Sophie murmured, "You are too kind, my lady."

"Rubbish! If there is one thing I am not, it is stupidly kind. I am a calculating, interfering old busybody and I always have a wonderful time." She chuckled and subsided into a silence that Sophie found faintly disturbing.

Sophie paid more attention to the passing scenery now, seeing sights that appeared familiar. She could not prevent a rising excitement from welling up within her. Whether it was the thought that her dear uncle might have remembered her in his will with a much needed bequest or the thought that very shortly she would see Jonathan again after four long years, she didn't know.

How hard she had tried to convince herself that she hated him—hated him for stirring her so, then casually walking off as though he had flitted her world. She had wanted to despise him for his splendid success in London, taking the *ton* by storm. She had read the gossip columns and had rightly guessed that he was the J-G referred to by the writers, and she had secretly reveled that she had once known him at all, for he blazed a trail through Society that was most spectacular. Dratted man! Beast!

"What a fierce look on your face, my dear. I pity the object of that expression," Lady Mary said, studying Sophie's determined countenance.

"Oh!" exclaimed Sophie, compelled to laugh at her own thoughts. "I was being foolish again, I fear. Perhaps it is this countryside that turns my normally sensible self into that of a silly girl?"

"Somehow I doubt it," Lady Mary murmured. She settled back against the beautifully cushioned squabs to rest, closing her eyes.

Sophie took advantage of the quiet to decide how she might best face her cousin—and the others in attendance. For all she knew every member of the family who had enjoyed her uncle's company on those lovely summer holidays would be here. In a way that would be excellent. She might avoid seeing anything of Jonathan, except from a safe distance.

It could not be helped. The coach at last turned through the impressive stone pillars upon which hung exquisitely worked iron gates. They proceeded up the avenue at a stately pace, much to Sophie's pleasure.

"My dear girl, when you said your beloved uncle was well-to-do, you did him a disservice. This is a magnificent setting for what appears to be an equally magnificent house." Lady Mary seemed most impressed, as well she might.

Looking ahead to see the familiar house, its central block rising above the two spacious wings on either side, Sophie felt a constriction in her throat. Uncle Philip would not greet her at the door with a generous hug and pats on her head anymore. Not that she would ever visit here again; Uncle Philip was now part of her past.

"I must say, that fountain is quite splendid," Lady Mary said, sounding reluctantly stirred.

Somehow Sophie managed to enter the house without disgracing herself. Newfound maturity prevented her from bursting into tears at the sight of the black cape draping the hatchment on the front door.

"Welcome, Miss Sophie," intoned Biggins, Uncle Philip's faithful butler of many years. "You will be in your old room and your guest"—he looked at Lady Mary with a measuring eye and continued respectfully—"will be housed in the Rose Room."

"Dear me, I quite forgot myself. This is Lady Mary Croscombe, Biggins. She is my employer," Sophie concluded, daring the old retainer to say a word about her new status.

"You will both be welcome guests. It is a sad time for all of us," he said with a knowing look at Sophie's eyes, brimming with tears.

"Is the new Viscount Lowell in residence?" she asked, although she guessed the answer.

"Indeed, Miss Sophie," the butler replied while ushering the two women over to the housekeeper, his good wife, Mrs. Biggins.

Sophie calmed her emotions while she and Lady Mary were ushered up the grand staircase to the first floor, then along to the east wing, where the guest rooms were located. The house was silent; even their footsteps were hushed by the thick carpet beneath them.

Lady Mary gave an approving glance at the serene luxury of the Rose Room when escorted there by the quiet Mrs. Biggins.

"Have James bring up our luggage, please," Sophie instructed politely. "He is still here, is he not?" she thought to add, for much could happen in four years.

"Indeed, miss. You are to go as soon as may be to the library. The will's to be read this evening. Everyone ought to be here by then." Knowing that Sophie knew the location of her old room, the housekeeper silently returned to the lower regions of the house.

After settling Lady Mary and the redoubtable Wickens in their suite, Sophie went along the hall until she reached the room that had always been hers when visiting her uncle.

"It is just the same," she said to herself, surprised that it was unchanged when she had altered so greatly.

An unfamiliar maid entered with a pitcher of hot water and an inquiry as to when Sophie might return downstairs, where she was wanted.

"Just give me a few moments to wash and repair the damage from traveling and I shall be there," Sophie promised. Why it was so necessary for her to present herself without delay puzzled her, but she knew better than to query a maid.

Placing her bonnet on the dresser, Sophie ran a comb through her curls, then removed her spencer. The white muslin had fared better than expected. Of course the skirt was creased from sitting, but there was no dust clinging to its folds. Splendid coaches appeared to guard well against excessive dust.

She trailed her hand on the reassuring solidity of the oak banister as she walked slowly down the curved stairs. Biggins gave her a nod when she reached the bottom, and she obediently went along the hall until she reached the library. Here, she paused before the closed door, noting her heart had begun to beat an anxious tattoo within her chest. It was merely a summons to appear. Perhaps the solicitor had a private bequest to offer before the others arrived on the scene. Curiosity high, she turned the brass knob to open the door and enter.

It was a high-ceilinged room filled with shelves containing a modest number of books—for a house this size. Her uncle had not been what you might call a great reader, but he had often pointed out books he thought might interest her. She had spent long hours here, especially on that last visit when trying to evade the others. Jonathan in particular.

The room appeared to be uninhabited at the moment. She was about to leave when a voice halted her flight.

"So you came after all. I made a small wager with myself."

Sophie reluctantly turned to face cousin Jonathan, seated in a high-back chair near the window on the shadowed far side of the room. "And did you win?"

He blinked, then slowly said, "I believe I did."

"Mrs. Biggins said I was wanted immediately in the library. I do not see the solicitor here. Did you wish to speak to me?" She felt so cold she ought to be shivering, yet she also felt as though she might melt at the nearness of the man she had once adored. She positively had to get away from him before she disgraced herself by doing something stupid. She had tried so hard to hate him and it had been all in vain.

Jonathan rose from his chair and strolled across the room until he stood directly before Sophie. "You have changed since I last saw you."

"One does eventually grow up. You are the same, I believe." Could air actually sizzle? Was it possible for tension to create sparks between people? Fireworks? Or was her imagination galloping away with her?

"I was sorry to learn of your father's death. I would have attended the funeral, but the news reached me some time after the event." He continued to examine her face with disconcerting thoroughness.

"We wished to keep it a simple affair with only close family." Sophie dared him to make a comment on her impoverishment. She thought she might crown him with that vase of summer flowers gracing the Sheraton desk were he to ooze false sympathy at her plight. She ought to have known him better.

"Lawrence is well situated, I believe. And your mother is living with Aunt Emma?" He was all politeness.

"Yes," she replied baldly, waiting.

"You look well. I trust you have, as usual, found yourself on your feet?" His gaze raked her from head to toe, not missing one wrinkle or mend in her gown.

"Indeed. I am companion to Lady Mary Croscombe. She is a very dear lady who enjoys traveling about the country. I am most fortunate in my position." She lifted her chin, daring him to make a slighting remark.

"Good girl," he said softly, then reached around her to open the door. "Dinner will be in one hour, should you care to change."

"I have no blacks, Jonathan. They remained behind when I left home." Again her cerulean eyes blazed with defiance, daring him to belittle her.

"I suspected that might be the case. I instructed Mrs. Biggins to place a selection of gowns in your room, should you wish to change into one of them. They might be a trifle snug. You are not as thin as I recall."

"As I said, people grow up. I changed." She hoped her eyes revealed the scorn she tried to summon.

"You certainly did, brat."

"Oh!" She gave him a scathing look, thinking it might be possible to hate him after all. She swept from the room and up the stairs, borne by her anger—at herself, for still loving that miserable man, and at him, for stirring things best left to wither on the vine.

In her room she opened the wardrobe to find three black gowns of impeccable taste and design within. Selecting one that looked as though it might fit with the fewest alterations, she slipped from her muslin and donned a soft bombazine of the most lovely weight and texture. He had guessed her change better than he'd thought, for the gown was not too snug. Rather, it clung nicely to her curves and yet had a proper decorum about it. She adjusted the lace-trimmed collar, thinking that she could spend three months in such garments with no great difficulty.

Mourning for an uncle depended upon how close one was to the deceased. It ranged from a proper three months for someone like Uncle Philip down to six weeks for an uncle not so cherished to three weeks for an uncle never seen.

A rap on her door was followed by the entry of Lady Mary, also suitably gowned in dull black.

"Goodness, but someone did well by you," Lady Mary commented as she circled her companion.

"It is a lovely dress." Sophie stroked the soft fabric with an appreciative hand. "My cousin provided several for me. I gather he suspected I might have need of such."

"Most considerate of him. Perhaps you will be able to endure this confrontation after all?"

Sophie thought of the meeting earlier and shook her head. "I doubt it."

At dinner she found herself at the opposite end of the table from Jonathan. With no wife to serve as hostess, he had requested that she substitute, since she had been so close to Uncle Philip. Not knowing how to avoid the inevitable speculation this would bring, she agreed and now could steal a glance from time to time at the man who puzzled her so greatly. The array of cousins was not as great as anticipated. The solicitor was hardly the dry, papery man she expected, but rather a youngish gentleman, a younger son of a fine family, no doubt.

When she signaled for the women to leave the table, Jonathan rose as well.

"I suggest we have the reading of the will at once. That will end fruitless speculation."

Hating to be grateful to him, yet thankful he had spoken thus, Sophie led the way, with Jonathan immediately behind her. When he lightly touched her waist to guide her to a library chair it was a wonder she didn't jump through the roof. This was what it must be like when described as being on pins and needles.

The will contained no great surprises. Jonathan naturally inherited the entailed estate. He also received an indecently vast sum of money, stocks, and other property.

Suddenly Sophie heard her name and fixed her attention on the speaker. "To my dear niece, Sophie Garnett, I bequeath the contents of my library." The solicitor gazed at her, waiting.

Books? She had inherited books—a library full of them? Had it not been a serious occasion she would have burst into laughter at the idea of a homeless girl inheriting a library of books. Precisely where was she to house them? In the air?

"You do not have to accept them, you know," Jonathan said wryly.

Sophie glared at him and tilted her chin in battle. "I should be pleased to accept, sir. I have loved many of my uncle's books."

Chapter Two

The following morning while walking amidst the shrubbery with Lady Mary, Sophie still could not understand the reasoning behind her late uncle's bequest. She had thought and thought about it and could not find a satisfactory answer.

"Do you suppose he had failed mentally?" Lady Mary suggested quietly.

"It is possible, I suppose. But would his solicitor not have taken that into consideration when such an outrageous proposal was offered?" Sophie exchanged a concerned look with her employer and now confidante.

"What will you do with all those books?" the ever-practical lady inquired.

"I shall not leave them for my odious cousin. Oh, he would have been delighted to have me give them to him. Now he will have to fill all those empty shelves on his own!" Sophie gave her ladyship a smirking glance.

"Do you have any doubt but what he will? He strikes me as a man of great resources." Lady Mary paused to examine a beautifully sculpted shrub in the shape of a bird on the wing, the centerpiece of the topiary garden.

"I believe I should like to begin packing the books," Sophie declared. "Why should I not take them to London and sell them to a book dealer? I daresay there are a number of expensive volumes in that collection. Perhaps it was his way of offering me a substance no one else would desire, knowing I would understand what to do with it?" Sophie's tone made it clear that she had no great assurance in her bold words.

"I do not know . . ." Lady Mary said with great doubt in her voice.

"Nor do I," admitted Sophie. "Nevertheless I shall examine those books and crate them up."

"Where do you intend to send them?"

"Well," Sophie said consideringly as she discarded the thought of the home she had once known and had no more, "I have a friend—Lady Anne, who sent me to you—who will tolerate them for a few days, I feel certain."

Lady Mary gave Sophie a dubious look but said nothing.

A short time later, the two women met in the library. With a mobcap tidily over her blond curls and an apron neatly covering her black gown, Sophie began to carefully fill the first of the boxes brought to her by James, the footman.

Lady Mary, watching from the same high-back chair that Jonathan had used the day before, said, "Those volumes look to be rather heavy. What are they?"

"These are a series about ancient Greece and Rome. It seems the ancients required a lot of words on paper to be presented properly. Dry as dust, most likely," she added in an undertone.

"Do take them one at a time, 'else I fear you may drop one and damage the spine. That might reduce its value at a book dealer's," Lady Mary cautioned.

She might as well have saved her breath, for at that moment the two volumes in Sophie's hands proved too awkward and both tumbled to the floor. Pieces of paper fluttered from between the now-open pages. Sophie stared, utterly transfixed by what she thought she saw.

"What is it, dear girl? You look as though you have seen a ghost." Her ladyship rose and crossed to Sophie's side, then bent to pick up one of the pieces of paper. Her gaze met an astounded Sophie's with equal amazement. "A hundred-pound note? What manner of book marker is this, pray tell?"

Sophie dropped to her knees to gather up the rest of the scraps. She turned her face up to see Lady Mary watching her intently. "All of these are also hundred-pound notes."

"Well! This puts a different complexion on the matter, does it not?" Lady Mary said while Sophie dazedly rose to face her.

"There were five hundred-pound notes in this book. You don't suppose . . . No, it could not be. Never. Who would do anything so foolish?" They exchanged looks, then knelt on the floor.

Both women pulled books from the partially packed box to shake them upside down and watched in stupefaction as more notes of various denominations drifted to the floor. They then attacked the other books in the box with the same results. An hour passed before Lady Mary sank down on the nearest chair to fan her face with a twenty-pound note.

"Gracious me, your uncle was a most quixotic man. How I would love to have known him. Do you see a pattern emerging? I think I do. Any book that has to do with the ancient world in any manner contains money. See here, a book dealing with agriculture has nothing in it, whereas this volume on Greek myths contained nearly three hundred pounds."

"I shan't take any chances. I intend to examine every book, no matter what," Sophie muttered. Then she realized what she had said and sat back to look up at her employer. "I do apologize, ma'am. I quite forget that I ought to be at your beck and call. Should you desire to leave here, I will simply pack up the books and ship them off."

"Rubbish! I am having the time of my life, dear girl. Besides, I want to know how much money dear Uncle Philip left you beyond that tidy bequest in the will."

"It was only slightly less than my other cousins received. They did look superior, did they not?" Sophie giggled at the thought of how condescending her now-dignified cousins had looked as they accepted their due, then left early this morning. Only she and Lady Mary had remained behind. And Jonathan, of course. He would be required to take up the reins of running Lowell Hall now. That is, if he could tear himself away from the arms of his latest flame—a red-haired widow, by the newspaper tattle.

"Well, we had best get to work on this. How I would like to see Jonathan's face if I waved all this lovely money in front of him." Sophie chuckled, then began the task of stowing the books in the depths of a box.

Lady Mary crossed to turn the key in the lock, smiling at Sophie's surprised expression. "We do not want anyone to know of this, do we? At least, I gathered you do not intend to tell your cousin of your discovery. May I ask why not?"

Sophie knelt by another box after the contents of the first box had been carefully examined and closed. "I think Uncle intended it to be a secret. Why, I cannot guess. But I intend to keep it that way. I want no one to hear a word of this. It is to be our secret. Promise me?"

"Of course, I will, if that is your wish. I must say that it does give this business a touch of spice and a dash of mystery. Lady Mary gave Sophie such an arch look that Sophie simply had to giggle.

The doorknob rattled, then the door was shaken by an impatient hand. "Hullo, in there. What the devil is going on?" Jonathan was clearly vexed at being denied entry to his library.

"We are packing books," Sophie called out in reply. "We do not wish to be disturbed at our task."

"Who is 'we'?" he asked in a strange voice.

"Why, Lady Mary is helping me," Sophie replied with a glance at that lady, who looked about to laugh.

"I have need of some papers on my desk."

"If we keep him out he is bound to be suspicious," Lady Mary whispered. "Conceal the money and I will let him in. Perhaps he will find the dust too much and leave us to our task?" She crossed to unlock the door, her tall, gracious mien preventing Jonathan from uttering words he obviously longed to say.

Sophie hastily gathered all the bills together and stuffed them in her reticule. When that was accomplished she nodded and Lady Mary flung open the door. She greeted his lordship pleasantly and he replied in kind. He glared at Sophie, looking as though he could cheerfully order her off the premises.

Seeming absorbed in her work, Sophie ignored Jonathan as he crossed to his desk to search for the papers he wanted. Then she picked up the feather duster and began to brush the tops of a stack of books, sending clouds of fine white dust about the room, particularly in the direction of the lovely Sheraton desk and Jonathan.

He sneezed and bestowed a nasty look on Sophie. She returned it with a limpid gaze of pure innocence—a feat made plausible by her angelic appearance, golden curls peeping from beneath a halo of a white mobcap and cerulean blue eyes wide with surprise. "Bless you," she said in sympathy.

"I suppose it is useless to think I might work in here," he grumbled. "I should think you would prefer to have a maid do that packing for you."

Seeing the suspicious gleam in his eyes, Sophie promptly said, "But I feel it important to examine every book. I am sorting them into two categories. I shall wish to sell a few, for it will be difficult to store all of them until such time as I have a home of my own in which to place them."

"I had no idea you intended to marry." He gave her a sharp look. "Is this a recent thing? Who is he?" At the widening of her eyes and the indignant rise of her bosom in justified ire at his interference, he added, "As head of the family, and since your father is no longer here to advise you, I stand to assist if I may."

"It is possible for a woman to have a home without being married, you know," Sophie explained in the manner of one speaking to a not-too-bright soul. "With no fortune to gain, most men think twice before offering hand and heart to a lady." She gave Jonathan a crystal-clear gaze followed by a smile so dazzling it sent Lady Mary into a fit of coughing. "I expect an inheritance from a distant aunt—on Mother's side of the family. It will permit me a living."

"I know that devious smile of yours, brat. I have seen it often enough over the years. I do not know what mischief you are up to now, but I will find out eventually." With that pithy summation, Jonathan picked up his papers and marched from the room, closing the door with exaggerated care.

"Dear girl, how glad I am that I elected to come along with you. I declare I have not been so entertained in ages," Lady Mary said while blotting tears of laughter from her eyes with a scrap of white linen. "Now," she said briskly once the handkerchief had been put aside, "we had best busy ourselves. Viscount Lowell may decide to return—merely to keep an eye on you. Unfortunately, that brilliant smile of yours raised his doubts. I suspect you may have been a bit of a scamp as a child."

"No one else thought so." Sophie shook her head, then sighed. "It seems as though he brings out the worst in me."

"I can see that," Lady Mary murmured as she shook a volume of *Sights of Ancient Egypt*. It contained six fifty-pound notes that Sophie quickly tucked into her reticule.

"I shall put the money in here immediately so that should Jonathan return we will not have any delay in opening the door again." She met Lady Mary's understanding look with raised brows and a shrug. "I do believe he is a trifle more suspicious of me now than when I was sixteen. I wonder why? He never used to be a snoop."

"That reminds me," Lady Mary said, crossing the room again to turn the key in the lock. "We do not wish the servants to accidentally enter the room either."

They continued in silence for a time, for as Sophie whispered, there were times when servants were not above listening at doors.

They had finished checking half the books by one of the clock when Sophie yawned and looked at Lady Mary with sympathy. "I believe we must take a rest. Perhaps you could go first, have a bit of nuncheon, and relax on the terrace. It overlooks the gardens where the cascade leads down to the fountains and there's a splendid view. I fear if you do not, it will raise Jonathan's suspicions even higher."

"What about you, dear girl?" Lady Mary said, seeing the wisdom of this logic. She rose and went to the door, pausing for a reply before leaving the library.

"I should be uneasy leaving here. What if Jonathan took it into his head to 'help' me by having a maid do the rest of the packing? What a jumble that would be! Perhaps you might be so kind as to request a tray for me in here? Something light, I think. And nothing greasy," she concluded, looking at her soiled hands. "I do not wish to damage the books in any way."

"Nor the money, either, I suspect," Lady Mary said, her eyes twinkling with amusement. "Although I think you ought to leave here for a bit, I understand your reasoning. From what I observed, your cousin might well do as you suspect. That would be dreadful. Expect a maid with a tray for you before long."

With that her ladyship left the room. Sophie followed to turn the key in the lock again and gazed at the shelves of remaining books. Just how much money had they found so far? Settling into the chair behind Jonathan's lovely desk she pulled the bills from her reticule and began to count. She was well into the thousands of pounds when there was a scratching on the door. Hastily stuffing the bills back into her reticule, Sophie rushed to open the door.

"Over there, if you please," she said to the quiet little maid, directing her to place the tray on a table near the window that looked out to the fountains.

After expressing suitable appreciation and denying anything more, the maid departed, leaving Sophie alone. A bowl of rose-scented water had been brought so she might rinse off her fingers. No doubt she had Lady Mary to thank for that. Sitting on the comfortable chair, she began to eat the dainty meal, a thoughtful expression on her face.

"What shall I do with all this money?" she said at last into the quiet of the paneled room. "If I carefully invest it, I could live—in a most quiet way—off the interest for some years." She ate a little more, then said to the marble bust of Plato on the top of the bookcase, "On the other hand, were I to take a portion of it, I could have that trip to London I have always dreamed of making. And clothes." She thought for a while longer, then brushed off her fingers before again washing them. She wiped her hands on the linen napkin, then returned to her task with renewed vigor.

Two hours later there was a gentle rap on the door, followed by Lady Mary's calm request to enter the room.

Sophie rushed to comply, then urged her ladyship inside with haste. "You will not believe all I have found. My uncle had some very strange notions of saving. Think of the interest he might have reaped from thousands of pounds!"

"Thousands?" Lady Mary replied, fastening on the most significant point in Sophie's words.

"After the rest of the books are packed we shall retire to your sitting room—no one would ever disturb us there—and count it." Sophie's eyes flashed with anticipation.

"Thousands," Lady Mary murmured, seemingly fascinated with the amount of money now stuffed into Sophie's reticule. Indeed, it bulged in a most satisfactory manner.

"Good thing I had my large reticule with me. What would I have done with that tiny mesh one I use?" Sophie grinned, then thought she probably was not acting much like a companion at the moment. But then, how many companions inherited a library crammed with money?

Lady Mary joined in shaking books before stacking them to be packed. After a bit she asked, "What do you intend to do once you have completed checking all these books? Will you still ship them to London?"

"I could ask Lord Lowell—I must be accustomed to using his new title—if I might store them in the attics. Or perhaps I will take them with me. As you must have anticipated, I wish to go to London and see the sights I've been denied. I would love to buy some lovely clothes, attend the theater, visit all manner of interesting places, do the lot." Sophie reclined, skirts tucked demurely under her, by the box of books, looking as wistful as a child who has just discovered she might have her heart's desire after all.

"Have you thought of the expense of renting a house, or possibly the cost of staying at a hotel? It would be dear, even out of Season, much less in Season." Lady Mary watched Sophie's face as she considered the words.

"No, I suppose it would eat into my funds. But I am determined to go. Perhaps I should take a few of the books along to sell? The ones we thought particularly old? They certainly were dusty." Sophie frowned, giving Lady Mary an inquiring look.

"I have a proposal to put before you. I have a house in London. It's a small house but in a good location. Mayfair is the place to be, you know. A good address is so important when establishing oneself in the City. Have you considered entering Society at all? As a baronet's daughter, you are entitled to a certain respect and position among the *ton.*"

"Use your house?" Sophie thought a few moments. "I could rent it from you." She returned to her checking of books, her efforts growing speedier with repetition.

"Nonsense. You can scarcely do that when I am there with you. If you think I am going to disappear after such an intriguing beginning to this adventure, you are badly mistaken. We could join forces, as it were. I know the best mantuamaker in London, likewise the best bonnet shop and boot shop. You have a good friend in Lady Anne Radcliffe and I know a few people in London as well."

"I should not wish to impose on your kind nature," Sophie protested.

"I believe I told you once before that I am not kind, but an interfering busybody who likes to get her own way far too often. And may I tell you right now that I fully intend to accompany you. Besides, think of the stamp of approval your residing with me shall bring you." Lady Mary rose to her full, imposing height and stared down at Sophie until she thought she must give way to laugher.

"You are a devious lady. How could I possibly refuse your offer with that lure attached? I do not know about entering the world of the *ton*. Is the Season not well advanced?" Sophie feared she sounded quite as wistful as she felt.

"There will be better prices at the mantuamakers now that all the chits have bought their gowns. And since you won't have to rent a house, you can use all that lovely money to achieve just what you want," Lady Mary said in an obvious attempt to entice Sophie. "Just because you will be in black gloves does not mean you cannot go about, providing you do so discreetly."

Sophie stared at the Turkey carpet on the floor so the perceptive Lady Mary would not see into her mind and determine what Sophie truly desired above all else. It was something money could not buy.

"Sophie, let me in, will you?" came an impatient voice from the other side of the library door.

Jumping up, she ran to turn the key, knowing that all the money so far discovered was safely tucked inside her reticule. There was no way Jonathan could know what had transpired in this room while he was elsewhere, and she was quite determined that he would never find out. He was entirely capable of spoiling her find—not to mention her fun—if he so chose.

"Ah, my pretty little cousin, eager to allow her lord and master into his own library. I wish I knew what was going on in that lovely head of yours. I seem to recall that expression as one that promised trouble." He walked into the room, looking over at the nearly empty bookshelves with a wry grimace before turning to study his young cousin.

His words had a cynical ring to them that angered Sophie. "You are scarcely *my* lord and master, for all you claim to be head of our family. Uncle Philip never touted himself so. And as to what is going on in my head, you might try asking," she said with mock humility and a voice that might be compared to silk.

"What ho? Sophie Charlotte is being agreeable? I see it surprises you that I recall your middle name. I know all about you, dear Sophie."

Why did his words seem to have a subtle menace to them? She didn't like the way he had said that, implying that he knew the secrets in her heart. *Those* he would never learn.

"My lord, Sophie is to go to London with me, nothing more," Lady Mary interposed smoothly. "It is hardly the sort of thing to make a fuss over. I have a house on Lower Brook Street. Since Sophie has never been to London and I am in need of some new clothes, I decided that it would be agreeable for us to go to my house in the city directly after we leave here."

"I shall be sorry to see you leave, my lady. I fear this house will seem oddly empty with everyone gone. When do you intend to go?" He cast a sidelong glance at Sophie, bent over the latest box of books, now half full.

Sophie noted that he had not included her in his reluctance to see them depart and hardened her heart against his enormous appeal. She explained tartly, "We shall leave as soon as I complete this packing. As you can see, we have made great headway. By tomorrow the remainder will be done. We shall depart the following day. If you are anxious to see the last of us, we could possibly leave tomorrow afternoon." She glared at him, finding odd comfort in disliking him a little.

"What a touchy creature you are, Sophie," he exclaimed with a laugh. "Well, if you are to go to London, perhaps we shall see each other there. As soon as I can have matters in hand, I also intend to go to town."

"I suppose there are certain things that must be done in regards to your accession to the title," Lady Mary suggested. "You will have to pay your fee upon introduction to the House, as I recall. You intend to do that now?"

"The House is still in session, so yes, I may as well be done with that."

"If our esteemed King decides to pop off, you will be able to wear our late uncle's robes to the coronation. How fortunate for you that robes require no fitting." Sophie glanced at her cousin, then turned her attention back to the books at hand. There were several volumes on travel that she doubted contained any money. Lady Mary had been proven correct—so far all the notes had been found in books dealing with the ancient past. She turned each volume upside down, giving it a surreptitious shake before placing it in a box.

"Looking for spiders or dust?" Jonathan inquired in an amused tone.

"Dust, mostly. It is shocking how the maids have neglected the books. Look at the top of this one!" She blew off the dust in his direction, sending a cloud of white powdery dust his way.

"I can see that you are determined to make me sneeze again, so I shall disappoint you by returning to my own interests."

He turned to leave the room and Sophie couldn't resist saying, "You have interests here? I thought they were in London. At least the newspapers imply such."

"Actually, I am going over the house with Biggins and Mrs. Biggins to see what may need doing. Later I meet again with the steward Uncle Philip employed to check expenditures for the home farm." He paused at the door to meet her curious gaze with one equally inquisitive. "I wonder why you wish to know. Could it be that you truly take an interest in my affairs?"

"Not in the least. I merely considered that life in the country must be deadly dull for someone like you." Sophie felt herself spellbound, her eyes trapped in his gaze.

"I shall look forward to seeing you in London, brat. Oh, I suppose I had best cease calling you a brat, for you must surprise me by behaving like a young lady once in Town." The mockery in his tone matched the look in his dark eyes.

"What a truly nasty person you are, my lord," Sophie said with a tone to match his in sarcasm.

"Well, once you depart this house, you need not worry about it again, will you?" He paused at the door as though wanting to say more and not knowing how.

"I do have a favor to ask of you." At the raise of his brows, she smiled, then continued. "You may well think me mad after the way I spoke to you. Could I store my books here for a short time? After all, I might snabble a husband while in London and it would likely be easier to transport them to a country home from here, don't you think?" She beamed a wry smile at him again, pushing her mobcap back on her head with an impatient hand, allowing the feathery blond curls to tumble about her face in charming abandon.

"Such an angelic face with such wicked thoughts. You will drive the gentlemen of the *ton* into a frenzy with desire when you appear on the scene. Best hire a guard, Lady Mary. I suspect you may have need of one." His expression and tone were equally dry.

"Perhaps," the lady replied with a smile. "However, I believe that Sophie can cope with anything that arises."

"If I cannot, I shall apply to you as head of the family to solve my dilemma. You'd not reject my plea, would you, Jonathan?" Sophie spoke in a mocking way, yet she was aware of the undercurrent of sincerity in her query. She desperately desired someone she might turn to if in trouble, someone she could trust and depend upon. "Whatever else you may be, I know you to be trustworthy and reliable."

"You heard the chit, Lady Mary," Jonathan said in a low voice that had lost its mocking quality. "She thinks me worthy and reliable." He cast a look at the woman kneeling by the box half filled with books and nodded. "I give you my word. If you have need of me, I will do my best to help you—cousin."

Sophie felt a wave of relief wash over her. In spite of her sparring with him, she really did not wish to alienate him completely. She merely needed to distance herself from the one man who had the ability to reduce her to a mass of quivering idiocy.

"I doubt it will prove necessary. After all, what could happen to a proper companion while in London?"

"You remain as a companion?" He looked at Sophie, then at Lady Mary.

"Indeed. At least for the moment. As Sophie said, some fine gentleman may wish her for his wife. I do think it would be a shame not to pass down those beautiful golden curls or those fine blue eyes. Cerulean, I'd call them," she concluded absently. "Would you not agree, my lord?"

"Heavenly, by all means. And that goes for her general appearance. Dress her in white and London will be certain that an angel has condescended to join its ranks."

"How cruel you are, cousin," Sophie said. "I am well aware that you believe me anything but angelic. Only your innate politeness prevents you from calling me the name you would prefer."

He gave her an odd look, then retorted, "You know nothing about what I'd prefer, Miss Garnett. Nothing at all. Now, if you will excuse me, I shall join Biggins and leave you to boxing books. Shall I tell James to bring you more boxes?"

"Please do," Sophie replied while deep in speculation about his words. What would he prefer? Quite obviously it was not to kiss her again. No, he must be wishing her to the ends of the earth.

Chapter Three

Jonathan frowned at the image in his mirror. Maybe—just maybe she was the angel she looked to be. Was there ever such an exasperating bundle of femininity? He had always suspected under that angelic face and body there lurked a core of pure granite. He'd observed over the years that she was as tough as old boots. When the other cousins had quailed at adversity, Sophie had plunged in to triumphantly finish the game. Uncle Philip had adored the little Sophie, with her big blue eyes and golden curls and so-winning ways. Only she wasn't a little girl anymore.

What a seductive little baggage she'd become—so demure in her garb as a companion yet retaining that aura of latent sensuality about her. He shook his head at the thought of Sophie let loose on the unsuspecting *ton*.

He had not forgotten that forfeit kiss. It had lingered in the back of his mind, forcing an unwilling comparison to the many successive and unsatisfying kisses that followed. What would a kiss from a more mature Sophie be like, he wondered. That would be like touching a flame to kindling, he concluded. Best left alone. He wanted no complications from his little cousin. Besides, he didn't quite trust her devious mind.

He had to admire, albeit reluctantly, her solution to her poverty. It had taken courage for the very cosseted daughter of the handsome Sir William to seek employment instead of latching on to one of the relatives. But as usual, Sophie had landed on her feet, finding a most extraordinary and forbearing woman to companion.

"Will that be all, milord?" Fyfield asked, standing to one side of his employer with a curious expression on his face.

Jonathan gave a start and responded, "Indeed. You may begin to pack my things. I believe I will go to London on the morrow. I ought to have matters well in hand here by that time. I can return later for the harvest and the necessary planning for the coming year."

The dismissed valet disappeared into the dressing room, leaving Jonathan to his thoughts once again. Only this time his attention turned to the matters that must be concluded this day. Picking up the papers, he ran down the stairs to the main floor, intent upon seeking his library before Sophie commandeered it again.

Why the girl wanted total privacy while packing those books escaped him. One of her idiosyncrasies, he supposed. As angelic as she appeared it was difficult to believe that Sophie had ulterior motives for anything she did.

"Jonathan!" she exclaimed as he entered the room. Her face was flushed with the exertion of moving the library ladder to where the last lot of books awaited on a high shelf. Poised on a step, her arms full of books, blond curls rioting about her face—the mobcap being absent today—her blue eyes were looking slightly guilty. Guilty? Sophie? How could an angel be guilty of anything?

"Oh dear, I so hoped I could have these books out of your way before you needed the library. I feel dreadful, interfering with your management of the estate. I know you must have a great deal to do." She gave him a look that begged forgiveness.

That explained the guilty expression. She was merely remorseful at causing him inconvenience.

"It's quite all right, Sophie. I can work here while you finish, if you don't mind. But first I shall have my breakfast." He placed the papers on his desk, then turned to leave. Courtesy prompted him to ask, "Have you eaten?"

"Goodness, yes. I was up with the birds. I have always been an early riser. One accomplishes so much more by rising early, you know. I will have the remainder of these books packed by the time you return. And may I have James store them in the attics if I decide to leave them? You never did agree to that."

He paused at the door, thinking that if she came to collect her books he had best be far away. He was much too old to be considering golden-haired sprites. "By all means, my attics are yours to command, whatever you choose to do. James is at your service." Jonathan had observed the admiring looks from the silent James. It was doubtful there would be the slightest complaint at toting boxes of books to the top of the house from that quarter.

Once Jonathan had left, considerately closing the door behind him, Sophie hastened down the ladder to deposit the load of books on the floor by yet another box. She was tired of packing, but marveled at the flutter of currency that continued to fall from between the pages of selected volumes. Hastily stuffing the bills into her reticule, she paused to note there were also a number of consols. That three percent income would be greatly welcome for her peace of mind. There was also a long-term five percent annuity. Uncle Philip had planned this all very carefully.

What an amazing man her uncle had been. Sophie felt remorse that she hadn't spent more time with him. She had come to see him when she was certain that none of the cousins might be there—particularly Jonathan. And that proved simple to do, for Jonathan was more and more occupied with life in London once he'd left Oxford far behind him. She'd had no danger of encountering him these past four years. And Uncle Philip had been quite delighted with her company, the dear man.

Working with concentrated speed, she had closed the lid on the final box of books when Jonathan opened the door. He paused, staring at her in a disconcerting way. She probably had a smudge on her nose and her hair must be going every which way. She gave him an apologetic look. "I shall be off once James has collected this last box. I shall spare you their presence and take them with us."

"You intend to leave this afternoon?" He advanced into the room, coming to stand by the fine mahogany Sheraton desk that stood in lonely splendor before the vacant bookshelves.

Sophie nervously wiped her hands on the apron that protected the black gown. "Lady Mary desires to make a leisurely trip of it. We shall likely take three days to travel. I am not certain where we stop this evening."

"You have adequate guards? The roads are not always safe for women—men, either, for that matter."

"My lady takes no chances." Sophie felt a twinge of anguish that she must leave him. "I may see you in London. If so, I must remember not to call you Jonathan. That would set tongues to wagging, I expect. Good day, Lord Lowell. I'll say a final good-bye before we depart."

He placed his hands behind him in the same sort of gesture Sophie used when she wished to control herself and not seize something she longed to hold. That was odd—unless he wanted to give her a shaking scold, and she couldn't think what she might have done to bring that on.

"Until then, Sophie—Miss Garnett." Jonathan bowed, his look inscrutable.

She paused at the doorway to glance back at him after summoning the footman. "It seems distinctly odd that we have the same last name when we scarce know each other."

"Indeed. The family ranks continue to dwindle. Any chance of Lawrence finding a wife?"

"Not that I know. Few fathers with pretty daughters are willing to permit a marriage with a lieutenant having no more than eight pounds eight shillings a month pay." She clasped her hands demurely before her and gave him a wise look. "Less than a hundred pounds a year is scarce enough to care for a wife, let alone a family. Uncle Philip kindly aided his path in the navy—having friends in influential places. Now that Uncle is gone, Lawrence must make his way on his own merits. But then, he is a clever chap and determined to make the navy his career. He'll do." Lawrence had made no effort to intercede on behalf of Sophie— leaving her on her own. She supposed that was not unreasonable. He had his life to see to, after all.

"Unless Lawrence has changed a great deal, he will overcome that difficulty if he finds a likely lass. He is almost as determined as you are."

"You think me determined?" Sophie resolved to make Jonathan see her as something other than a silly sixteen-year-old cousin, an age and viewpoint she'd left years ago.

"Let me say that I'd not wish to stand between you and something you truly wanted. *Is* there something you want, Sophie Charlotte?" His gaze was watchful, eyes narrowed, face serious. He was not joking as was so often the case.

"Oh," she countered lightly, "what woman does not have wants? Perhaps a miracle will occur and I shall have mine. Until then, it is a secret."

She smiled at him, her heart aching just a trifle. He was older, wiser, and far too handsome for her peace of mind. He was also as far removed from her as the moon. How could she—an untutored miss from the country, daughter of a late baronet—compete with the likes of the women whose names were linked with his. They were women of wealth, position, and beauty. In their midst Sophie would seem like an insignificant peahen surrounded by glorious peacocks—never mind that those creatures were male. It was the idea of comparison that mattered, and in that she failed.

"You never used to keep secrets," he said, his face relaxing into a smile.

"I grew up," she said simply with a shrug and a wave of her hands. Deftly transferring her reticule from her arm to the safety of her hand, she whirled about and hurried to the stairs, leaving Jonathan staring after her.

Rushing down the hall, Sophie tapped on the door of Lady Mary's room. Upon being bade to enter, Sophie found her ladyship standing by the window overlooking the cascade and fountains.

"How lovely it is here. This must bring back many happy memories for you." Her ladyship turned to observe Sophie standing with the reticule clutched in her hands.

"I am done with the books," Sophie said, a triumphant note in her voice.

"Shall we count?" Lady Mary quickly walked to the round table near the window and cleared off the top of it. Once seated, she commanded the reticule's contents be dumped out to cover the surface.

"Goodness me, but that is a lot of money. I wonder how many years he spent squirreling notes and consols away in those volumes?" Sophie murmured as she settled down to place the various bills in the proper piles.

Sometime later the two ladies looked up from the paper upon which Sophie had kept record. Pencil held aloft, Sophie stared at the final total.

"I cannot believe so great a sum would come to me. And to think my cousins laughed when I inherited the library of books. If they but knew!" Sophie exchanged a smile with Lady Mary as she handed over the paper for her edification.

"How do you propose to explain this sudden influx of riches? Is there any danger that a creditor might try to claim any of this money?"

"All father's debts have long been satisfied," Sophie replied softly. "The sale of the house and its contents covered everything." It had been hard for her to see all her beloved treasures sold under the hammer to the highest bidder. Her mother had gone with Aunt Emma, not able to stand the sight. Sophie had remained; she had wanted to learn who purchased the pieces she cared for dearly. Someday in the future she intended to buy a few, if possible.

"So . . . ?"

"I shall say it is an unexpected inheritance. Who will be able to argue with that?" She gave Lady Mary a shrewd look then added, "I would feel better were I paying for my housing."

"Nonsense. The house stands empty. It would be foolish for you to rent a place of your own. Besides, it would be considered odd for an unmarried woman to do so. You will find it costly enough to fit yourself out with the wardrobe you have been dreaming about."

"I shall be in mourning, you know."

"It is not as though you mourned a husband or parents."

"Well, as to that, I wore my blacks for a very short time for Father. I had no desire to come to you so garbed. But will not Society expect a full three months' mourning?"

"It varies a great deal for uncles. I believe under the circumstances that three weeks will be proper."

Sophie wondered what the circumstances might be that would limit her period of mourning for her dear uncle. Yet would he wish her to be garbed in deepest black when he had always referred to her as his sunshine girl?

When she packed her belongings, she studied the dresses that Jonathan had ordered for her. They were far more stylish than anything she presently owned. The fabric might be a soft black, but it was excellent quality. She decided to take them along. It would be better to appear in a fashionable black gown rather than those outmoded and carefully darned dresses that had been her present garb.

James arrived to remove her case along with the ones from Lady Mary's room. She followed him down the stairs, wondering if she would find her cousin in the library. "James," she said decisively. "Would you bring the boxes of books out with the baggage now, please? They should fit in the boot quite well with the rest of our things." The books could easily go with the trunks and traveling impediments a Lady Mary deemed necessary. Sophie could sell the books and claim that was where she got her money!

"We shall have a nuncheon before leaving," Lady Mary announced in a firm voice.

"I remembered and spoke to Cook about it," Sophie said quietly. She gestured toward the breakfast room. "It will be on the table in there. I shall join you in a minute." She wondered if she'd find her cousin in the library.

With a knowing look on her face, Lady Mary walked ahead while Sophie crossed the broad entry hall to the library door. She found it ajar and peeped around the door to see whether Jonathan was at his desk.

"I have come to say good-bye," she said when assured he was still working on his papers.

He rose, walked around the desk, and came to stand before her, causing Sophie to take a step back.

"You will be careful," he admonished like her uncle used to do. "And listen to Lady Mary when in London. I suspect she is well up on correct behavior."

"She says that because of circumstances I need wear my blacks no more than three weeks. Does that seem correct to you?" Sophie hated to ask him, but she suspected he was even more up to snuff than Lady Mary.

"Circumstances?" He considered this word, studying Sophie all the while. Then he half smiled and nodded. "Aye, we would not have all of London plunged into mourning as it were. Does Lady Mary intend to go about in Society while in Town? If so, you will need some clothes."

"If she does, I shall do well enough." She gave him a defiant look, daring him to offer her charity. It was enough that she had accepted the black gowns he had ordered for her. Since they had been provided she'd have been a fool to refuse them.

"As I recall you always gave Uncle Philip a farewell kiss. Do I not rate that as well—as the new Lord Lowell?"

Sophie caught her breath. Swallowing with care, not wishing to seem to place more importance on the matter than would be logical, she bravely smiled. "Indeed—cousin." Stepping forward she stretched on her toes to place a butterfly kiss on his cheek. At least that was what she'd intended to do.

Somewhere along the line Jonathan moved; since her eyes were closed she'd not noticed. The firm warmth of his mouth shocked her as it had four years ago. For seconds she yielded, then she pulled away, her lashes flying upward in surprise. "I'd not meant to do that," she whispered, utterly overwhelmed.

He smiled at her. "You have improved, Sophie Charlotte. There is hope for you after all."

Spinning about in confusion, she set off to the breakfast room. What Sophie ate was a mystery, no doubt something nourishing and not too surprising, for Lady Mary made no comment on her selections. When replete, Lady Mary suggested departure.

Jonathan escorted them to the traveling coach, handing each of the ladies in with characteristic address. He glanced at the coachman and outriders, noting their weapons and sturdy equipment. Nodding with approval, he said, "I will see you in London, I expect. Do not forget your promise, Sophie."

She gave him a puzzled look and faintly shook her head. It was no wonder she could not think; her head was all of a muddle after that kiss, brief though it was.

"If you have any problems, be sure to contact me. I'll see what I can do to help you."

"How like Uncle Philip you sound. Very sedate and fatherly," she added with an impish smile.

Jonathan smiled in return, then watched the coach head down the avenue toward Oxford and London, followed by the baggage carriage. Jonathan shook his head as he returned to his library, now devoid of books and rather lonely. She thought of him like an uncle. And so he could be had his father been a bit more precocious. As it was, he was far too old for the chit, even though he was not fatherly in his feelings for her at all. It had taken considerable restraint not to gather her in his arms and do that final kiss properly.

With a sigh, Jonathan Garnett, Viscount Lowell, turned his attention to estate matters, welcoming his inherited steward into the library for additional discussion.

"That went well, I believe," Lady Mary said as they bowled along the road that led through Cheltenham, then on to the east. "You were blessed with opportunities to holiday at such a lovely home with an indulgent uncle. What a pity all good things seem to come to an end."

"Indeed, they do," Sophie replied wistfully. Should she see Jonathan in London all would be altered. He would be in his milieu and she would be the little companion given a treat in the City.

"I have a fancy to stop at one of the quaint inns that dot this countryside. See what you can find in the book, Sophie."

Obediently picking up the well-worn copy of *Patterson's Roads,* which was their guide to roads and establishments along the way, Sophie puzzled over the pages for some time. At last she said, "I believe the George in Burford is what you wish, my lady. I think it the most acceptable between Cheltenham and Oxford. Although I must confess that when one is not traveling *from* London the routes are quite confusing."

"The George it shall be, then. It is but a village, is it not?" Lady Mary inquired while adjusting her pelisse.

" 'Tis said to be a very pretty place. There is a market building not far from the inn where sheep are sold. I trust there will be no market day when we arrive."

The thought of a village full of sheep did not appear to unduly upset Lady Mary and she leaned back against the squabs to rest her eyes.

Sophie took advantage of this to gaze out the window at the passing fields and green hills. Well—she had seen him and escaped unscathed, unless one could call that wisp of a kiss damaging. Pity it had happened. It had stirred her even more than that first forfeit kiss. But then, she was older now. 'Twas a shame she wasn't wiser as well.

Burford and the George were much as expected. The landlord was gracious to Lady Mary, as well he might be. The sight of her imposing traveling coach was enough to gladden the heart of any host.

They strolled about the tiny village before dinner, then went to bed early after eating an excellent meal in their room.

The next morning saw them at a leisurely pace on the road leading to Oxford. *Patterson's* was scarce any help at all regarding an inn, but Lady Mary had her own ideas.

"We shall stay at the Mitre in Oxford; I always do."

And they did, welcomed with warm hospitality by the landlord of the ancient inn. Sophie envisioned the stately progress of a monarch of old, so did Lady Mary travel. She expected the best and she certainly obtained it. When they left Oxford, with Sophie wistful for sights unseen, it was with the promise of seeing the spires and views of London by that evening.

Their arrival in London was an anticlimax. The late day traffic was horrendous. The smells were horrid, as were the street criers and vendors. Sophie marveled at the ease with which the coachman guided the horses through the town and up to the house on Lower Brook Street.

Lady Mary marched ahead to enter the house while Sophie rushed to keep up with her. The butler seemed totally unsurprised at his mistress suddenly appearing without notice when she ought to be away in the Cotswolds. The Georgian-style house gleamed with polish and the scent of roses drifted about them. The spacious entry was sumptuous, with great mirrors and vases of flowers on the narrow marble-topped tables. Lady

Mary swept along the black-and-white marble floor to where the stairs rose in stately splendor.

Sophie glanced about her as she ascended the stairs. It was clear that Adam had been hired to do the interior decoration. His inimitable style was evident everywhere. She glimpsed the first-floor drawing room and thought it most elegant. The small house Lady Mary claimed as her own was scarcely mundane.

"There is a morning room, just behind the library—a water closet as well." They climbed to the chamber story, which was quite as elegant as the floor below. "You will have the room at the front while I am in my room to the rear of this floor," Lady Mary explained. "The other room will be reserved for a guest, for one never knows. With no window, it is a trifle gloomy, but in that case, the guests do not tarry."

Sophie didn't linger over the light repast served in the lovely dining room. Both ladies declared they would have an early night of it. When Sophie tumbled into bed it was with a vague feeling of anticipation for the morrow. She could begin her wardrobe and see some sights before her three weeks of mourning were finished, surely.

The following morning she learned that Lady Mary had her own ideas.

"We shall stop by to see Madame Clotilde and have her take your measurements. You may select the fabrics if you please, but otherwise you should leave everything in her capable hands. Then I believe we ought to leave my cards at a number of homes—my friends will wish to know I am returned to Town. After that, I confess I would like a drive in the park. Of course, we shall have to eat sometime during all this. "Oh," she said, drawing a deep breath, "do you not feel the excitement in the air? We are in London, dear girl, the center of the world!"

It might be the center of the world, it was also rather dirty and noisy to a country-bred girl. Sophie kept her mouth closed and her eyes open as they took a small town carriage to Madame Clotilde's elegant shop.

The mantuamaker might have hair of an improbable red

shade, but her mind was as sharp as could be. She listened to Lady Mary's demands, then quickly took the measurements of her customer. She kept glancing at Sophie from time to time, muttering words in French, among which the word *angélique* figured prominently.

"You shall take the *ton* by storm, mam'selle. The palest blue, most delicate pink, and cloud white—most suitable for one who is an angel."

Sophie smiled and agreed to the number of garments to be made, leaving the styles to the woman, who seemed to believe she could make something wonderful of Sophie.

Shopping was followed by pauses at various houses at which the footmen took visiting cards indicating that her ladyship was back in London, to be placed on small silver trays. The last house belonged to the Radcliffes.

Here, the footman returned to the carriage with the news that Lady Anne desired that Lady Mary and her companion enter.

"I hoped she would be home," Lady Mary murmured to Sophia. "Anne always serves the best nuncheons."

"Lady Mary, how lovely." Lady Anne exclaimed when they met. "And, Sophie! I am so pleased to see you in London. What fun we shall have. How long will you be in town and do say you will come to dinner while here. And is there any way in which I may assist?"

"Feed us, first of all," said the forthright Lady Mary while Sophie attempted to stifle a smile at this boldness and failed.

"Indeed, it will be my pleasure. I well know how much you enjoy my cook's offerings." She summoned her butler, then sat back to enjoy a comfortable coze. The news of Sophie's inheritance was received with delight. "And for you to have the cachet of Lady Mary as your friend and sponsor—for you will do that for our dearest Sophie, will you not?—is above all things wonderful."

"I will have you know that I would not miss a moment of the coming weeks. I have a feeling that London does not know what it's in for—if you know what I mean," Lady Mary said with a significant glance at a puzzled Sophie.

Lady Anne studied Sophie and slowly smiled. She was

about to say something when the butler entered bearing a card on a silver tray. Lady Anne took one look at it and grinned. "By all means, I am to home."

In short order a young man entered the room. He was tall and thin; his sandy hair carefully groomed into a windswept style. While the cut of his clothes was unexceptional, his waistcoat blazed with the glory of embroidered birds. A peacock, Sophie thought.

"Lady Mary and Sophie, I should like to present Mr. Peter Antrobus, a good friend of my husband. Peter, you inspiring bird with your marvelous waistcoat, this is Lady Mary Croscombe and a dear friend of mine from school days, Miss Sophie Garnett."

"Any relation to Viscount Lowell?" the dashing young gentleman inquired with flattering attention to Sophie. Actually, he looked a trifle dazed, but that could have been the snug fit of his pantaloons.

"He is my third cousin, Mr. Antrobus."

After acknowledging the luck of some gentlemen, Mr. Antrobus fell silent, simply regarding with some bemusement the heavenly beauty sitting across from him. He finally noticed she was in blacks and offered his condolences.

"There will be but three weeks mourning, for her uncle did not wish excessive display, you know," Lady Mary intoned with stately aplomb.

"Would a carriage drive be acceptable, my lady?" At Lady Mary's regal nod, he turned to Sophie and begged, "I should deem it wonderful if you would give me the pleasure of taking you for a drive in the park."

"Well," Sophie began, looking to Lady Mary for guidance.

"I think it would be simply lovely. Dearest Sophie does not know a soul in Town, other than Lady Anne. It would be the greatest kindness if you would show her that small favor." Lady Mary beamed a smile at the gentleman, who straightened up and positively glowed.

The way Lady Mary looked at Mr. Antrobus one would have thought him to be a shining knight, Sophie thought, stifling an urge to smile.

"This afternoon at five of the clock—if I am not too presumptuous, that is?"

Sophie took matters into her own hands at this point. She gave him a blinding smile and nodded ever so gently at him. "That would be lovely."

Quite dazzled, Mr. Antrobus rose and walked from the room with a murmured farewell.

Lady Anne went into whoops once she knew he was gone from the house. "My dear, I predict you will take all of London without waging a battle. I salute you. You certainly are not the little girl I knew at school."

"Who is?" Sophie replied softly.

Chapter Four

When Mr. Peter Antrobus arrived a few minutes before five of the clock he carried a small but exquisite nosegay of delicate pink rosebuds. Sophie gave him an enchanted smile of thanks, thinking that Mr. Antrobus displayed rare taste and was a gentleman to be cultivated.

He also revealed a nice skill with the ribbons as well, she reflected while they made their way to Hyde Park. As the fashionable hour for driving and strolling in the park was just commencing, the press of carriages was not overwhelming. However, it was sufficiently crowded for Sophie to appreciate his ability.

"You do well, sir," she said at last as he neatly skimmed around a curricle that was being handled by a cow-handed driver more frustrated than a hen whose chick had strayed.

"Thank you, Miss Garnett. Cannot hold a patch to your cousin. Garnett, that is, Lowell—keep forgetting he must be called that now—is a top-of-the-trees driver."

Sophie digested this bit of information in silence while wondering if there was anything in this world that Jonathan did not do well. Apparently he was much sought after in Society, having the power to turn an ordinary party into a smashing success merely by attending for a bit, lending his suave presence to the occasion. He'd never married, so she couldn't know what sort of husband or father he would be. Most likely he'd be the best. Reflecting a bit longer, she decided there were any number of things she did not know about her cousin. And likely never to know if he had his way.

"I believe I should like to have a rig of my own," she said

pensively to Mr. Antrobus, offering a smile when he turned to give her a startled look.

"A carriage? You are familiar with handling the ribbons?" His voice tended to squeak when taken aback.

"I was used to drive in the country. I fancy it would take a time of early morning forays into the park before I could begin to cope with this half as well as you do," she said, allowing her admiration for his skill to show in her voice.

The gentleman straightened up and held his reins at precisely the proper angle, urging his fine pair of chestnuts to a spanking trot. "I imagine such a thing would be acceptable."

"I understand that a lady cannot attend the auctions at Tattersall's. Would you be so kind as to purchase a horse for me in the near future? I should like to study the papers first to see if there is a nice carriage available. I have not the patience to wait for a coach builder to make me one."

"No need. There are always carriages for sale. If you will allow me, I . . ." His voice faded away as he saw the approach of Miss Garnett's most excellent cousin astride a magnificent black steed. Peter drew his chestnuts to a halt and gave his acquaintance a wary nod.

"Antrobus," the viscount said politely by way of greeting. Then turning his gaze to his pretty cousin, he took note of her nosegay and said, "Out and about so soon, Sophie? You have scarcely settled in, I imagine." Glancing around him he noted the interest his attention to Sophie was garnering from the passing peers. With a hint of deviltry in his eyes, he reached over to take her hand, which had been resting on the rim of the carriage. Bringing it to his lips, he placed a lingering kiss on the neatly gloved surface.

"Cousin, I believe you are a tease," Sophie said with a glinting look in her eyes.

"Tease? Never. How do you go on, my dear?" He released her hand with a show of reluctance that was not as pretended as might have been.

Sophie looked back at him and placed her hand in her lap. She sniffed the rosebuds before replying. "Quite well, I believe. Lady Mary and I are doing all the expected things one must upon arriving in London. Mr. Antrobus has graciously offered to assist me in selecting a horse and carriage. Is that not most kind of him?" There was a challenge in the flash of eyes in Jonathan's direction, of that he was certain.

"No need for that," the viscount found himself saying, to his surprise. "I shall be pleased to oversee that task for you, cousin. After all, as head of the family that is more or less my duty."

There was nothing feigned in Sophie's startled look at him. She had not expected him to offer his assistance and Jonathan smiled with satisfaction that he had actually caught her out for once.

"I should not wish to impose on your time," she insisted. "I understand you are much in demand, cousin." She studied the nosegay clutched firmly in her hand and then slanted a look at her impressive relative. "However, if you insist, I fancy I can rely on Mr. Antrobus for lessons. I shan't wish to drive at this time of day until I feel comfortable with being in Town."

"I imagine I could oversee that as well. You must do the family credit, my dear girl." Jonathan noted the angry flash of her eyes and smiled. Was he actually thwarting her interest in the insipid Antrobus? "I insist, Sophie. Antrobus doesn't know what he would be letting himself in for should he agree to guiding your driving."

"And you do?" she asked sweetly, with a melting smile that undoubtedly had a core of steel in it.

"I believe I do," Jonathan replied, backing away from them as his mount was becoming restive. Then it occurred to him to wonder where Sophie was to obtain the funds for such a rig-out. "However, I shall discuss this with you this evening. You will be to home?"

"I believe we are to attend the theater. Lady Mary said it is quite acceptable to see something by Shakespeare while in mourning for my uncle."

"I shall join you, if I may."

Sophie noted the determination in his voice and decided it would do no good to deny him. "If you please. Lady Mary insists we go a trifle early. She said if she paid for the entire play, she wishes to see it."

"Wise lady. Until later."

Sophie turned her head to watch him thread his way through the growing throng of riders and carriages. "I must apologize, Mr. Antrobus. My cousin is rather spoiled and accustomed to having his own way. If you wish, we can still have our drives together. I'd not want you to believe I prefer his teaching to yours."

"You do well to accept him, for he is the best around," Mr. Antrobus said with reluctant honesty.

"I had no idea. I'd have not said a word had I known, believe me," she concluded earnestly.

This left Mr. Antrobus to wonder why she would not have said a word—because she favored his company or because she would have preferred her cousin as a teacher in the first place.

The remainder of the drive passed with comments on the various carriages, comparing the merits of one horse against another. Mr. Antrobus made it plain that he had never encountered a young lady like Miss Garnett, who preferred to discuss these topics instead of noting who sat in said carriages or rode which horses.

Sophie well concealed her anger at her cousin's high-handed manipulation of the situation. Why he should interfere with her entrance into Society, she didn't know. Having come to the conclusion that she could never be his, Sophie with great practicality had decided that she had best find a nice gentleman with whom she might spend her declining years. It was a most agreeable alternative to being a companion the rest of her life. This gloomy reflection occupied her the last of the drive back to Lower Brook Street, where she bid good day to Mr. Antrobus with true regret.

A short time later at dinner Sophie related all that had occurred while driving in the park. Her gown of rich gray satin was utterly plain, depending upon interest by the clever draping of the lustrous fabric. Around her neck she wore a strand of pearls with pearls also at her ears. The effect of the pearls against the gray was lovely and when combined with her blond curls and amazing blue eyes, proved to be quite out of the ordinary to say the least. Light from the chandelier and the wall sconces reflecting from the satin gave Sophie the appearance of an angel who only lacked a halo to be quite perfect.

"I suppose you must agree to your cousin's interference," Lady Mary said at last when Sophie had given vent to her ire. "Does he know you intend to purchase the rig and animal yourself? Perhaps Lord Lowell thinks he—as head of the family—is expected to foot the bill?"

Sophie dabbed her napkin at her mouth, then leaned back in her chair, considering the matter. "I doubt it. For one thing, I would never allow Mr. Antrobus to spend so much as a farthing in that direction. Nor do I believe he would be so unhandsome as to offer such a thing. And I gave my cousin not the slightest hint that *he* might be expected to pay the amount required."

"Then I wonder what your cousin's motive might be," her ladyship mused as they rose from the table to head for the entryway. Their maids stood ready with their evening cloaks. Sophie's was of gray velvet lined in a cloud white satin. Lady Mary's pale green evening gown contrasted nicely with her cloak of forest green.

Sophie looked in the mirror, then said, "We make a good pair, I believe. I am looking forward to the play. I have never seen one, you know. I suppose I ought to be grateful to Jonathan for accompanying us this evening—even if he means to read me a scold. Think of the consequence of being seen with *him* at the theater!" She laughed just as a rap sounded on the front door.

Turning, she watched Jonathan enter and walk along the hall to where she and Lady Mary waited.

He offered each lady a dainty bouquet of flowers. Lady Mary received a nosegay of golden roses, while Sophie had a collection of creamy white blooms. Giving Sophie a narrow look, he said, "White is for innocence, I believe."

"So I understand," Sophie replied demurely in a voice that would melt butter. "Shall we depart? Lady Mary . . ."

"Of course. You and I will discuss the matter of the carriage and steed eventually. Antrobus is not to be involved. The very idea that you would go to him is beyond belief. I shall see to the matter," he promised in a low tone meant for her ears but of course overheard by her ladyship.

"I do not see what the trouble is," Sophie insisted. "You seriously do not imply you believe I would accept such a *gift* from anyone, surely you don't! And I shan't expect you to pay for it, you know. I am well able to assume my own expenses." She glanced sideways at him, satisfied at the stunned expression on his face.

Once seated in his fine equipage, he stared across the carriage at her and inquired, "Since when do you have the funds to do all this?"

"That is none of your business, other than to know it is all perfectly legal and I have done nothing wrong in acquiring the money," she said in a soft reply that struck Jonathan as oddly seductive. How could this minx put her hands on so much money—legally? He rubbed his jaw while pondering the matter.

Lady Mary inserted a few comments on the play to be seen and the actors who portrayed the roles. "I am pleased to offer Sophie her first opportunity to see a theatrical production," she concluded.

"You have not been to the theater before, brat?"

"No, and I wish you would not call me brat," she said, her ire clearly revealed for a moment as she flashed her blue gaze at him. "You said you would not." She eyed the lovely flowers held tightly in one hand and continued. "Some people might believe it imparts greater intimacy than is warranted with our distant connection. Indeed, it is perhaps foolish of you to venture to come with us this evening—it gives way to such speculation, you know."

"I imagine Sophie has confided to you the true reason for her coming to London, my lord?" Lady Mary said with a lift of one aristocratic brow.

"No, she has not," the viscount replied with a curious look at a now-silent Sophie.

"It is all well and good to be my companion, but I shan't always need the darling girl," her ladyship said. "It is best for her to marry. I should like to see her married well—an income of several thousand a year at the very least."

"Content with so little?" he said in mock dismay.

"I have never had a great deal of money in the past," Sophie reminded him.

What his lordship thought of this prospect was not revealed. The carriage drew to a halt before the theater and his lordship exited to hand the ladies down—first Lady Mary, then Sophie.

The flambeaus outside the theater cast beautiful shadows on the gray velvet cloak. Sophie laughed at something said by Lady Mary, tilting her head upward.

The light captured the joy in her face and another gentleman just arriving caught his breath at the sight.

Jonathan noticed this and gave the chap a grim look. His foolish action was rewarded by the fellow joining them.

"Lowell, my good man, introduce me to your companions," the Earl of Chessyre said with a gallant bow in the direction of Lady Mary, then Sophie.

With an obvious reluctance that immediately caught Sophie's notice, Jonathan performed the duty as politely as possible, then froze when Lady Mary spoke.

"Do join us if you are free, sir. I feel certain you would be a delightful addition to our little party," her ladyship said with a glance at Jonathan.

Chessyre gave Jonathan an amused look and bowed over Sophie's hand with the sort of careless grace that was his trait. "Nothing would give me greater pleasure. I cannot say an angel has ever been one of my acquaintances."

Sophie's chuckle was the sort to appeal to the earl, not terribly impressed with the subservient attitude of many of the young ladies entering Society.

In the crush of going into the theater, Sophie and Jonathan became separated from the earl and Lady Mary.

"I do not see why those people had to insert themselves when they could clearly see we are a party," Sophie softly complained to her cousin.

"Do not think for a moment it was that. I held you back because I want a word with you in private," Jonathan growled in her ear. "In the morning we will discuss the matter of your finances as well as this notion you have of finding a husband this Season. Do not think to leave for the mantuamaker's before I meet with you," he cautioned.

"I will be occupied in studying the papers for a carriage," she fired back at him. "I suppose whatever I like will be on sale at Tattersall's. I must say I think it vastly unfair that I should be deprived of examining the carriage myself. I do have brains, you know."

"I give leave to doubt that, my dear," Jonathan muttered as he guided her to rejoin Lady Mary and the earl, who was looking far too amused at the sight of Jonathan hovering over his angelic cousin.

The stage production was secondary to the action taking place in the theater box, with Sophie seated with the Earl of Chessyre, Lady Mary, and Viscount Lowell. Evidently the earl had decided to honor Sophie with his attentions, paying court to her with a deference that would have turned the head of anyone but the practical Sophie.

Her levelheadedness was at variance with her angelic mien—one that appeared to be so ethereal she couldn't have a sensible thought in her head. She merely chuckled at his encomiums, giving him sidelong looks that said clearly how amusing she found his regard.

Lady Mary observed this exchange, alternating her attention between the stage—which clearly had the lesser appeal—and Sophie.

Viscount Lowell hovered at Sophie's right side, shamelessly listening with simmering wrath to the bon mots and little pufferies tossed off by his polished opponent.

None of this performance was missed by those who could see the box where Sophie's party was seated. At the first interval swarms of gentlemen converged on the box, forcing Jonathan to allow just a few he personally knew well to enter.

Sophie sat in her gown of rich gray satin, looking her most angelic and flirting like anything but an angel.

"Ease up, old man," the Earl of Chessyre advised as he stood with Jonathan at the rear of the box. "I do not think Sophie is the sort of girl who responds well to a tight rein."

"She has no money," Jonathan muttered. "Where she is obtaining the money to finance her wardrobe and all the rest is a mystery to me. But I intend to learn."

"Why? She strikes me as a total innocent. Perhaps there was a bequest? Did your uncle not die recently? Maybe he . . ." he halted when Jonathan directed a withering look at him. "Well," he said lamely, "she simply is not the type of girl to take money from a man."

Jonathan could scarcely tell his friend that Sophie was about as innocent as a wildcat. Her flirting was but a pale reflection of her kiss and that ability had improved considerably from that first forfeit four years ago.

In the front of the box Sophie was having the time of her life. Never had she expected to entertain the likes of these gentlemen—two earls, one marquis, several barons, and a goodly number of esquires paying her court. They were all a trifle foolish, of course, comparing her to an angel. She had heard that nonsense until it ceased to have the slightest meaning to her. Anyone more down to earth than herself she couldn't imagine. It came from having to do without and make her own way in this world.

She might appear angelic—but that was a mere twist of fate that combined blond curls and blue eyes in an ordinary oval face. True, she wasn't given to spots or freckles, and she carried herself as she had been taught, tall and straight. Certainly the men who flattered her offered charming prospects.

However one glance at her cousin told her that he was furious with her and would likely read her a scold come morning. She had best make use of her abilities now.

In less time than would have been believed, she had sorted them out, arranged drives and party dates with each, and had sent them on their way.

"Miss Garnett, I fear you will not have a moment to grant me, so busy will your coming days be," the earl complained with gentle amusement when he resumed his place.

"Nonsense," Sophie replied with a genuine smile. "I saved a waltz for you at the Hethering ball and if you wish you may take me driving come next Tuesday."

"Done," he murmured as the play resumed—not that anyone

paid the slightest attention to it. "I shall await the moment with great anticipation."

"You cannot waltz with him," Jonathan muttered in her other ear, not without satisfaction. "You have not been granted permission by a patroness."

"Lady Mary assures me that I will by then. She is a great friend of Lady Cowper. Besides, Lady Mary knows everyone. I cannot imagine that there is a patroness who would deny me that privilege when I am under her wing, so to speak."

"I shudder to think of what you will do next," Jonathan said, but without heat. Keeping an eye on his charming cousin while she resided in London was becoming an obsession with him. He'd not intended to go near her, fearing the consequences. Now here he was at her elbow, hovering over her like a father, for pity's sake.

At the second interval a repeat of the first occurred. Lady Mary turned when the door to the corridor opened to reveal the first of the gentlemen.

"Dear me, and I had wanted a lemonade," she whispered.

"I imagine you both could use something refreshing. I shall battle my way on your behalf," the earl replied, earning a heartfelt smile from Sophie.

When the evening concluded, Jonathan was most relieved. He sat opposite Sophie in the carriage, staring at her with a hooded gaze.

"Well, I believe the evening went splendidly from one point of view," Lady Mary offered.

"Yes, if Sophie is thinking of becoming a byword in Society, that is true," the disgruntled viscount added.

"I do not have the option of a second Season," Sophie reminded him. "As Lady Mary pointed out, I must find myself a husband. My father is dead, as is Uncle Philip. My brother is off in the navy. That leaves no one else—unless you are interested in finding a match for me, my lord."

"I?" he queried, sounding utterly aghast.

"You have stated that you are the head of our family, that I am obliged to listen to your counsel. Who better to vet my possibilities? Tell me, would your friend the Earl of Chessyre be a potential husband?"

"No," his lordship said with a decisive snap.

"Think about it and perhaps you can offer some suggestions in the morning. You are still coming over to talk to me, are you not? I might wish your counsel regarding a carriage while you are there. Or here, as it were," she added when the carriage came to a halt before the house on Lower Brook Street.

"Expect me by ten o'clock." He escorted both ladies to the door, giving Sophie a fulminating look that was quite lost in the dim light.

Once inside, Lady Mary walked with Sophie to the landing of the second floor, where she paused. "You were a trifle hard on your poor cousin, were you not?"

"Nonsense, he deserved it. He did not wish to introduce me to that perfectly charming Lord Chessyre, nor did he wish the others to make themselves known to me. Do you know I persuaded one of the gentlemen to take me to the British Museum and another is to conduct me around the Tower of London? I believe I can persuade yet another man to take me to the Exeter 'Change if I try," Sophie said with a grin. "I shall see all the things I've longed to see while deep in the country and yearning to come to London."

"And a husband?"

"As to that, I shall put my overbearing cousin on the spot. I intend to seek his wisdom and guidance. Is that not proper? Can he complain? I will ask his advice on every man who seeks my hand, should some impulsive man who does not need a fortune be so brave."

"Your poor cousin," Lady Mary said, her eyes twinkling with mirth.

"He did ask for it," Sophia reminded. "He said I was to consult him if there was ever a problem. And I suspect that a suitor might very well be just such a problem." She gave her ladyship a virtuous smile that belied the mischief in her eyes.

"Oh, how thankful I am that I found you. How deadly dull life would have been had you not crossed my path," her ladyship declared before retiring to her room at the back of the house.

Sophie proceeded to her own room that overlooked the street far below. Here she removed the gray gown with the help of her maid, Anna. Then, after things had been put away, she dismissed the girl.

Curling up on her comfortable bed, she considered the evening. It appeared to have been productive. If only Jonathan's behavior had stemmed from a touch of jealousy. She knew better than that. He was merely being his autocratic self. What he would say come morning would prove interesting. She meant to be ready for him, and with that thought in mind she said her prayers and drifted off to sleep.

During breakfast, while perusing the morning papers, she settled on an advertisement in the *Morning Post* regarding a fashionable curricle to be sold. It had been the property of a lady and used but a few months.

"It is painted patent yellow and the seats are covered with light blue cloth, *and* it has patent axel trees. There is also a barouche landau, painted yellow and black, the owner deceased and the carriage to be sold at one-half value," Sophie read over toast and tea. "However, the barouche would require a driver and I wish to drive myself."

"I noticed on the same page that Tattersall's has one hundred fashionable carriages for sale—among which are a high-perch phaeton and a crane-neck phaeton, not to mention gigs and whiskeys," her ladyship offered between sips of her favorite chocolate.

"Those phaetons are a trifle risky for me to consider," Sophie began, only to be interrupted by the entrance of her cousin.

"I am profoundly happy to hear such sentiments from your lips, little cousin. After last evening I despaired of ever hearing a sensible word from you again." He pulled out a chair and sat down.

"Do join us, Jonathan. Coffee? Perhaps toast or maybe a slice of ham with buttered eggs might suit you?" Sophie said sweetly, her eyes glittering at his appearance.

"Yes to all mentioned. Of a sudden, I am famished," he responded.

There was a hasty flurry of activity while his lordship was supplied with all the food he desired. Once finished, he pushed his plate aside and reached for the paper she had studied. "A curricle? I must say, I thought you would hold out for a crane-neck phaeton."

"I do hope I have some sense, dear Jonathan," Sophie said, mocking him as he had mocked her earlier. "Although what business it is of yours is beyond me."

"Where did you obtain the funds?" he quietly demanded.

Lady Mary choked on her chocolate and had to be thumped on the back before she recovered.

"I do not intend to reveal my source at this time, sirrah," Sophie said, that touch of steel in her voice again. "Now, will you purchase the carriage for me, or do I go to inspect it myself?"

He shuddered and said, "I will do it, for no other reason than that I fully believe you will do as you threaten."

"I have no doubt you will obtain me a better bargain, anyway," Sophie said with a saucy grin.

His frown dissolved into a reluctant smile. "You are a minx. Wonder I did not see that when we were growing up."

"You never saw enough of me to know anything at all."

Jonathan might have disputed that, but it would have involved a complicated explanation he would prefer not to make now or ever, if truth be known.

"I trust you to do all that is proper, Jonathan," Sophie said. "A horse as well. I am told your taste is outstanding when it comes to nags. How much money do you think it will take for everything?"

He named a sum he thought was fair. If he exceeded it, he had decided to take that amount from his own pocket.

"Excellent," Sophie said, exchanging a look with Lady Mary. "One moment and I shall fetch the bills for you."

"You intend to pay cash?" he queried, sounding as surprised as he felt. "In that case I might fetch you an even better price."

"Cash, it is," she said lightly, pausing at the door before going to her room.

When she handed him three hundred-pound notes he gave her a quizzical look that said more than words could at the moment. "One day you are going to tell me."

"Perhaps. Promise me that if it comes to more than that amount you will tell me. I'll not be beholden to you."

"Independent to a fault, aren't you," he snapped back, then strode from the room in high dudgeon.

"My, my," Lady Mary commented.

"Indeed," Sophie said quietly.

Chapter Five

At Madame Clotilde's, while patiently being pinned for fittings on her new gowns, Sophie wondered at her reasoning regarding Jonathan. Why was it so vital that she not reveal her source of income to him? Did she actually fear he might take it away from her? He did not seem to be a niggardly person, coveting what another possessed. As a youth he had always been generous.

"Turn this way, please, Miss Garnett," Madame requested, then stood back to look at the effect. "Miss has an excellent figure. These willowy styles well become you." She adjusted the skirt of the cloud white gown of soft Florence satin and nodded. "This can be ready soon."

Sophie's thoughts returned to Jonathan. Really, he was not her *problem* in a sense. But he was the one person who broke through her easygoing nature to touch that stubborn streak deep within her.

Submitting to a change of gowns, she tugged at the carriage dress of soft violet challis and gently requested, "I would like this dress ready as soon as possible, if you please."

"For so well-bred a lady it will be done." Madame paused by the door and looked with respect at Sophie. "It is appreciated when a customer not only is pleasant but pays in cash. For such a woman, much can be accomplished."

Practical to her core, Sophie could quite understand that cash in hand was far better than airy promises of future remuneration. "Every garment will be paid for upon delivery, you may be sure. I have a horror of debts," she concluded softly, thinking of her father. "In fact, I shall give you something on account, if I may." She turned to pick up her reticule and pulled a one-hundred-pound note from it, then handed it to the astounded madame.

The improbable red hair was smoothed back with a trembling hand. "Miss Garnett, I shall create such gowns for you as have never been seen before. They will truly make you look like the angel you are." She paused a moment, then continued in a strained voice. "There have been clients of late who have failed to pay their bills to such extent that I have been pressed for funds. Now I can arrange things more to my liking. Bless you." The mantuamaker flushed at this uncharacteristic unburdening of her problems and left Sophie to stare at the reflection in the looking glass. Her thoughts returned to her cousin.

Jonathan's trouble was that he was a perfectionist. And that natural reserve he wrapped about him did not make it easy to know him well. Surprisingly, he was a good listener, analyzing problems, offering dependable advice—usually. But his dignity must have been offended at the crush of men who had sought her out last evening. The Earl of Chessyre had been amused. Not so Jonathan. He had run a frustrated hand through his carefully brushed dark hair and his very dark eyes—almost black, they were—had snapped with annoyance.

This morning he had been pleased, however. True, he was as pessimistic as ever, thinking she would select the most inappropriate carriage, but he had rallied, cheered by her good sense, she supposed. And he did like to do the purchasing. She'd have liked to have gone with him. What, she wondered, would be the outcome of his shopping?

After approving several more designs and fabrics, Sophie, along with her maid, Anna, left Madame Clotilde's with a list in hand, complete with fabric swatches for matching, of slippers, shoes, bonnets, and reticules that Madame insisted necessary for her fashionable appearance.

"Ah, the perennial woman shopper, I perceive," came a voice from behind her.

Sophie turned to greet Lord Chessyre with a warm smile. He was such a genial man in spite of that look of ennui he cultivated. That was all a sham, she was convinced.

"Good day, sir." With a raise of a brow she indicated to Anna that she could step back a trifle. Sophie would not come to harm from this man.

"May I walk with you to your next shop, my angel?" The earl said, laughter lighting his eyes.

"Lord Chessyre, I am most certainly not your angel, nor anyone else's come to think on it," Sophie scolded, her reproving tone spoiled by her amusement.

"Then I have hope," he answered.

"I suspect you will hope for a long time to come. I doubt you are ready for wedlock." She flashed him a keen look, aware that while he might say flirtatious things, marriage was the last item on his agenda. She wanted a gentleman ready to settle down in an agreeable arrangement. She didn't want to believe she was too particular, but it was unfortunate that every time she tried to imagine what a husband might look like, he strongly resembled Jonathan.

She paused before the door of a recommended shoemaker. "I shall take leave of you now. I doubt if you have the slightest interest in slippers."

He bowed gallantly over her hand, saying, "It all depends on whose feet are in the slippers, ma'am. I trust I shall see the results at the Hethering ball?"

"Perhaps. I shan't forget I promised you a waltz. All I must do in the interim is to snag a nod from a patroness."

"Tiresome, but please do. I look forward to our dance." His smile struck her as most genuine.

Sophie permitted herself a last glimpse of him as he strode off along the narrow street before entering the shoemaker's shop. It took some time to be measured for her slippers, then to select the leathers she wished. No Denmark satin for her, she wanted something that wouldn't fall apart in one evening.

By the time she had selected suitable bonnets, reticules, stockings, and other items on the list, she was worn to a flinder and only too happy to summon a hackney. Satisfied that every item had been paid for in cash, she leaned back against the squabs with a contented sigh. This afternoon she was destined to explore the Tower of London with Henry Somerset. He was a younger brother of a peer and apparently not only well liked, but financially secure as well—an unusual situation for a younger son.

While Sophie sought out Lady Mary, Anna took the pile of parcels to Sophie's room.

"Well, you look as though you could do with a change of occupation," her ladyship observed when Sophie found her in the small sitting room.

"Not having stood for fittings, selected slippers, reticules, and bonnets by the half dozen before, I am not accustomed to such tiring activity," Sophie replied while sinking onto a cushioned chair.

Lady Mary rang for tea and sandwiches, then turned to face Sophie. "There is a message from Lord Lowell. I suppose it has to do with your carriage."

Sophie accepted the folded note, broke the seal, then read with amusement. "I have a curricle, but not the one that was on sale by the lady who rarely used it. He says it was obviously in an accident. Rather, he found an excellent buy at Tattersall's. The carriage is dark blue, picked out in white, and has blue leather upholstery. He also adds that the horseflesh is top-notch. A chestnut of rare gentleness yet with good spirit." She glanced up, then added, "It seems he has done well."

"When are you to have use of them?"

"He says he will bring them around tomorrow. Mr. Antrobus has offered to instruct me in city driving."

"Not Lord Lowell?" her ladyship queried with a raise of her expressive brows.

"Oh, Jonathan indicated he would, but I put no dependency on that. I would put him in a huff in no time, I think," Sophie observed with understanding of her cousin.

"Yet, I would not wish you to cross him," Lady Mary began, but ceased when Sophie waved a hand.

"Pooh. He fancies himself head of the family and as such makes all manner of pronouncements. He is far too much the perfectionist to be bothered with fussing over my driving. I might drive him . . . to distraction," she concluded with amusement.

A glance at the mantel clock reminded Sophie she had best change for her outing.

"You are off somewhere today. Who with and what is it to be?" her ladyship asked lazily from the comfort of her chaise longue which was covered in a particularly pretty print. A novel, marker tucked inside, sat close to hand on a pie crust table.

"Mr. Henry Somerset has promised to escort me around the Tower of London, dear lady. I vow it will be entertaining, for he is reputed to be most knowledgeable."

"Is he that young chap in the House of Commons who has been making a name for himself?" Lady Mary asked with an intent look at Sophie. "Fancy yourself as a political hostess, do you?"

"I am merely taking a look about the Tower, not interviewing a candidate for marriage today. And 'tis Mr. Fane who sits in the House of Commons."

"Remind me to pay attention when you come around to doing interviews," her ladyship said before settling back on her many cushions and picking up her novel.

Sophie laughed, then hurried to her room. Considerate of others, she did not wish to keep the gentleman waiting. So it was that within half an hour she presented herself in the entry, garbed in a pale gray lutestring carriage dress trimmed with a violet Vandyke border edged in black. It was most suitable for one who was at midpoint in mourning. She checked the tilt of her bonnet in the looking glass positioned across from the bottom of the stairs, pushing the neat jockey design back a trifle. She didn't wish it to obscure her vision. Anna stood silently by.

Promptly at two of the clock Mr. Somerset arrived and blinked when he noted Sophie was not only ready but waiting.

They wound their way through the press of traffic until they reached the east end of the city, just below London Bridge. Mr. Somerset courteously assisted Sophie from the carriage while she absorbed the scene before them. During the drive he had refreshed her memory of the Tower's history. She studied the moat as they crossed it via the stone bridge. Considering how accessible the Tower was now, the moat seemed rather a nuisance, what with the odors that arose at low tide.

It was an agreeable afternoon, although Mr. Somerset seemed more taken with Sophie's golden curls than with the Tower.

They strolled about the inner ward, then paused before each cage belonging to the animals of the royal menagerie. Sophie was surprised when told that the animals born in captivity were more ferocious than those who had been taken from the wild.

The cages appeared clean and the animals healthy, which was more than she might say for the children she had seen along the streets in the vicinity.

Her favorite was not the apartments where prisoners awaited their executions, but the Jewel Office where she saw the imperial crown, the golden orb, and other regalia belonging to the monarch. "When," she inquired of the patient Mr. Somerset, "do you think these may be used once again? The King grows worse daily and our Prince is most impatient to assume the throne."

"There are those who wish to do away with the monarchy, considering the behavior of our noble Prince and his wife. I am not one of these, however. As to when he becomes George the Fourth is anyone's guess. His father is a rather tough old fellow. He may linger for years."

"Poor man,' Sophie murmured, but whether her sympathy was directed at the ailing King or his anxious son was not revealed.

Mr. Somerset returned her to Lower Brook Street with all due propriety and praise. "I have escorted many a lady through the Tower, and I must say you asked the most sensible questions and listened more carefully to my answers than any to date. I congratulate you, Miss Garnett. I do, indeed."

She bade him farewell, then headed for the drawing room. Upon leaving the entry hall she discovered Jonathan coming down the stairs.

"Another swain conquered, I suppose," he said with a slight edge to his voice.

"Mr. Somerset is a very nice man; do not disparage him. Would you have patiently answered all my questions at the Tower of London?"

"That is where you spent the afternoon?"

"Indeed, sir. Now I must change to go driving with Mr. Antrobus." She made to pass him on the stairs and he put out a detaining hand.

"I shall deliver the carriage at ten tomorrow morning. I trust you will be here then? Or are you off exploring another part of London?"

"Lord Crewe has promised to obtain tickets to view the British Museum. He is good friends with one of the trustees, it seems," Sophie quietly explained.

"It is to be hoped that you will be allowed time in which to view the objects within instead of being hustled through the place at a rapid pace. At any rate, I shall see you in the morning." He ran down the remaining steps and through the arch to the entry hall, crossing the black-and-white marble squares in a rush, as though anxious to leave.

It was a thoughtful Sophie who changed into a pale violet dress. Looking at herself in the glass, she decided it would be a good thing to have all her new clothes soon. She was becoming tired of alternating amongst her current wardrobe. She gathered up reticule, parasol, and gloves before walking down to the entry.

Jonathan had worn not only a superb corbeau coat over neat biscuit pantaloons but an expression she had not seen before. Something bothered him, she could see that. She hoped he was *not* mulling over ways to make her tell him where all the money had come from. Apparently three hundred pounds had been sufficient for the curricle and the horse—at least she hoped it was.

"Mr. Antrobus, do you think three hundred pounds would cover the expense of a curricle plus a horse to draw it?" she inquired once they were past the busier part of Mayfair and driving through the leafy glades of the outer portion of the parkland.

"I should think so. Depends on the condition of both. You are concerned about your purchase?"

"I worry that my cousin will conceal the price from me. Perhaps I have not given him sufficient funds. I will not be owing him money," she quietly insisted.

"You must allow a gentleman to make a lady, particularly a pretty cousin, a gift if he so chooses," Mr. Antrobus chided. "Trust your cousin to do all that is proper. I cannot think so dignified a gentleman would consider anything beyond the pale, you know."

At which gentle rebuke Sophie dropped the subject. Instead she requested that Mr. Antrobus show her the finer points of driving a pair.

"If you wish," he agreed mildly. He carefully explained what she was and was not to do, then handed over the reins to her.

Intrepid man, thought Sophie as she neatly guided the horses along the lane, putting them through their paces with great delight. "Excellent beasts," she complimented.

They entered a crossroads at the same time a gig approached at great speed. Sophie did her best to control the horses, not wishing to cause them any harm, yet wanting to avoid a collision with the gig whose driver appeared to be well foxed—judging by his erratic course.

What happened was purely accidental, but it caused laughter for months to come whenever called to mind. The gig dashed directly into their path, tangling carriages, horses, not to mention occupants in a truly Gordian knot. Sophie doubted if the most clever lacemaker could have devised a more difficult web to unravel. Fortunately, no one appeared to be hurt badly.

"I cannot believe this," Sophie muttered to the driver of a dray who stopped to help. He was aided by a gentleman from a passing landau, whose ladies silently stared in horror at the debacle. Another carriage drew to a halt and that gentleman came to assist as well. Before long the roads in all directions were blocked with carriages. Some helped, others gawked. Poor Mr. Antrobus looked at though he wished he had never heard of Sophie Garnett.

Eventually it was all straightened out and miracle of miracles, the carriage belonging to Mr. Antrobus had but minor damage, which Sophie offered to cover. Of course her suggestion was declined.

"I feel dreadful, sir," Sophie said as Mr. Antrobus tooled the carriage at a sedate pace in the direction of Lower Brook Street. "I should have been able to avoid the mishap."

"Fellow was a fool, driving when three sheets to the wind," muttered the much-tried Mr. Antrobus.

"I thank you for trying to teach me," Sophie said meekly. "I only hope my cousin does not hear of this."

Lady Mary was of the opinion that the accident might be talked about, but that Sophie would escape censure since the driver of the gig had made such a fool of himself.

"What a pity that the carriages required so much help in untangling. However, I am simply glad you were unhurt," she concluded.

Sophie was not so sanguine about the chances of escaping reproof, particularly from Jonathan. "We shall see if anything is said this evening," she declared.

The ladies went up to dress for the Hethering ball.

Sophie found the new gown of cloud white Florence satin spread out on her bed for display. She popped into the hall and called to her ladyship, "Did you see the offering from Madame Clotilde? How lovely! I shall be able to wear something new after all. I did not especially look forward to wearing my black." She returned to touch the exquisite fabric with reverent fingers.

So it was that they entered the Hethering ballroom with Sophie wearing the heavenly creation of softest satin. It rustled gently as she walked at Lady Mary's side to meet one of the patronesses, Lady Sefton.

This lady could not fail to be impressed with the dazzling creature presented to her by the stately Lady Mary. Her ladyship's regal appearance nicely offset the ethereal beauty of her companion. And Sophie's lovely manners were such that Lady Sefton soon gave permission for Sophie to waltz. How could anyone so divine commit any sin in public?

They were approached by Lord Crewe and Mr. Somerset. Both gentlemen desired to stand up with the vision in cloud white. Before long a throng of superbly groomed gentlemen descended upon Sophie, determined to obtain a dance with the most heavenly creature seen in ages.

At this point Jonathan entered the ballroom and grimaced at the sight of several gentlemen he knew well making a cake of themselves over his little cousin. Quickly elbowing his way to the center of the throng, he made the crowd melt away at his casual look of disdain.

Lord Chessyre ambled up behind him and said in a scolding manner, "Jonathan, how could you spoil your cousin's court? A beautiful girl deserves no less." Turning to Sophie, he added, "I trust you have saved a waltz for me?"

"Of course," Sophie replied steadily without looking at Jonathan. "I always keep my promises."

"Well, I do not in the least care who commanded your first dance, I shall claim it by right of seniority," Jonathan said with a look at Sophie that boded ill.

Her program had every dance spoken for and she did not know what to say when Lord Crewe appeared to claim his minuet.

"Sorry, Crewe. I fear you will have to be satisfied with escorting my cousin around the British Museum. I need to speak with her. Matter of some importance, you know."

His lordship didn't know, but he was far too much the gentleman to argue with Sophie's cousin.

"What is it that you must needs tear me away from my partner?" Sophie demanded quietly under her breath while trying to look as though nothing was amiss.

"I understand there was a bit of a tangle in the park today. The tale was all over the club when I stopped by there. Seems a young woman who should have known better was trying to drive a pair of prime chestnuts when a very drunk driver of a gig decided to cross her path. Would you know anything about this?" He gave her a meaningful glance.

Sophie chanced a look at her cousin and replied when they drew close once again, "You know very well who that lady was. It was unavoidable."

"You were dammed lucky you were not killed," he said in a ferocious whisper.

"Jonathan, there is no need for that sort of language," she scolded before slipping away in the pattern of the dance.

"You expect me to turn over that fine carriage and a pair of splendid horses to a cow-handed driver tomorrow?" he said when next they joined hands.

"I paid for them," she replied tersely, flashing him a winsome smile that had the gentlemen nearby sighing.

"You will take lessons from me, my girl, before I release them into your possession." This was said with a firmness Sophie had not previously associated with Jonathan.

"Very well," she agreed with a sudden capitulation that surprised even her. Jonathan gave her a suspicious look, then sighed.

"Stubborn wench. You never fail to amaze me. Be prepared come morning to learn how to drive a pair of high-stepping chestnuts."

"You are the best of cousins," she replied lightly, glad to be over the ground so easily.

At the conclusion of the minuet Jonathan paraded with her along the edge of the ballroom to where Lady Mary was seated with Lady Sefton.

"I suppose you conned her ladyship into permitting you to waltz," he muttered in her ear.

"She so graciously suggested I might enjoy that dance, yes." Sophie looked up at her cousin with a sweetness of expression that belied her anger. "You are determined to think and believe the worst of me, for some reason. I cannot imagine what I did to you to make it so. But know that I will not tolerate a heavy hand. I intend to find an agreeable husband before the Season is over. If necessary, should two gentlemen who both seem worthy seek my hand, I might wish your opinion. But otherwise, do keep your nose in your own affairs. I feel certain they will benefit from your attention more than I will."

He did not reply immediately but gave her a hard stare that was most disconcerting. "Agreeable?" he said, latching on one word that had struck him as impossible. "There is no such creature where you are concerned."

"Lord Crewe, Mr. Somerset, and even your good friend, Lord Chessyre, are all that is agreeable—to my knowledge. If you know something to their detriment, you may speak of it and I will listen. Otherwise . . . ?" She paused, turning to gaze into his eyes, now black with feeling. "We once were friends."

"I doubt we can be that again, if we ever were," he said with a thoughtful frown.

Sophie sensed a rise in the tension that lately had been near palpable whenever they were close. She didn't know what to make of it.

He reached for her wrist to check her program. "Antrobus has bravely requested the supper dance." He drew a line though the gentleman's name, earning a protest from Sophie. "I have a prior claim," he said, daring Sophie to argue with him.

"I do not see why," she replied, taking a step in the direction of Lady Mary.

"We need to talk," he said by way of explanation before handing her over to Mr. Somerset in front of Lady Mary.

Sophie gladly walked away with Henry Somerset, glancing back to see Jonathan deep in conversation with Lady Mary.

That poor lady had not the slightest idea what she was letting herself in for when she'd agreed to come to London with Sophie. Oddly enough, she seemed to enjoy herself a great deal, listening to the tales Sophie relayed and appearing to relish the confrontations she had with Jonathan.

Sophie relished them as well, in a way. They made her feel alive as nothing else did. She was usually a quiet person not given to argumentation, but Jonathan seemed to bring out the stubborn streak deep within her that she deplored. Her papa had always praised her for her tact. That skill seemed to fall by the wayside whenever she encountered her cousin. How could she have been so blunt when telling him to mind his own business? Because, a small voice within replied, he would pay you no heed otherwise. True. Too true.

Mr. Somerset was grace itself when it came to a cotillion. Sophie performed her part with equal elegance, an ability noted by many. When they retired from the dance, it was to the eager besiegement of gentlemen not given a place on her program. Sophie was chagrinned to find she was enormously pleased to have Jonathan see her as such a success.

When it came to the supper dance Mr. Antrobus was nowhere to be seen. Sophie toyed with her ivory fan, wondering if Jonathan had truly disposed of the kind gentleman who had in vain attempted to teach her how to handle a pair.

"I trust you are not looking for your erstwhile instructor," Jonathan said from her side, suddenly appearing like one of those specters in a Gothic novel.

"Lord Lowell, I believe you overstep the boundaries," she said, trying to scold him and failing miserably.

"Come—before the lobster patties are gone. I find I am dashed hungry."

"I have not observed you dancing. And I had not realized that talking could produce an appetite."

"That shows how little you know, cousin," he quipped.

"You say that in the same manner that you used to say 'brat.' I do have a name, you know. Use it," she urged sweetly, smiling while gritting her teeth.

"Now, Sophie Charlotte, do not climb on your high ropes with me," he admonished with a sudden grin. "I have known you since you were in leading strings. Indeed, before that. I seem to recall peeping into your cradle in the dim, dark past. You were an enchanting baby—you scarcely ever cried." His smile was almost paternal, odiously so.

"There is a distinct disadvantage to having known someone from that age," Sophie complained. "How could I ever hope to impress you when you can recall me in infant clothes?"

"You wish to impress me?" he said with a quick glance at her face.

"Never," she denied firmly. "Do fetch me something to eat before I collapse from dire hunger."

"Surely," he said. "And then we will have our little talk."

At which point Sophie's appetite flew out the window. What manner of scold did he intend to bestow on her now? It seemed to her that he had said quite enough already.

Chapter Six

"Here," Jonathan said, plunking down two plates filled with delectable food on one of the dainty tables Lady Hethering had provided for guests, "settle down and we can have our little session."

"My lord, do you have any notion how ominous that sounds?" Sophie said with constraint.

He ignored her comment and continued to speak, while handing her the necessary cutlery and summoning a footman for glasses of the delicate white wine for which Lord Hethering was famous. "I will deliver your carriage and the horses in the morning as promised. However, there has been a slight change of plans." Jonathan reflected that if someone had told him two months ago that he would offer to give Sophie driving lessons he would have certified them daft. "I will teach you to handle the equipage and cope with the horses in London parks."

"Not in traffic?" she inquired, her tone dulcet.

"Given time, I expect you could do anything you pleased—even cope with London traffic. But do you truly wish that? A chair would be faster and safer."

She ignored the chair remark and thought a bit while chewing something she had popped into her mouth in an absent moment. Then it struck her. He had said the word *"horses."*

"Tell me, why two horses? I should think that one would do admirably," Sophie asked while stabbing a lobster patty and wishing it were Jonathan.

"The beauty of two is that should one go lame, the other will bring you safely home again," he replied with perfectly good sense.

"How could I possibly argue with that?" she wondered aloud. "Of course, that presupposes that I will be driving in the country for such a need to arise."

"Even in the parks, one can encounter trouble." His dark eyes searched her face, then he added, "Afraid to try it, my girl? I'd not thought you a coward."

"Never!" Sophie snapped back before considering what all was involved. It would mean daily drives with Jonathan and that would be more punishment than she deserved. Groping for excuses, she said, "I would have thought that teaching a mere woman would be a task you'd never do."

"So did I," he admitted—to Sophie's amazement.

"What? Then why offer, my lord?"

"Because I fear for the public should Antrobus try to instruct you. And stop 'my lording' me all over the place. I'd far rather you called me Jonathan."

"I fear that would not be proper. Even if I called you Cousin Jonathan, you and I know that it is a distant connection—third cousins to be precise. It would never do." She slanted a mocking look at him, then returned her gaze to her plate, knowing it a far safer object. "Besides you have ever been known for your reserve. Think of the proprieties."

"You worry about proprieties? What about the source of your money? Is Lady Mary helping you?"

"She kindly insisted upon my sharing her house with her, but she ceased to pay me some weeks ago. We are merely friends at this point." Sophie gave him a frank look, then added, "Living with her saves money."

"Where *did* you obtain the money, cousin?" he growled at her, inching closer in his determination to find out the truth.

"You may style yourself as head of the family, but that does not mean I must reveal my personal life to you. How that money came to me is none of your affair—as I believe I have mentioned on more than one occasion. My source is secret. Leave be, Jonathan," she said quietly, her cerulean blue eyes gazing directly into his.

He swallowed hard, noting that those eyes could never appear more innocent than now, nor more enticing. Her flawless skin, that rose-tinted mouth, not to mention those beguiling eyes, capped with the riot of blond curls—somewhat ashen in hue and glinting with silver accents, given the candlelight in the room, served to make him forget all the resolves he had made about keeping his distance from his young and beautiful cousin.

"Yes, well, I shouldn't wish to make you uncomfortable with persisting in this vein. But I shall find out, one way or another," he promised.

"That is guaranteed to give me sound sleep," she countered without humor.

"May I join you or is this a private party?" Lord Chessyre asked in a bantering tone, yet his gaze seemed serious.

Realizing that others might consider his interest in his cousin to be inappropriate or worse, Jonathan nodded a welcome he didn't feel. "By all means."

Looking as relieved, as though rescued from a dire fate, Sophie stretched out a hand. "Please do. I was so interested in what you were telling me earlier about your home in the country. My cousin is preparing me to drive on country roads. I am to have two horses for my curricle, if you please."

"That is not precisely accurate, my dear," Jonathan said in an aside.

"You are to give this angel lessons?" Chessyre said, almost choking on his wine. "But you never . . ."

"Into each life a situation like this must fall. And, having known my cousin since the cradle, I can vouch that she is not nor ever was an angel. Tormentor might be a better word for it," Jonathan responded, thinking he had never spoken a truer word.

"I can see you are too close to the matter. If there is anyone on earth who more deserves the title of angel I have yet to meet her," Lord Chessyre gallantly replied.

"I shall be an excellent student, you may be sure," Sophie assured them both. "For, as soon as I have reasonably mastered the skills required, I shall be free."

"There is a groom's seat attached behind the body of the curricle. I'd not have you driving without protection," Jonathan insisted.

"Did the sum I handed you cover it all?" Sophie asked in a

low voice. "And do not think to lie to me, for I shall find out soon enough."

"Actually, I believe there are a few pounds left over. Do you wish them now or later?" he said with a mocking glance at Sophie.

"Beast," she hissed at him. "You . . . you . . . Oh, I cannot think what more to call you."

"I shall call for you at ten in the morning," Jonathan said, then rose, knowing he could not tolerate sitting so close to Sophie another moment. "I leave her to you, Chessyre. Handle with befitting care."

Sophie watched her cousin stride through the growing throng of guests who were gathering about the table laden with delicacies and frowned.

"It ought not be too bad," Lord Chessyre said in a comforting tone. "And if you like, you can practice driving with me." He bestowed an amused look on her hopeful face.

Sophie considered his offer. How angry might Jonathan be were she to accept Lord Chessyre's kind proposal to help her? "That is most generous of you, my lord. I shall take you up on your kind offer and then I shall be done with the teaching all the sooner."

"Is it such a very bad thought—to be under your cousin's direction?" Chessyre asked thoughtfully, studying Sophie's face until she wondered what he found there.

"Not really, I suppose," she temporized. "We have always been at odds, ever since I can recall." Particularly since that forfeit kiss four years ago, she added to herself. The farewell salute at Lowell Hall had not helped matters, either. The memory of the warm touch of his lips against hers had not disappeared as hoped.

"Whatever intriguing thought is running through your head now?" his lordship teased. "No, do not say, I fear it has nothing to do with me. Now, to change the topic, would you consent to go driving with me tomorrow?"

Sophie gave him a startled look. He had been described to her as a man who preferred widows and birds of paradise, not young unmarried women. He assuredly was not on the lookout for a wife. "I would be delighted, sir."

Whatever prompted his decision to enlarge his circle, she would welcome his attentions. He was handsome; blond where Jonathan was dark, and gray-eyed where her cousin had a midnight gaze that seemed to pierce her heart. Both men were tall and powerfully built. However Lord Chessyre made her feel protected, whereas Jonathan made her feel hunted in more ways than one.

"As I recall," he said with a glance at the doorway, "you promised me a waltz at this ball. May I claim it? I believe one is to be played after supper."

"That would be lovely," Sophie said with enthusiasm, ignoring the food remaining on her plate, only drinking the last of the delicate wine. It seemed to go straight to her head. She accepted Lord Chessyre's hand and gave him a blissful smile of joy. She adored dancing, particularly the waltz. She had learned it just before Papa died and life had changed forever. To think she might waltz again was pure magic.

He proved to be an excellent dancer, holding her with tender regard at just the precise distance demanded. Sophie closed her eyes, giving herself up to the wanton rhythm of the music.

"May I not see your lovely eyes?" he teased as he whirled her into another turn, going round and around the room in slow revolutions. "You seem to enjoy the waltz."

Sophie considered his remark. "I do enjoy waltzing and you are particularly good at it. I should guess that you are good at anything you choose to do. You have that look about you. Not that you are the perfectionist that Jonathan is, but rather someone who knows what he wants to do and does it." She gave him a contented look, one of warm regard and happiness at doing something she enjoyed.

"I must say you do well at conversation. I had no idea that young ladies were so delightful." He gazed down at her as the waltz drew to a close.

"And you are so ancient," she scoffed. "You are no older than Jonathan and he is but a few years beyond me."

"Sometimes it is more than age. Experience can make a great difference, my pet." His face assumed a serious mien for a moment before relaxing again when he looked at her.

She didn't take umbrage with his endearment as she might

have with Jonathan. Rather, she gave a little laugh and promised she looked forward to seeing him on the morrow.

As was customary, he returned her to Lady Mary upon completion of their little promenade following the dance.

That dear lady watched Lord Chessyre walk away to the card room with a considering expression. "He certainly is a handsome chap, is he not?"

"Not only handsome, but enormously thoughtful. He offered to assist me with the driving lessons so I can be rid of Jonathan all the sooner."

"And that is important? To be rid of your cousin?" Lady Mary surveyed Sophie with a frown, quite as though she could not believe her ears.

"What if he learns about the money and is advised by his solicitor that because the money was found in Lowell Hall it legally belongs to Jonathan? I fear that I might have to give it up to him. My uncle's quixotic sense of humor is known to us, but a solicitor might see matters differently."

"I suppose it is a possibility. You think he might do such a thing?" Lady Mary inquired with concern for her little friend and erstwhile companion.

"I sense he wishes to be in control of me, for whatever reason that might be. I suspect he will want perfection from me in driving the curricle and that terrifies me."

"You fear that he might intimidate you to the point where nothing goes right?"

Sophie sighed. "True. That is why I am pleased to accept Lord Chessyre's suggestion that he assist me."

"Take care. He is not some young puppy up from Oxford, you know. He is a mature gentleman who has been on the Town for some years. I hope you know what you are doing, my dear."

"So do I," Sophie confided with a sigh.

"I am pleased you do not give up easily. What a tenacious little thing you are," her ladyship said with a chuckle.

The topic was closed when Mr. Somerset returned to claim his second dance.

It was almost the time Lady Mary had set for their departure when Jonathan appeared at Sophie's side.

"You have enjoyed a pleasant evening, cousin?"

"I have," Sophie agreed. If she had to leave London this moment she would have known more pleasure than she had expected for some long time.

"I claim your last dance." His voice and manner brooked no opposition, least of all from the young sprig of nobility who dared to step forward at this moment. Jonathan gave him a look and the lad faded into the guests with nary a whisper. That it was his third dance with his cousin, Jonathan ignored. She was a relative. That made things different in his book.

"That was rude, cousin. I'd not thought you uncivil," Sophie scolded gently.

"But then, do you know me all that well?" Jonathan escorted her to the floor with a flourish.

Sophie was dismayed to hear the strains of a waltz, the last of the evening, drift over the assembled throng.

"I promise I will not bite you. Smile at me," Jonathan ordered as he placed his hand at her waist.

She did as bade, finding the warmth of her hand in his almost overpowering. She discovered him to be an excellent partner. Perhaps she did not experience the lighthearted joy she had with Lord Chessyre, but then, his lordship did not touch her as did her cousin.

Jonathan knew he was courting disaster, but a waltz was an acceptable way he might hold his dangerous little cousin in his arms. Did she have the slightest idea how her smile affected him? Did she comprehend how impossible was his interest in her? Or did she even guess there was an interest? Every time they drew close to one another a spark ignited a quarrel. She probably thought he disliked her. Goodness knew he wanted to.

"I adore waltzing," she murmured to his cravat.

"You are most adept at it. I suspect you have a natural talent for the dance. Some do. Graceful as a willow, some would say."

"You know better. More likely to climb the willow, I fancy you are thinking. I am beyond that now, Jonathan."

"I believe you, cousin. I believe you."

They exchanged no more words, but circled in silence until

the dance came to an end. Jonathan paraded her along the edge of the room, then escorted her to her aunt.

"It is time we leave," Lady Mary said, noticing the wall that seemed to separate the two at her side. "Come, let us thank our hostess and hope our carriage will not be too long arriving."

Jonathan and Sophie obediently followed her ladyship, said all that was proper to Lady Hethering, then walked to where the carriage awaited. Tom Coachman had judged the time to a nicety, knowing his mistress well.

Sophie feigned sleepiness and leaned back against the squabs, watching Jonathan from beneath her lashes. The light from passing houses and lampposts cast interesting shadows on his face. He disturbed her greatly. And he must never learn that little fact. How she would endure the lessons she didn't know. But she would. And pass with flying colors.

"You smile, Sophie," he said. "Anticipation regarding your curricle and team, I trust?"

"Yes," she answered, thinking that in a way he was right, only not quite the way he believed.

In the morning she dithered in selecting her wardrobe for the drive. Another box had come from Madame Clothilde, holding the violet carriage dress she had requested be finished as soon as might be. She looked at it with longing. It was dashing, the latest mode. Jonathan would notice that, she suspected. Would it bring him to the topic of money again?

But she truly did not wish to wear the black, nor the other garment he had seen on her.

When she joined Lady Mary in the morning room that dear lady gave an approving nod. "I can see the touch of Madame Clotilde in that dress. What a lovely shade. My, it came sooner than I expected."

Sophie smoothed down the pretty violet cloth, thinking that she was a vain fool. She'd not been able to resist looking her best. "Thank you, I do like it. I felt I needed a bit of a boost this morning."

"You make too much of a little lesson. I am certain your cousin will not expect a great deal of you. After all, you have driven before, have you not?" Lady Mary set aside the morning paper she enjoyed reading at the breakfast table.

"Only in the country and I fancy it is much easier there than in the city. Actually, I am more worried he might try to winkle out the truth of the money at a time when my mind is otherwise occupied."

"I see what you mean. But then, will you not have a groom along? Or Anna at the very least? She is a most sensible woman."

"I hope it will be the new groom."

"How does the money go? You do not overspend, do you?"

"I placed the consols and annuity in the bank along with a sizable amount of the cash. I have kept just enough to pay my way as I go. I must say, the man at the bank nearly had a spasm when I entered and told him I wished to open an account. Women"—she flashed a look at her ladyship—"do not manage their own finances. Had I not known that there were other women who had accounts at this particular bank, I'd have left. Lady Anne, bless her heart, directed me."

"Well, at least I do not have to worry you have tucked the money under your mattress."

Sophie nodded, then poured out tea and buttered her toast. She managed to eat that, but little else. Her stomach was tied in knots.

Promptly at ten, Jonathan presented himself at the front door along with a groom. She said good-bye to Lady Mary as though parting from her forever, then joined Jonathan. She inspected the carriage, approving all she saw. It was modest in looks yet appeared to be good quality. The horses were fine chestnuts and she walked forward to become acquainted with them.

Jonathan watched her in silence for a time, then directed her to climb up in the carriage. The groom moved to hold the reins and Sophie prudently left the whip—a most excellent one, she noted—in the socket until she had settled in place.

Then it began. If she thought she knew how to handle a horse and carriage she soon discovered she had a great deal to learn about the matter.

He handed her the whip and instructed her precisely how to

hold it in her hand about the top ferrule, her thumb pointing slightly upwards and at the same time holding the point of the thong—which ought to lap around the stick three or four times, not more—about a couple of inches below the top of it. Sophie complied, wondering if they would ever leave the front of the house on Lower Brook Street.

The sun peeked through the clouds, cheering her immensely. It was like a benediction, encouraging her to believe she would succeed.

At last Jonathan told her to head for the park. He was alert, as was the groom seated behind them. The top of the curricle was down and the groom had an unobstructed view. It also meant that Jonathan would be most circumspect in what he said to her. Or asked of her.

With polite ruthlessness, Jonathan put her through her paces with the horses time and time again. There was nothing he did not demand of her—corners to be mastered, paces to be gone through. She could feel the sweat on her hands inside the durable leather of her driving gloves. When he finally ordered her to return to the house on Lower Brook Street she could have cried with relief.

Yet she had to admit she found it exhilarating to control two such prime bits of horseflesh. They truly were high-steppers, dainty and perfect for a lady to drive in the park.

"I would prefer the carriage and horses to be in my stable," Jonathan said, interrupting her thoughts. "It is asking a great deal of Lady Mary to make room for them in her small stable in the mews. I have plenty of space."

Sophie accepted the truth of his statement without ill will. Even if she paid the bill for the feed and care of her horses, it crowded the others, not to mention that the large traveling coach left little space for a vehicle even as small as the curricle.

"I may summon the carriage and pair anytime I please? There will be no restrictions, other than sensible ones like not going out in a rainstorm or some such silliness?" Her voice was commendably quiet and her manner tactful, but she longed to be able to tell him to jump in the Thames.

"Practical girl," he replied in approval of her acceptance of his suggestion. "You have good hands and a light touch with the horses. By the time I am done with you, you will be a first-rate driver, my dear cousin."

Too astounded to answer this encomium, Sophie could only stare at him when he picked her up and swung her to the ground. She glanced at the groom, now standing at the horses' heads, a mild grin on his face. Apparently he also felt she had done well.

Never had Sophie in all her life felt quite as victorious as at this moment. Jonathan approved of something she had accomplished. Would she ever recover?

"I cannot take you out tomorrow morning because of a previous appointment, but if you agree, I shall be here the following morning. Is that satisfactory?"

"Indeed, yes," Sophie replied with heartfelt pleasure. Perhaps she would muddle through the driving lessons after all.

Jonathan gave her a small packet, admonishing her to have a care for it, then took his place in the two-wheeled carriage. Sophie watched with admiration as he drove the shiny blue vehicle along the street and around the corner.

Inside the house she slowly walked along the hall, then up the stairs until she reached the drawing room where Lady Mary sat in expectation of their return.

"Well, I see you are in one piece, at any rate," her ladyship remarked in a dry tone.

"He said I had good hands and a light touch," Sophie repeated, still somewhat dazed by those words.

"I gather that is high praise, indeed."

"Indeed," Sophie echoed in a whisper.

"Well, far be it from me to say I told you so, but I did say it might not be as bad as you first thought," her ladyship pointed out.

"He is a dragon," Sophie said, stripping off her gloves to accept the small glass of sherry Lady Mary offered. "I never thought I would survive all he put me through today. Those poor horses—how patient they were."

"Have you thought of names for them?"

"Well, I was not told if they already have names, but I should call them Patience and Virtue. They are probably called something more appropriate like Gimcrack and Little Nell or some such thing."

"You have a packet, something your cousin wished you to have?"

Sophie turned her attention to the small package she had tossed on a chair when she entered the drawing room. Impatient, she broke the string, then unfolded the paper to see a note atop a number of pounds. She glanced at Lady Mary in astonishment. "What on earth?"

"Best read what is written on that slip of paper. Guessing is so futile." Lady Mary allowed a small smile.

The words were hastily absorbed, then reread. Sophie grimaced, then turned her gaze to her ladyship. "This is the money remaining from the sum I gave him. Since the carriage was used and in excellent condition, it didn't need a great deal of work to it, and the two horses he obtained from a stable he knew well. I suspect it is his own, although he does not say so. At any rate, the price is so low I find it difficult to believe. So . . . he returns the money and advises me to pay my other bills."

"He does not know your habit of paying as you go, then?" Her ladyship picked up the piece of needlework that had lain in her lap during this conversation, preparing to resume her occupation with needle and yarn.

"I suspect that if I were to tell him, he'd not believe me," Sophie said ruefully. "I will never permit debts to accumulate as did my father and so Jonathan should expect."

A little later in her room, Sophie counted out the pounds, then put them in her reticule. It was a greater sum than she had first thought, and she'd have returned it if she thought Jonathan would accept it.

"You wish to change, miss?" Anna inquired upon entering the room.

"Please freshen this carriage dress once I remove it. I shall be driving out come five. In the meanwhile, I will wear something else."

Anna selected one of the lovely black gowns that Jonathan had provided for Sophie at Lowell Hall. Grimacing at the funereal color, but allowing that the design was exquisite, Sophie joined her ladyship in a bit of luncheon. She was starved after eating practically nothing earlier.

When Lord Chessyre arrived shortly before five, Sophie was again dressed in her violet carriage dress, only this time with an appropriate parasol and gloves, and a delicate twilled bonnet that permitted her blond curls to peep in tantalizing charm from beneath its brim.

Lady Mary was away visiting one of her friends, so Sophie was left with Anna as attendant when Lord Chessyre arrived. They met his lordship at the foot of the stairs, then walked with him to the door, which Jenkens opened with great assurance. Anna watched as his lordship escorted Sophie to his high-perch phaeton, looking relieved she was not required to go along with them.

"How did the lesson go this morning," Lord Chessyre inquired after handing Sophie up to the open carriage, then settling beside her.

"Better than expected," Sophie said politely. "He seems an excellent teacher and certainly put me through my paces. I was happy to finish for the day, however."

"He is a noted whip, you know—member of the FHC and all that. Were you aware that he has never taught anyone, let alone a woman, to handle the reins before this? You must rate very highly in his book." He studied her as though to learn the precise relationship of this unusual pair of relatives.

"I have seen little of my cousin in the past four years. I had thought he'd forgotten me altogether. For some peculiar reason of his own, he insists upon teaching me to cope with the carriage and pair. I trust that when he has me off his hands he will head for more interesting pastures," Sophie said, hoping that her words might make it so.

Lord Chessyre smiled. He directed his team to the park and made it evident to one and all that he held Miss Sophie Garnett in no little esteem.

Sophie decided that she could learn to like this man very much if she tried.

Chapter Seven

"Would you like to try my team?" the earl inquired when they had reached the far end of the park and the throng of carriages and riders had thinned considerably.

"I would feel better were I to drive my own pair under your supervision," she replied, then gasped before adding, "What a coil. My cousin insisted upon stabling my team and housing my curricle in his mews. I have no doubt I'd not be permitted to take them out without his permission at this point. How vexing." She shared a look of exasperation with Lord Chessyre.

The earl chuckled. "Precisely what I would have done, my dear lady. However, he need not know if you practice with my team. They are prime goers and respond to a light touch. If Lowell said you have a light touch I am confident my team will come to no harm."

Sophie accepted the reins from him, thinking her soft, thin gloves were unequal to the task of protecting her hands from the reins. She need not have worried. A sweeter pair of horses couldn't have been found in all of England, she was sure. They were most responsive and very obedient and she drove along, gathering self-assurance with every yard covered.

At last, suddenly aware that they had been traveling along the park road for considerable time and had nearly reached the farthest point, she drew the carriage to a halt and handed the reins back to the earl.

"How kind of you to permit me to practice. At least now I know how a very fine carriage and pair ought to handle. Although I must confess I was a bit tense on that last corner," she admitted. "Thank you so very much, Lord Chessyre."

"I would rather hear William from your lips, but I daresay I am not on the same informal footing your cousin enjoys. And as to the driving, as soon as you had passed that first carriage with such aplomb I knew I had nothing to fear."

He smiled at her with such charm that she felt a constriction in her heart. Could it be possible to fall in love with two men at the same time? Lord Chessyre had the distinct advantage of not being a remote relative and he was certainly not trying to order her life.

"How gracious of you to say so," she said in a soft voice, her customary tranquil manner coming to the fore.

"It is unusual to find one so feminine in every way who can also control spirited animals," the earl said, his admiration for Sophie revealed in his gaze as well as his words.

"Jonathan says I have talented hands and that I am too stubborn to admit I cannot do everything I wish," Sophie said with a sigh.

The earl wisely made no comment regarding Jonathan, but turned the conversation into other channels. Sophie found her liking for the tall, quiet gentleman growing exceedingly on the drive to Lower Brook Street. Once there he handed the reins to the groom, then helped Sophie from the carriage with great courtesy.

"I look to see you this evening, perhaps?" he politely inquired, hinting for her plans but not actually asking where she might be going.

"To tell the truth I do not recall what Lady Mary intends this evening." Sophie gave him a look that unconsciously revealed her inner distress and desire to see him again.

The earl smiled, seeming well satisfied with the impression he had made on one deemed an angel by all who saw her.

Sophie entered the house, intent upon learning precisely what she was to do that evening. It said much for her state that she couldn't recall one thing about it.

Placing her parasol on the hall table along with her bonnet and gloves, Sophie went in search of Lady Mary, finding her at last in the morning room, perusing the papers.

"Well, how did the drive with the earl go, my dear? By the looks of it you are well contented."

"He is so well mannered and very handsome. I must say I am fortunate to have caught his eye. And he allowed me to drive his team for a short distance. He is a most obliging man." Sophie exchanged a look with her ladyship that indicated there was another man who was less than obliging in some ways.

"Do you remember we are pledged to the Seftons for dinner this evening?" Lady Mary rose from her chaise longue and swept Sophie along with her from the morning room. "We must dress for the occasion. I have a gown of gold tissue that well becomes me. What shall you wear? Not the blacks, I believe."

"Was anything delivered from Madame Clotilde while I was gone?" Sophie asked while hurrying along the hallway.

"Let us find out," her ladyship suggested, urging Sophie up the stairs ahead of her with a gentle nudge.

Placed across Sophie's bed was a strange-looking garment that seemed to be nothing more than a length of silvery tissue. "How odd," Sophie said, gathering up a handful of fabric to note its fragility. "It is like silver cobwebs."

"Anna," Lady Mary ordered politely, "help Sophie change into this new gown and pray that it is acceptable, 'else it must be the cloud white again."

Seeming as much puzzled by the length of fabric as the others, Anna set to work. Lady Mary went off to don her gold tissue with the assistance of Wickens. In a reasonable time she returned—to stand in the doorway as though transfixed to stone.

"My dear girl! Do you suppose Madame wishes to give a heart attack to every male in London?" She walked forward to examine the gown that hung in deceptively simple folds from beneath Sophie's bust. She turned and Lady Mary gasped in delight. The fabric drifted about Sophie's lovely form like a mist of silver, clinging, then floating away—mysterious and alluring. A single strand of pearls graced Sophie's neck and simple pearl ear bobs peeped from beneath her blond curls. Her hair was ornamented with a coronet of flowers tucked into her curls like a halo of white and gold.

"I do believe this is going to be an interesting dinner party. I wonder who else attends?" Lady Mary said after thanking

Anna for her skills. The ladies descended the stairs with care, Sophie observing how her gown seemed to have a life of its own.

"I cannot accept that image in the looking glass. I do think it is someone else there, you know," Sophie whispered lest she be overheard by their escort.

When she turned to the entry hall she found herself staring into Jonathan's face. He looked as though he had just received a blow. Sophie was about to inquire if he was all right when Lady Mary stepped forward to greet him.

"Dear sir, how kind of you to join us. I always feel so much safer with a gentleman escort while in London. One never knows about footpads and the like. Shall we?"

Jonathan appeared to recover his poise and bowed over her ladyship's hand with his customary grace. He then took Sophie's gloved hand in his and they began to walk to the front door.

"You had a pleasant drive with Chessyre this afternoon?" he asked in a rather subdued voice.

"Indeed. He is a very nice person," Sophie said warmly. She did not mention that she'd been allowed to drive his lordship's team. Let Jonathan think her improvement was due to him alone.

He handed Lady Mary up into the carriage, then offered Sophie his assistance. Pausing, he looked at her with what seemed to be a troubled gaze. "May I say that you are in stunning looks this evening. I can truthfully state that I have never seen anything to equal you. You are truly a vision of loveliness, cousin."

"Thank you, Jonathan. For once it did not sound like you would rather have used the word 'brat,' " Sophie said, twinkling a mischievous smile at him.

He said something under his breath. Although it didn't sound like "brat," it was doubtless a word she would rather not know. She found his stare disconcerting and gazed out the window in an effort to avoid his watchful eyes.

Lord and Lady Sefton greeted Lady Mary with pleasure, then turned to speak to Sophie. The earl appeared to be struck dumb but Lady Sefton had no such difficulty.

"I see the tales that have reached my ears are true. London is indeed graced with a celestial beauty."

"Just do not make the mistake of thinking there is anything angelic inside that exquisite package, my lady," Jonathan replied in a teasing manner. "I know otherwise," he said with the ease of one who was accustomed to the vision at his side as well as being a relative.

"Nonsense. You are simply familiar with your cousin, I imagine. She will make a splash, if I make no mistake."

"A seraph who swims—how novel," Jonathan muttered as he guided Sophie from the entry hall into the drawing room, where a number of others gathered.

The misty silver gown garnered the same reaction here as with Jonathan and the earl. Every man present was transfixed at the image that floated at Lord Lowell's side, while every woman appeared willing and ready to tear Sophie from limb to limb. An exception was Lady Anne Radcliffe, who, with her husband, Cecil, walked over to join the newcomers.

"How droll. Trust Sophie to turn the *ton* upside down. Shall I tell them of your girlhood escapades, dearest Sophie? I distinctly recall several that were most creative." Lady Anne grinned at her school chum.

Sophie laughed, a low musical sound that captured the hearts of the gentlemen fortunate to edge close to the little group. "Rubbish," said the very down-to-earth Sophie in reply to this suggestion.

"*I* should like to hear the tales," Jonathan inserted, looking annoyed at the expressions on the faces of the gentleman in the room. Even Cecil looked a trifle dazed.

This plan was foiled by the arrival of the last of the guests and the announcement of dinner.

All was done according to precedent—almost. Instead of the Duchess of Portland walking in at the side of the Earl of Sefton, the large Irish earl had walked over to Sophie, declaring that angels from heaven took precedence over mere mortals.

Embarrassed by the attention, Sophie threw a beseeching glance at the duchess. She was a lady possessing a good sense of humor and smiled in return. Emily Molyneax, Countess of

Sefton, might be the highest *ton* but her husband was a gamester of the topmost sort and not above creating a bit of silliness if he chose.

Actually, the dinner was delightful. The earl paid her far too much attention and Jonathan, seated far down the table, looked extremely vexed whenever she caught his eye. But the food was marvelous.

"Nice to see a gel who enjoys her food," the earl said.

Since she had learned that he prided himself on his gastronomic expertise she suspected that the earl had checked the menu as well as his wife.

"How could one not enjoy such excellent food?" Sophie said pleasantly. "For example, the sauce on the cod is outstanding and as to the harrico of mutton . . . well, I cannot recall when I have tasted such quite as flavorful." She took another bite of the ragout, savoring the flavor.

The earl perked up. "By Jove, a gel who not only has looks but can speak with intelligence. I should say you ought to be able to pick a husband wherever you please!"

After that unfortunate remark, one that drew far too many eyes, Sophie confined herself to her food and quiet replies to the earl as well as the gentleman on her other side, the Earl of Erne, another of the Irish peers.

The Duchess of Portland, seated across from Sophie, studied her off and on throughout the meal. When Lady Sefton signaled that it was time for the ladies to leave the dining table and retreat to the drawing room for their tea and conversation, Sophie found Her Grace strolling beside her.

"Do you have this effect all the time, my dear? Or is it simply that Madame Clotilde has outdone herself?"

Sophie grimaced at the outrageous question. Well, a duchess could say anything she pleased and get away with it.

"I fancy Madame's talents exceeded previous efforts, Your Grace," Sophie said modestly.

"Well, whatever it is, you certainly captured the heart of every gentleman here this evening. I wonder what would happen should you wear that gown at Carlton House? At least you most likely would not have to worry about being overheated. The fabric looks to have little ability to warm you."

"Neither do most muslins," Sophie reminded her. She was a bit tired of the not-so-subtle comments on her gown and looks. What woman wouldn't make the most of what was given her?

The duchess raised her brows in surprise, then welcomed Lady Sefton and Miss Tewksbury. The conversation became general and Sophie did her best to ignore any comments on her personal appearance. It was one thing to know you looked your best. It was quite another to be the object of dislike because gentlemen were fascinated with what they saw.

They left very early, Jonathan nudging her toward Lady Mary and then saying that Sophie had an early appointment on the morrow. Unfortunate, but there you were.

"I do not have an appointment in the morning, early or otherwise," she whispered angrily after they had bid their host and hostess good evening. Lord Sefton had gazed after them with obvious regret.

"You do now," was the terse reply.

Nothing more was said on the way home and Sophie worried about what Jonathan was going to do or say next. He looked frightfully angry. Even when she had done something dreadful as a child he hadn't looked this furious.

Lady Mary stood beside Sophie in the entry, preventing Jonathan from uttering anything other than generalities. At least he possessed that sense, to know that her ladyship would not tolerate a dressing down while she was there.

Sophie flicked a glance at the front door after it had closed behind the departing Jonathan and sighed. "It would have been better had you let him boil over now."

"Nonsense," her ladyship declared as she marched up the stairs with Sophie. "Let him simmer and stew all night. By morning he ought to be well done and perhaps his equilibrium will be restored. Or at the very least his common sense. What rubbish, to be upset *merely* because you displaced a duchess and captured the eye of every male attending the dinner. Well done, my girl. I never thought to see the likes of it."

"You know I did not seek the attention. It was this gown." Sophie whirled around in the drawing room, the misty fabric swirling about her figure, making her look like a nymph from Olympus.

A sound on the stairs brought their attention to the drawing room door. Sophie's eyes widened as Jonathan marched inside and up to where she had paused, towering over her like an avenging specter.

Sophie stood her ground and faced him, hiding well her trepidations. "Cousin Jonathan, what a surprise. I thought you had left."

Lady Mary chuckled and withdrew to a favorite cushioned chair, prepared to enjoy the battle—if there was to be one.

"You are not to wear that gown again," he began.

"Who is to prevent me from doing so?" Sophie asked sweetly. "My brother is at sea and I do not think you have that power."

"It is indecent," he muttered, running his hand through his hair to totally destroy what remained of the carefully achieved windswept his valet had created.

"I am well covered, certainly as well covered as any woman at that dinner this evening and better than Miss Tewksbury, whose neckline plunged so low I was nervous all the time we chatted.

"That is her mother's problem."

"Agreed," Sophie replied reasonably. "Jonathan, understand you do not have the right to dictate to me. I appreciate your escort, I value your instruction in driving, and I am proud to be your cousin. But you do not rule me!" She whirled about and paced to the fireplace, then turned again to see Jonathan staring at her in the same manner he had earlier—transfixed. He looked for all the world as he had when, as a child, the sweet tray had been brought out for the children to enjoy. He had loved sugarplums. However, Sophie was not a sugarplum!

"Lady Mary?" he turned to her for support.

"I am on her side," her ladyship said. "Sherry, perhaps? Or would you prefer something stronger?"

"Stronger, if you have it." He continued to look at Sophie, standing quite splendid in her lovely gown and looking somewhat defiant.

Her ladyship instructed Jenkens, who quickly brought his lordship a glass of amber liquid. Jonathan downed it in one gulp, then gasped. Looking at the empty glass, he turned to Lady Mary. "Liquid fire, madam?"

"Well, my stepbrother seems to think it serves on occasion."

"Jonathan, hear me out," Sophie pleaded, taking several steps in his direction. "I intend to have a wonderful time in London. I want to see as much as I can, do as much as I can. To be invited to the lovely homes of members of the cream of Society is beyond what I'd hoped and very much enjoyed. Madame Clotilde has created nice gowns for me and I fully intend to wear them. Cease your fussing. You remind me of my nanny!"

"Nanny! By heaven!" As though Lady Mary were not there, Jonathan swiftly crossed to confront Sophie and stare down at her face, framed by golden curls and possessing the most beautiful blue eyes ever seen. "I doubt this is like your nanny," he muttered. Then he kissed Sophie with all his expertise—short but most effective.

Sophie broke it off, stepping away from Jonathan and glaring at him like a cat whose tail had just been stepped on. "Enough, my lord. Go home. I shall see you in the morning—if you feel it is necessary. Now, good night for the second time." She crossed her arms and tapped her foot, tilting her head to give him a wicked look.

Apparently deciding he had lost his first battle with his cousin, Jonathan glared at her, then strode from the room, not even bothering to bid Lady Mary good evening.

"Insufferable man!" Sophie declared. His kiss had been tinged with the drink, tasting bitter, yet sweet. It had taken all her strength to resist his appeal. Oh, how she loved the dratted man, and how utterly furious he made her!

"I had no idea that whiskey could have that effect," Lady Mary said mildly as she guided Sophie along with her up the stairs to their bedrooms.

"I apologize, my lady," Sophie began.

"Do not, I beg you. I am having the time of my life."

Morning brought the two ladies together over the breakfast table. Lady Mary sipped her customary hot chocolate while Sophie consumed a third cup of strong tea.

"I gather you slept well?" her ladyship inquired.

"Amazingly, I did," Sophie replied. After all the tumult, she'd expected to be awake all night. In reality, after Anna had reverently taken away the gossamer gown, she had tumbled into bed and fallen promptly into a deep and refreshing sleep.

"Will your cousin show his face this morning?"

"I hope not. Perhaps he will have a loss of memory and forget all about last night?" Sophie said with a wry expression.

"At least he has not queried you again about the source of your fortune," Lady Mary said by way of comfort.

"As to that, wait until the day is over," Sophie replied with what she felt to be justified pessimism.

Jenkens brought in a lovely bouquet of flowers and handed them to Sophie, who checked the card. "From the Earl of Sefton. Mercy, I did not expect this." She glanced at Lady Mary, who was trying not to laugh.

The first bouquet was immediately followed by a dozen others. Lord Chessyre's offering stood out from all the rest, being a petite bouquet of rosebuds with a wreath of dainty starched lace around them. Sophie was sniffing their fragrance when Jenkens ushered Jonathan into the room.

"Thinking to open a flower shop, cousin?" he said, looking quite as though that fiery kiss of last evening had never occurred.

"I might, if necessary." There had been no floral offering from Jonathan. She had half expected one of apology. Not so.

He didn't comment on her provocative reply. Rather, he paced back and forth in the breakfast room until Lady Mary ordered him to sit down, he was making her dizzy.

"I have heard a number of disturbing remarks about you, my little cousin," he said at last after accepting a cup of coffee and pulling a chair from the table to seat himself on the edge of it.

Sophie waited to see if her gown had caused comments and wondered what could have disturbed him.

Lady Mary looked up from her paper and said, "What could anyone have to say about Sophie that would give you that expression, my lord?"

"Several chaps seem to be under the impression that Sophie has inherited a considerable fortune." He gave his cousin an expectant look and waited for her reply with obvious interest. If he expected her to disavow the gossip as utter rubbish he was doomed to disappointment.

"How interesting," she said at last, after sniffing the posy of roses one more time.

"Who sent you those?" Jonathan was sidetracked into asking.

"Lord Chessyre," Sophie responded, with what she fervently hoped was a dreamy smile. "He is such a handsome gentleman. I believe he is coming to call later this morning— at the appropriate time for calling, of course." She directed a sweet look at her cousin, her remark reminding him that he had come far too early in the day to be proper.

"If I knew where all that money came from, I could set the fellows straight." A crafty look briefly crossed his lordship's face before he resumed his expression of polite interest.

"That is true," Sophie replied most unhelpfully. "What a pity that since it really is none of your affair you cannot do that."

"Dash it all, Sophie, we are cousins!"

"That is certainly true," she said with maddening calm.

He threw up his hands and glared at Sophie. Resting his hands on the table before him, he continued, "Do not blame me if a rackety bunch of fortune hunters come sniffing at your door."

"Would I do such a thing, dear cousin?" Sophie said, her eyes a limpid blue.

"Are you prepared to go driving this morning?"

"I thought you had an appointment?" Sophie said, giving Lady Mary an alert glance.

"It has been changed. I imagine you are most anxious to have the carriage and pair at your command."

"That is also true. My, Jonathan, I am quite in charity with you this morning."

"You agree with me but do not tell me a thing."

"How frustrating for you," she said in her most soothing manner.

The look he gave her was indeed frustrated. He was ready to do violence, yet there was not a thing about which he could argue, really. She had made it quite evident that the source of her fortune was none of his business, no matter that he was titular head of the family. Sophie made her own rules regarding that. As to her behavior in public he could find no fault. From all he'd observed, she had put Miss Tewksbury and those other women last evening to shame. Her manners were impeccable. She was simply the most stubborn woman he had ever met.

"I shall wait here for you to change. You do still wish to drive out with me, do you not?" His eyes narrowed with speculation. Perhaps Sophie would change her mind after all that had happened last evening, particularly that kiss. He'd not been proud of his behavior, but never in his life had he been driven to such a point. Frustrating? That didn't begin to cover it.

"Allow me to finish my toast and I am yours to command— at driving, that is." She did as she indicated, put the last of her toast into that rosebud mouth, drank the remainder of her tea, then blotted her mouth daintily with her napkin before rising from the table.

Jonathan rose as well, waiting for any comment.

"It should not take me long to change into my carriage dress. Perhaps you will remain with her ladyship and peruse some of the morning paper?" So saying, Sophie quickly left the room.

Jonathan sank down on the chair once again and sighed while glancing at the papers in front of Lady Mary.

"Here, have one." She pushed several papers his way. "There is nothing in them half so interesting as what goes on in this house but that cannot be helped."

"You do realize that she is enough to drive a man mad."

"Of course. But think how dull life would be without Sophie to lighten things up."

" 'Dull' is a word one would never associate with Sophie. Not in a million years."

"You might have thought differently had you seen her the

way she was when I first met her," Lady Mary said in a casual manner.

"What do you mean?" Jonathan said, frowning at her ladyship in concern.

"Her clothes were dreary, life was without hope at the time, no money, no future. What man would marry a pauper, no matter how pretty? Pity it took a reading of a will to bring a bit of help and hope into her life."

"She was your companion," Jonathan reminded.

"True. And as such she did extremely well. She is an incredibly efficient young woman blessed with understanding far beyond her years. She handled paying my bills, arranging my transportation and traveling—rooms at inns and so forth. I shall miss her."

"Sophie is going somewhere?" Jonathan said, again feeling as though he'd been kicked.

"Oh, I feel certain that some intelligent gentleman will come along and see what a paragon exists beneath the lovely exterior. Not every man is blinded by beauty."

Jonathan made no comment to her observation, but waited with rising impatience for Sophie to return.

Lady Mary shook out her paper and scrutinized an item. "Fancy that, a fourteen-old-chit ran off with a chaplain. Went to the Chapel Royal, then took the air to Barnet. From there they dashed to Gretna Green. Both were children of baronets. The girl's mother hadn't the faintest notion as to what was going on. Her ladyship eventually caught up with them but not until they were wed." Lady Mary laughed, adding, "Says the young lady will have a very large fortune. I wonder if the chaplain would have looked at her otherwise?"

"Surely fortune is not the only reason for marriage," Jonathan found himself saying. He would have accepted Sophie without a shilling, had it been possible.

"It is for most. Tell me, do you truly think there will be fortune-hunting chaps haunting our doorstep?"

"I would not be surprised."

"Well, it will make life interesting." Her ladyship buried her nose in the paper again, leaving Jonathan to rise and wander toward the stair hall.

It was but a few minutes when Sophie came skimming down the stairs. "I am ready, if you please, thanks to Anna."

Jonathan looked at the angelic face and wondered again precisely how she had obtained all that money. Somehow he had to find out.

Chapter Eight

"Lady Mary says will you please come down to the drawing room at once," Anna said with breathless urgency as she entered Sophie's bedroom.

"At once?" Sophie looked up from the little writing desk where she sat composing a letter to her seafaring brother. She had included a reference to Jonathan's teaching her to drive a pair, but did not touch on all that had happened when he took her driving. That would never survive telling in a mere letter. Jonathan had been pleased with her improvement, but had somehow learned of her drive with Lord Chessyre, so discounted her progress—to her annoyance.

"If you please, miss. She says to tell you the first of the hunters are come."

"How diverting," Sophie said with a surprised lift of her brows. She wiped her pen point, then capped the ink bottle and placed the pen on the desk before rising. This would make another paragraph for the letter.

"Do I look well enough to face a hunter, Anna? Like an heiress, perhaps?" She grinned at the maid's confusion, then took pity on her. "Some fool has put it about that I am a great heiress. Did you ever hear such nonsense? Now I shall have to listen to all manner of silliness."

Anna inspected Sophie's appearance, tucked a curl in place, then watched her leave for the drawing room.

Entering the room, Sophie found Lady Mary in a state of bemusement. Turning slightly, Sophie discovered the source. There was a veritable tulip of the *ton* propping himself against the fireplace.

The gentleman was arrayed in a delicate-looking coat of a

lilac-patterned-print fabric with a waistcoat to match. It seemed he had selected tapestry for his garments. His breeches were an unexceptional biscuit color, and lilac clocks in his hose bordered on outrageous. Returning her gaze to his coat, she noted that he sported a posy of silk lilacs on his lapel—an enormous posy that threatened to overwhelm everyone who came near the chap. However, they blended with his coat quite nicely.

Taking note of her inspection, he preened, straightening his languid pose. Sophie could see why the fellow remained standing. His breeches were so tight he couldn't possibly have sat in them. Even his bow was limited in scope.

"Reginald Montegu, at your service, my dear Miss Garnett," the tulip gushed in fluting tones.

"Good day, sir," Sophie said, groping for a chair that she might contemplate his magnificence in comfort. Of course the reason he would seek out an heiress was readily apparent. That splendid array must cost a horrendous sum, even if it did make him look ridiculous.

"I trust you were not occupied in a significant task," the tulip continued. "I saw you in the park yesterday and desired to make myself known to the newest incomparable. Dare I say that your beauty puts the sun to shame, the moon to hide, the very earth to rejoice?"

"That is certainly a novel compliment, sir," Sophie replied, not daring to look at Lady Mary lest they both go into whoops.

"I rather thought so as well," he said absently. Then without regard to the ears of his listeners, he continued to spout similar fustian for another ten minutes. Had he thought to earn a place in the heart of the newest heiress, he was far and away off the mark.

Never had Sophie been so grateful for the dictum of Society that a proper call should be limited to fifteen minutes. She glanced at the longcase clock on the far wall and bless his tulipy heart, he got the idea that it was time for him to depart. He did so with commendable brevity.

Jenkens ushered in her cousin before she and Lady Mary could compare opinions on their first guest of the day.

"What on earth was that I encountered on my way in?" Jonathan asked, his dark eyes sparkling with mirth.

"That, sirrah, was none other than Mr. Reginald Montegu, come to pay a call," Sophie replied, her eyes clearly revealing her own amusement.

"Yes, he informed me that he wished to get a jump on all the other chaps," Lady Mary added.

"Did he now?" Sophie said with a shake of her head.

"I did warn you," Jonathan inserted.

"So you did," Sophie said with a curious look at her notable cousin. Unlike the tulip, Jonathan was garbed in a sober deep blue coat of excellent cut over a pale yellow waistcoat and gray pantaloons that tucked into highly polished Hessians. If anything, he had the look of a Corinthian, with his windswept hair and casual air. No matter when she saw him, he always looked splendid.

"Did Sophie tell you how well she did this morning?" Jonathan inquired of Lady Mary.

"No. She merely said all had gone nicely and that she had managed not to frighten a single driver. How well *is* she doing?" Lady Mary asked with a significant look at him.

"She did not frighten anyone, least of all me," he replied with a darted glance at where Sophie sat in frozen expectation. "Actually she is coming along splendidly."

"That is high praise, indeed, from a member of the Four-in-Hand Club," Sophie replied with a smile. She thawed visibly, deciding there would be no more queries regarding Lord Chessyre. She had not appreciated Jonathan's questioning on that score in the least.

"I do not resort to fulsome flattery as some," he retorted with justification, considering the nonsense with which their ears must have been assaulted not long ago.

Sophie would have thanked him for his compliment when Jenkens ushered in Lord Chessyre. He gave Jonathan an odd look, then walked to where Lady Mary was seated to make his bow to her before turning to Sophie.

"I saw you this morning. May I offer congratulations on how well you progress?" His eyes held a private message for Sophie, one she was not certain how to answer.

"Cut line, Chessyre," Jonathan said abruptly. "I know all about your private tutelage in the park."

"I daresay it is impossible to be unseen in London," Chessyre replied with good grace. "I merely wished to assist Miss Garnett in attaining her goal. No harm done, my dear fellow. You must admit she is a fast learner."

How Jonathan might have answered that was never to be known as another gentleman was ushered in by Jenkens. Mr. Somerset crossed to do just as Chessyre had—make himself pleasant to Lady Mary before turning his attention to Sophie.

She tossed a pleased look at Jonathan. Here was a man who was well off financially and had no need of an heiress. He was here simply because he wished to see her, nothing more. And he was a delightful conversationalist.

The gentlemen chatted easily with Sophie, Lady Mary, and between themselves until near the time to depart. It was then Jenkens escorted in a gentleman who most assuredly gave Sophie pause.

There was nothing obviously wrong with him. He had a military bearing and wore acceptable clothes. He knew the other gentlemen and was obviously accepted by them. It was more a feeling she had. Unease at his warm look. Discomfort in his glance about the room. She exchanged a glance with Lady Mary, who also appeared to be troubled. Outwardly, however, she was calm poise.

The other men may have entertained mixed feelings regarding Oliver Fane but such was their address that one would never know it. They exhibited cool courtesy and before long Chessyre and Somerset bore him off with them, leaving Jonathan behind.

"There was something about Mr. Fane that made me uneasy," Sophie admitted to her cousin.

"He is a member of the House of Commons and a promising politician," Jonathan said slowly. "However, I suspect that he would be glad for a bit more of the ready."

"He needs money?" Lady Mary asked bluntly.

"How curious," Sophie said with a smile at Lady Mary. "Does not everyone desire more? Except Jonathan, perhaps. How did our dear Uncle Philip leave you fixed, cousin—if I am not being presumptuous in asking," she asked with hope he might actually answer her.

"I have the estate, as you know. It is most productive, thanks to his implementing many of Coke's agricultural ideas. Management was a strong point of Uncle's, so all is well there."

"You sound as though something was not right elsewhere, however," Lady Mary prompted.

"I'd expected more funds, to tell the truth. Since I took over, sufficient money has come in to show me there ought to have been more in the accounts than was there. I am wondering if there might have been some underhanded business or perhaps fraud by his steward."

"I hope you have not charged Mr. Wood with any crime!" Sophie said, alarmed that an innocent man might be accused of misdealing with her uncle's money when all the time Uncle Philip had been having fun, stashing it away in books for Sophie.

"Such interest on my behalf is encouraging, Sophie," Jonathan said with an arrested look at his cousin.

"I have known Mr. Wood for ages and he has seemed such a kindly person. His wife is a dear lady and with two children just as nice. I should hate to think him capable of any wrongdoing." Sophie hoped she had eased Jonathan's mind on the steward.

"Perhaps our uncle had other means of spending money that is not recorded in the books," Jonathan mused.

Fortunately he was not looking at Sophie at that moment, for he might have received a clue to the source of her fortune. She had nearly jumped out of her chair and only a warning glance from Lady Mary had kept her silent.

"I believe your uncle was a rather unusual person. Is it not likely he may have had concerns that would not have been listed in the accounts book? While he'd no reputation as a gambler, he may have indulged in other pursuits, spending sums upon them," Lady Mary said slowly, as though considering what those pursuits might have been.

Jonathan agreed, although he wore a frown, possibly wondering what sort of interests his somewhat eccentric uncle might have had.

He left shortly after that and when Sophie was satisfied that he was no longer in the house, she turned to Lady Mary in distress.

"You do not think he will press Mr. Wood for an explanation, do you? Poor man, he is as honest as the day is long." Sophie twisted the handkerchief she carried, worry clear in her voice.

"Let us hope that he will be sufficiently satisfied with the sums coming in at present to leave the past alone," her ladyship said thoughtfully. "You do realize that it is possible he may learn the truth, one way or another?"

"The way he spoke just now gives support to my fears that he would believe that the money ought rightfully to be his," Sophie said hesitantly. How *could* she love a man who might take away everything given her? "What am I to do?"

"I suggest you continue as you have begun. Pay all bills as you incur them. It truly would be difficult for him to recover the money, you know. Besides, how could he possibly guess the amount?" Lady Mary concluded with the attitude of one who has just discovered a surprising fact.

"I had not thought of that. No one, other than you and I, know the actual sum contained in all those books!"

"Has he asked you if you sold the books?" Lady Mary suddenly inquired.

"No," Sophie said quickly. "Perhaps I ought to seek his advice, ask him to go with me?"

"Well, you would be more inclined to receive a fair price were his lordship to be with you," Lady Mary admitted.

"There are a great number of books on agriculture I might offer Jonathan—sort of an appeasement, if you like."

"Splendid idea," Lady Mary said. Then she rose and gestured to Sophie to come with her. "Now, I should wish to drive with you in the park."

"You trust me to drive?" Sophie asked with a smile.

"If you are approved by Jonathan and Lord Chessyre, I feel certain we shall manage nicely."

Pleased with this show of confidence, Sophie agreed. She requested Jenkens to send someone with the order for her carriage and pair to be brought promptly, then joined Lady Mary in changing for the drive.

Another carriage dress had come from Madame Clotilde that morning. The woman must have several seamstresses sewing without ceasing to finish garments so quickly. Sophie was thankful to have a different carriage dress to put on. Heavens, if she was supposed to be an heiress, wearing the same carriage dress would give rise to speculation that she was actually impoverished! She grimaced at the thought. Perhaps she would do better to wear the old one!

But the sight of the pretty dress of corded muslin in a soft shade of blue and piped in black pleased her so that she set aside her reservations. There were little black buttons on the closing above the lower-than-usual waist and a high, pointed collar. A hat of the same fabric had also been sent that had a riband to match the one that tied at the waist. She felt very smart when she drew on her driving gloves and surveyed the results in the looking glass. She'd certainly not look poor while wearing such handsome garb.

By the time Lady Mary joined her in the entry, the curricle and pair was standing before the house. Whoever was at the mews had been prompt, indeed.

"Now I trust you will drive as usual," Lady Mary commanded. "I'll not have you poking along simply because I am with you." Lady Mary nodded to an acquaintance as the curricle and pair were guided into the park.

Sophie was enjoying her moment of freedom enormously. Then she spotted Jonathan astride his black steed and chewed her lip in vexation. Why couldn't the dratted man have ridden somewhere else today? But then, this was Hyde Park at the height of the promenade, or strut, as some wags called it. Where else would he be?

Naturally, he made his way to her side. "I decided I would watch your entrance. Well done, cousin," he said quietly.

"Thank you, Lord Lowell," she said politely, while maintaining firm control of the pair of chestnuts. "I must ask you to thank whoever it is that cares for my rig. The carriage was polished to mirror brightness and the horses are well groomed, too."

"Ever think of a name for them? It is possible that Castor and Pollux might not agree with your taste."

"I am neither an athlete nor a mariner so I do not claim their protection as patron saints, but the names are appropriate, for the animals do resemble twins." She eyed with apprehension the approach of a high-perch phaeton driven by one who looked more terrified than anything else.

"Best move ahead," Jonathan counseled as he also took note of the less-than-skilled driver.

Jonathan was right, she mused. It was better to keep moving, one presented less of a target that way. He rode at her side for a short distance, long enough for her to make her offer.

"I believe there are a number of books Uncle left me that might be of interest of you. Would you like to look them over?" And, she added inwardly, forget about the discrepancy in his funds.

"What sort of books?" he asked, obviously curious.

"Mostly agriculture, but a few others as well. Also, I would value your help if you could see your way to assisting me in selling the remainder, save for a few I cannot part with, ones I remember reading as a girl."

"When would you like me to go over them? I would be pleased to dispose of them for you." He effortlessly controlled his restless steed while examining Sophie's face.

"Tomorrow?" she replied. Was he a little too eager? she wondered. She had no opportunity to pursue that line of investigation as Jonathan elected to join some friends and she forged her way through a crush of traffic that required every bit of her concentration.

"He seemed anxious to have a look at those books, I must say," Lady Mary said, echoing Sophie's train of thought.

"Well, he may have them for all I truly care," Sophie answered after clearing the knot of carriages, "except for a few that I prefer to keep. It will be good to rid your basement of those boxes."

"They are occupying space in the beer cellar. Jenkens has placed the servants' keg in the wine vault for the time being. There is no problem with keeping them for now."

"I appreciate your forbearance," Sophie said, immediately resolved to rid the basement of the books as soon as might be.

"Do you realize that with one thing and another, it has been three weeks since we arrived in London?" Lady Mary said, not by a quiver revealing any of the trepidation she had felt on the drive through the park.

"That had occurred to me. Madame Clotilde should be sending over an evening dress today, I believe. Shall we go to the theater?"

"Well, I have a surprise. We have received vouchers for Almack's from dear Lady Sefton after your attendance at her dinner party. She said she thought you a pretty behaved young lady and as a relative of Lord Lowell's quite acceptable for her select little group come Wednesday." Her ladyship dropped her bomb with the casual manner of one accustomed to such elevated realms of Society.

"My," Sophie said, not betraying the excitement this news conjured up within her, "in that case, I hope that the dress will have arrived while we are gone."

"When do you think your cousin will come over to inspect those books?" Lady Mary inquired, returning to the matter that lurked in the back of both their minds.

"Who can say? I had best have Jenkens bring up the ones marked agriculture. Thank heavens I boxed them much as they were shelved—by topic—and thought to crayon the contents on the outside of each box." She restrained her team to permit another to pass before her and took a moment to share an appreciative look with Lady Mary.

"Well, we will worry about that later. Now, we had best return to the house and inspect our wardrobes. I would that you look your best for this evening."

They continued at a brisk pace—for the city. As they drew up before the house on Lower Brook Street, Lady Mary placed a detaining hand on Sophie's sleeve. "I want you to know that I am very well fixed and that should your cousin succeed in stealing away that which your uncle left you, I will assist you so that you may have your dream of a come-out. I never had a daughter, you see," she added, as if that explained everything.

An astounded Sophie thanked her ladyship and went so far as to give her a hug once they were in the entry hall.

The ladies walked up to Sophie's bedroom to find the longed-for evening gown had come as promised. It was a creation made in rich white moire trimmed with raspberry-colored ribbons stitched in diagonal lines across the dress. The tiny puffed sleeves also had the diagonal trim and there was a ruche of raspberry lace around the low neck, to which Sophie gave a dubious look once the dress was on her.

"Now, do not fuss," Anna said in a motherly way, removing Sophie's hand from the lace. "I have seen lower necklines than that and you have a splendid bosom, miss. Not all ladies are so blessed, if I may say so," she concluded shyly.

All went well at the prestigious assembly rooms at the beginning. Sophie made her curtsies to the patronesses attending this evening. Lady Sefton gave her a smile of approval, while Lady Jersey studied Sophie with speculative eyes. Mrs. Drummond-Burrell said nothing, merely giving Sophie her usual disdainful stare.

It was when Jonathan entered the room that Sophie felt a constriction in her chest and wished she was somewhere else. He looked so handsome and dashing, dressed in a coat of deepest blue above white breeches and stockings, with black patent dancing slippers. Even his waistcoat was a miracle of understated elegance.

The gaze of every unattached and attached—for that matter—female attending fastened on him. Wearing ensembles that revealed great taste and expense, young ladies flirted with him, nearly begging him to seek them out.

What chance did she have with her cousin when there were so many others available? Sophie had quickly observed that she was a very small fish in an enormous pond. Of course he did not seek her out. He spent some time with several of the young ladies who were in their second and third Seasons, avoiding the girls making their come-outs like the plague.

Sophie was about to request they leave when he came up to her in a purposeful manner. Was he actually going to ask her to dance with him? Sophie held her breath.

"It is well known I never dance with the entrants to the marriage game," he said quietly to Lady Mary, thus explaining why he'd avoided Sophie. "I would not single her out for undue attention *this* evening. What time shall I present myself on the morrow at Lower Brook Street to inspect the books?" he concluded with a look at Sophie.

It was as well he didn't expect her to say much. She was seething with annoyance. He ignored all the young women who made their bows to Society? "I am flattered you condescended to speak with me," she managed to utter with a straight face. "Perhaps ten of the clock if that is not too early for you, my lord." She made an exquisite curtsy, then turned to her ladyship with an air of dismissal. "Perhaps we should leave now? I find this somewhat tiring."

If Jonathan thought her behavior odd, he was too much the gentleman to say anything. Sophie and Lady Mary turned in the direction of the main exit only to find Lord Chessyre approaching them. "Wait," murmured Lady Mary quite unnecessarily to Sophie, who had darted a glance from one gentleman to the other.

"Dear Lady Mary and Miss Garnett," he said with exquisite courtesy. There was no flaw in his appearance, his beautifully fitting corbeau coat over garb similar to Jonathan's attire was remarkable. "Never say you are about to leave us? I had hoped for the pleasure of at least one dance with Miss Garnett this evening."

"She will be pleased, my lord." Lady Mary gave Jonathan an admonitory look, then stood back to watch Sophie grace the assembly floor with the very handsome gentleman. "They make a splendid pair, do they not?" she said to Jonathan from behind the protection of her fan.

"He is showing particular attention to Sophie," Jonathan commented with a slight frown.

"I believe he is interested in her, yes," her ladyship said with commendable restraint.

"Fine chap, none better," Jonathan grumbled, seeming reluctant to pay a compliment to his best friend. "But he is my age," he added, as though that were a detriment.

"A perfect age—just right. We look forward to seeing you

in the morning," Lady Mary said in a most dismissing way with a wave of her fan.

Jonathan, clearly unaccustomed to being so rejected, stalked off in high dudgeon to watch Sophie from a distance.

Mr. Somerset, who had entered with Chessyre, begged a dance with Sophie when Lord Chessyre returned her to Lady Mary.

Eyes sparkling, lips quirked in a mischievous smile, Sophie glanced at her glowering cousin and demurely walked with Mr. Somerset to take a place in a Scots reel. She had taken great care to be circumspect in her behavior. How amusing that it was Jonathan who had caused comment this evening. Even Lady Jersey seemed to take note, for she sauntered to his side to chide him on his lack of partners. Sophie heard a word or two while passing them and inwardly grinned. Her cousin seemed almost churlish, a word she was certain had never been applied to him in the past.

Lord Chessyre, upon learning the ladies intended to depart, insisted on attending them home. He was so solicitous in his attention that a good many of the watching matrons took note and much whispering ensued.

The following morning Sophie contemplated the nosegay of delicate blooms brought to her, smiling at her ladyship.

"Your cousin wonders if Lord Chessyre is paying particular attention to you, Sophie," Lady Mary said, returning an amused look. "I informed him I thought you a splendid pair, and that Lord Chessyre was the perfect age for you, even if he is an age with Jonathan. Your cousin said his lordship is a 'fine chap, none better.' "

"High praise, indeed. I thought Jonathan looked as though he'd eaten a sour pickle." Sophie glanced at the clock, then jumped to her feet. "Do I look presentable? He will be here in a few minutes, for he is rarely late."

As though to reinforce that statement, Jenkens entered the breakfast room to announce Jonathan's arrival.

Hard on the butler's heels, her cousin entered the room and all her ladyship could do was to give a discreet nod of her head in reply to Sophie's question.

"I requested the boxes to be placed in the dining room," Sophie informed him following the usual exchange of greetings. "It will be easier for you to cart them out to the front that way."

"Most considerate of you, cousin," Jonathan said with a mocking tilt of his brow.

"Your cousin is most practical, is she not?" her ladyship said. "I find her common sense most refreshing."

"Is it common sense to encourage Chessyre? Unless you are serious?" Jonathan asked, seeming casual, but with an intent look in his eyes.

"Whom I do or do not encourage is of no matter to you, dear cousin. I'd not have you worry your head on my account," Sophie said in a very soothing manner, sounding all consideration and sisterly concern. "Now as to the books . . ." She motioned him to follow her along the hallway until they reached the dining room.

Jonathan gave her an exasperated look, then opened the first of the boxes, pulling out a recent publication on the rotating of crops—quite controversial to some.

"Here is an empty box so you may place the books you wish to keep aside and put the others on the table. I can put them back later," Sophie said in an effort to speed up the process.

It was difficult to stand by and watch her cousin go through the books one by one. If anything, he was more handsome than last evening, were such a thing possible. A lock of his hair flopped down over his brow as he delved into the box to pull forth two more volumes. An amazing number were going into the box of books to be kept. Sophie wryly wondered if there would be any left to sell.

On the other hand, if things had been normal, all those books would have come to Jonathan as a matter of course. He inherited Lowell Hall and those books had been a part of the library. It would not be too surprising if he wished to have a few of them back on the shelves. She said nothing as he continued to pull out book after book.

Sophie was about to leave him to his task when he took one of the last volumes from the box. It slipped from his hands and he grabbed it before it landed, but the pages flew open and a paper fluttered to the table.

She gasped with dismay. A one-hundred-pound note!

"What an unusual book marker," Jonathan said, picking up the note to examine it. "A printing date some years ago, so it has been here for a time. Pity you did not shake this volume before me, cousin."

"If that is a book you wish, you may have the marker Uncle Philip must have placed therein," Sophie said with commendable rein on her nerves.

"I insist it is yours. You inherited the books, after all," Jonathan said with courtly courtesy. But he gave Sophie a speculative look that made her itch to flee.

Could he read guilt in her face, never mind that she had obtained her money because of Uncle's scheming? What would Jonathan do now?

Chapter Nine

From the doorway Lady Mary observed the scene with a bland expression. "What have we here? A book marker, you say?" She walked closer to the table, eyeing the note.

"It seems my uncle was given to using an expensive form of such, ma'am. I insist that Sophie accept it, even if it's in a book she consented to give me. The books were left to *her*, after all," he concluded with a glance from Lady Mary to Sophie.

"Do as your cousin wishes, Sophie dear. I am sure he knows best," her ladyship admonished.

"What woman could not use an extra hundred pounds?" Sophie quipped, reluctantly accepting the money.

"Well, perhaps we ought to check the others," Jonathan said while bending down to retrieve the final book. He thus missed the look of dismay that flashed between the women.

"I hardly think that necessary. Jenkens will bring up more of the books—perhaps the ones I wish to sell—and you might take a look at them. If you could sell them, I would be grateful," Sophie said politely.

Jonathan spent another hour going through the contents of several boxes of books before ordering them all to be carried to his carriage. "I will sell what I do not want. I know of a bookseller who is quite fair in his dealings. I shall bring you the money when done, if that is agreeable."

"I suppose you do not wish me to go with you?" Sophie said hesitantly. The way he'd been behaving, it seemed that he would be glad to see the last of her.

"That would scarcely be proper," he said with a dismayed expression on his face.

"Oh. Of course. Proper," Sophie said while fiddling with the handkerchief she carried. If he cared the least for her, he'd desire her company, even to the bookseller's.

He paused in the entry hall, seemingly intent on studying the black-and-white marble squares before he spoke to her. "We may be cousins, but there is always the matter of propriety and what people might believe. You would not wish to have others think you poor and needing to sell your assets?"

"But . . . Whatever . . ." Sophie floundered for a moment, then bowed her head. "You are right, of course. Until later, my lord."

He raised a brow, giving her a rather odd look before taking his leave.

Sophie walked back to the morning room, where Lady Mary awaited her. "He's gone. I do not think he was suspicious, although there was a moment after he suggested we ought to look in the other books that I wondered if perhaps he nurtured a few doubts."

"We will have to wait and see what develops. I did warn you that he might learn the truth somehow. This was a close call. What a good thing he did not happen to look up to see the expression on your face—it would have given all away. At least he insisted you keep the hundred pounds."

"I suppose I had best place it in my account at the bank. It bothers me to keep so much money in my room."

The ladies debated the matter of how one could spend such a sum of money over lunch, coming to no one conclusion.

"Bonnets and boots, chemises and night rails, gowns and carriage dresses—I have enough. I do not wish for more at the moment. I had best hand this back to Jonathan to compensate for his keeping my horses and the carriage."

"He might be insulted," Lady Mary cautioned as she led the way to the drawing room with the hope of a pleasant afternoon even if it did look to rain before long.

When Jenkens entered later with the information that Lord Chessyre had come to call, both women were pleased. The quiet had begun to pall.

Evidence of rain on his coat brought Sophie to her feet and over to the window. "It rains after all. I had hoped the day might improve." The gray sky looked to be the sort that brought an all-day rain.

Jenkens entered with a tray of refreshments, lit a branch of candles to cheer the room, and added a scoop of coal to the fire that took the chill from the air.

Lord Chessyre joined her by the window, looking down at Sophie rather than at the tiny yard behind the house. "You mind the rain so much?"

"In the city, yes. It is different in the country with the scent of the rain-washed gardens and fields, the feeling of renewal. Here, it brings mud and worse smells."

"It helps mitigate a few of them," his lordship said with a smile.

"True. We are ever surrounded by smells—some worse, some better. I thank you for the posy you sent me this morning. *That* is treasured fragrance," she said, liking the strength she saw in Lord Chessyre's face. Standing this close to him, she could detect costmary and his lotion—a lemony sort of scent that was very pleasing.

"Mr. Somerset has come to call, my lady," Jenkens said with a questioning look at her ladyship. Sophie and Lord Chessyre exchanged a glance before turning to the butler.

"A welcome addition to our group," Lady Mary said.

"Indeed," Chessyre politely responded. But it was clear to Sophie that his lordship was not pleased to see Mr. Somerset enter the room to do the pretty to Lady Mary and then Sophie. If anything, his lordship stood a trifle closer to her, as though to reveal a claim he had—which he did not at this point.

Sophie wondered if she would be averse to marrying this man, should he ask her. He was kind as well as handsome, well-off financially, and inclined to indulge her, she thought, judging by his behavior in the carriage matter. But he was not Jonathan. However, since that connection appeared doomed, it would be wise of her to look elsewhere. Whether it would be fair to Lord Chessyre or right for her was another problem altogether.

The two gentlemen carried on polite conversation with the ladies, regarding the conditions in London and sights to be

seen. Over biscuits and tea Mr. Somerset offered to escort Sophie and Lady Mary to view the panorama at Leiscester
Square whenever they might choose. Lord Chessyre countered
with a suggestion they join him at Vauxhall Gardens for a
party that would include his sister and her husband.

Pleased with both suggestions, tentative dates were arranged
and the gentlemen shortly left at the same time, a chilling politeness between them.

"I have been wishing to view that panorama," Lady Mary
mused after the men had left.

Sophie looked out at the falling rain. It was a good thing
they had not planned to go anywhere that evening. "Vauxhall
will be a treat," she said, recalling how she had longed to view
the famed pleasure gardens with Jonathan at her side. Well,
she was not one to repine on what was not to be.

"I wonder what your cousin will think of these invitations?"
Lady Mary said with a curious look at Sophie where she again
stood by the window, staring out at the rain that continued to
fall as the day drew to a close.

"Who can say?" Sophie replied with a shrug of her shoulders meant to convey that she didn't care in the least, when of
course she did.

They dined early, the rain giving the dining room an atmosphere of gloom in spite of the extra candles Jenkens lit for
them. He served them fish covered with a special new sauce
Cook had contrived, along with a simple boiled beef dinner,
quite fit for two ladies who were not entertaining.

Following a plain dessert of custard pie, Sophie retired to
the drawing room with Lady Mary, intent upon playing a game
of cards for two.

She found it impossible to concentrate. Giving Lady Mary a
concerned look, she said, "I vow that something I ate must
have disagreed with me. How do you feel, my lady?"

"Not at all well. Ring for Jenkens, will you?"

Sophie clutched the bellpull with an anxious hand. She was
feeling worse by the moment.

When Jenkens poked his face around the door it was clear
from his ashen visage that he also had eaten whatever it was
that had made the ladies ill.

"How are the others?" Lady Mary demanded, rising from her chair by the card table with the intention of going to her bedroom.

"Right bad, my lady. Anna and Cook are felled flat on their beds, moaning something fierce. And I expect I'll be next," he concluded, then rushed from the room, leaving Sophie and Lady Mary clinging to the backs of chairs, staring helplessly at one another.

"Let me help you upstairs, my lady," Sophie insisted, making her way to her ladyship's side with haste. "I wonder if there is any means we might find aid? Clearly neither one of us—nor the servants, for that matter—will be able to brave the rain."

It was slow going, both women clutching their abdomens and wondering quietly whether they would reach their rooms in time to be really ill.

Lady Mary sank on her bed with a sigh of relief.

Holding one hand to her face, Sophie found a basin for her ladyship should she have need of one, then paused at the doorway on her way to her own room.

"I would remain with you, but I fear I will be worse than useless." Then the force of the malady hit her and she dashed down the hall to her own bed and a basin.

All too soon Sophie ceased to care whether she lived or died. She thought it likely that she would not see the morrow, nor would anyone else in this house. Tainted food had killed far too many people to make it a rarity. Before long she lapsed into a semisleep, rousing to be ill, then falling back on her bed with the hope she might be taken soon, for never in her life had she felt so miserable.

Jonathan drove toward his home from the party, which he had found dashed dull. He'd taken a hackney, as his coachman was laid low with a bad leg. On an impulse, he ordered the jarvey to go by the way of Lower Brook Street. He would tell Sophie of the success he had found with the bookseller that afternoon. No doubt she would be pleased to have so many more pounds at her disposal. He'd not seen Chessyre at the party, although the fellow had said he might be there. Jonathan wondered if he elected to visit Sophie instead.

The house was shrouded in darkness, which was odd. He dismissed the jarvey after handing him a generous sum. This might take time and he didn't wish to be obliged to anyone.

Normally there would be light visible through the fanlight above the door. As well, there ought to be light from the drawing room windows on the first floor. He stepped back to look to the top of the house, where he knew Sophie's room to be. Dark. Something about it all bothered him. Something was not right.

There was no answer to his repeated use of the door knocker. Another mystery. Where was the estimable Jenkens?

Jonathan tried the door and found it unlocked. Worse and worse. He opened the door and cautiously stepped inside.

"Sophie?" Silence. The house appeared abandoned, so eerily silent was it. He paused to light a branch of candles before proceeding to the stairs and up to the drawing room. Here he looked about for evidence of occupation. A deck of cards was tumbled on the card table, as though hastily left. With no sign of life found in the dining room or the morning room, he continued up the stairs.

He did not want to disturb Lady Mary in the event they had simply retired early. Instead, he walked to peer into Sophie's room and halted, stunned.

Moaning and looking miserable, Sophie lay twisted and tangled in her garments. Whatever she had eaten for dinner was no longer in her stomach.

Jonathan ignored that and felt her forehead. She was damp with exhaustion, her lips looked parched, and she moaned when he touched her cheek.

Dull eyes, so unlike those incredible cerulean orbs normally seen, opened to gaze at him. "Jonathan, my love? Don't stay. I'm wretched," she murmured. She licked her lips and groaned. "Water."

Jonathan guessed there would be little point in telling her that he would be right back. He went to the other end of the hall to check on her ladyship and found her in slightly better shape, but hardly in a condition to help Sophie.

Dashing down three flights of stairs, he hunted around that level to find all the servants in a serious condition. There was no help to be found from Anna or the others.

Sophie was by far the worst and she merited his care before he considered anyone else. He quickly discovered what he needed, prowling through cupboards and shelves with a fine disregard for leaving things as he found them.

Shortly, he headed up the stairs to Sophie's room with a basin of water and a soft cloth as well as a glass of cooled tea. He wasn't sure what best to do—whether to try to find help and where, but he'd an idea she needed him right now. He wondered if it was too late for the ipecac to work on her.

He set the things down, surveying her again. First of all those garments that so restricted her must come off. She'd rest better when more comfortable. Dare he? There was no one who could help him, not unless he took precious time to go looking for propriety.

Propriety be hanged, he decided, pulling off his coat and tossing it aside. This was urgent. He rolled up his shirtsleeves and went to work. With great difficulty, Jonathan tugged the dress and petticoat from Sophie, wincing every time she moaned. Had she actually called him her love? Or was that the raving of a very sick woman?

Part of him observed her delicate form draped with the sheer shift that was all that remained of her clothing. Her body was even more perfect than he'd imagined. The rest of him went to work to relieve her discomfort. After administering the ipecac, he sponged off her face.

He took no notice of the passage of time. He held her head over the basin when the ipecac did its work of clearing out her stomach of any remaining food. Then he sat on the edge of her bed, holding one of her hands and willing her to be better, to live. Never in his life had he felt so helpless, so devoid of power.

The night was black and the eerie silence of the house pressed in on him. The candles flickered in a draft from the window he had opened to bring a breath of fresh air in the stale room. He stared at the face of the woman in the bed.

Even ill, she was beautiful. His throat tightened. Dear God in heaven, let her be spared, he pleaded.

Dawn came and Jonathan still sat slumped by her side, wondering how anyone could survive such a terrible onslaught. She had writhed and moaned in her distress, then she had sunk into an ominous quiet as she dozed. She must have an excellent constitution to have made it to this point. He had heard that the hour before dawn was the worst of the night, claiming more lives than any other time. Sophie had lived past that dangerous hour. Now if she could manage to hold her own.

"Jonathan, what are you doing here?" she said, her voice a wispy thread of sound, her eyes mere slits of blue.

"It seems you ate some tainted food yesterday. You and everyone else in this house." He leaned over her to study her drawn face. Did she look a trifle less pulled? Dare he hope she was over the worst of it?

"Lady Mary?" Sophie managed to whisper.

"Better than you are. A drink?" he urged, not wishing her to exhaust herself in trying to talk, let alone think. If she began to think, he could find himself in trouble.

"Umm," she replied, obediently opening her mouth to sip thirst-quenching cold tea.

Jonathan mopped off her face where water had trickled down her chin, then resumed his watch. He rubbed his chin with his free hand, realizing he would likely give her a fright should she open those eyes and see him with his growth of beard. Right now, he'd welcome a screech.

Another thirty minutes and Sophie opened her eyes again. "More tea," she begged.

Jonathan obliged, again mopping her face with a damp cloth and helping her to settle in bed.

"You should go," she urged weakly. "Mustn't stay here."

"I'll not leave you at the moment, Sophie. You have been very ill and I'll not be responsible for your demise should you take a turn for the worse."

"I shall be all right. All I need is sleep," she countered in a slightly stronger voice.

It was amazing how stubborn she could be, even when she needed help, he reflected. He didn't reply but offered her some

of the tea into which he had stirred some powdered willow
bark.

"Ugh," she said with a grimace. "That is worse than being
sick." She dropped her head back on the pillow to survey him
from beneath half-opened eyes. "You look terrible."

"I suppose I do," he agreed.

"Never say you have been here all night?" she softly demanded.

"I have," he admitted, wondering what was coming next.

"If you do not leave this instant, someone may see you and
think the worst," she murmured drowsily.

"And what would that be, dear Sophie?" he dared to tease.

Her eyes flashed open and she stared at him a moment before saying, "Why, that I'd invited you to my bed. You are a
very handsome man, you know," she concluded in that wispy
voice that he'd worried about earlier. Her eyelids drooped
until almost closed, then she murmured, "I shall never forgive
you for seeing me at my worst."

"Pulling you from the muddy creek does not count?" he
said, even though he suspected she was drifting off to sleep
again.

"My clothes?" she mumbled.

"Do not worry about a thing. Just have a nice little nap." He
watched as she finally shut her eyes and seemed to drop into a
restful slumber.

The door opened and Anna peered in, looking only margin-
ally better than her mistress. "Sir?"

"She is better. Do you know what you all ate that caused
this malady?" he quizzed as the maid slowly went about
straightening the room.

"It might have been the fish . . . or the custard . . . or maybe
the sauce. We all tried them. Only, Lady Mary ate very little of
the custard pie. Cook was disappointed to see her dish come
back half full."

"Custard. I suppose it is possible." He glanced to the bed
where Sophie now slept more deeply. "Can you manage if I
leave her now?"

"I believe so, milord. It's a right good thing you came to
look in on your cousin when you did," she offered as Jonathan

picked up his coat and walked to the door after giving Sophie a final inspection.

Lady Mary was in her bed and since the door was open Jonathan paused outside to inquire if she needed anything.

"Come in, come in," she said, sounding much better than Sophie. "A little bout with indigestion the doctor will call it, I suppose."

"Tainted food, more likely," Jonathan countered. "You ate little of the custard and had the mildest case of this ailment. Sophie must have enjoyed her dish, for she was by far the worst."

Lady Mary eyed his unshaven chin, his crumpled cravat, and tired eyes. "We owe you a great deal, Jonathan. I would not like to lose Sophie, nor would you, I suspect. We shall keep you posted on our recovery. And, thank you, dear boy."

Jonathan walked wearily down the stairs to the entry hall. He had not been called a dear boy since he could remember. He caught sight of his reflection in the hall looking glass and shuddered. Had he been on an all-night binge he could not have looked much worse. Rather than go out the front door and risk being seen by anyone, he elected to exit by the rear of the house, letting himself out of the garden gate into the alley behind. It was a simple matter to walk to the end and around to where he espied a chair. In minutes he was deposited at his door.

Fyfield did not say a word, but Jonathan sensed a reproach for the crumpled attire, if nothing else.

"I stopped by my cousin's house and found everyone extremely ill. Tainted custard, I think it must have been. I could not leave her—them, you know. But I'm dashed tired after being up all night."

With that explanation, he divested himself of his clothing and fell into bed and an exhausted sleep.

Some hours later Sophie again opened her eyes to a tidy room, the small nosegay from Lord Chessyre providing a faint scent of roses. She felt wretched. Her stomach seemed to have been twisted into a knot and now grumbled with emptiness.

"A cup of tea, miss? Lady Mary says as how it would be just the thing. Perhaps a bit of toast?" Anna inquired, having improved as the day had progressed.

"It sounds heavenly," Sophie agreed, wondering just how much of what she thought she recalled was real and what was fantasy.

When Anna returned with a tray bearing a pot of tea, a cup and saucer, and a plate with a slice of toasted bread, Sophie hesitantly inquired, "Everyone was ill last night?"

"Every last one of us, miss. Lady Mary the least, because she ate little of the custard. Or so thinks Lord Lowell, your cousin."

"Jonathan was here? Last night?" Perhaps she hadn't dreamt it after all. She'd thought she had been wildly out of her mind.

"Yes, miss. I dunno when he came but he was here with you this morning and looking a fright in his shirtsleeves and not having shaved and all. He seemed that worried about you, miss," Anna concluded.

"He watched over me? Took care of me?" Sophie demanded. Then she recalled that she had awakened without her dress and petticoat. "Did you put away my dress? I fear it needs a washing."

"I found it crumpled on the floor over in the corner along with your petticoat. You must have been in a rare state to toss it there," the maid said, busy with her tasks.

Digesting that remark, Sophie realized that Jonathan must have helped her from her clothes, put her to bed, and nursed her through the long hours of the night. While it was far more than she would have expected of him, it presented her with a dilemma. How could she face him again?

If word of this seeped out Society would demand a marriage between them. She couldn't bear to be wed to Jonathan when he did not love her as she loved him. That would be far worse than marrying someone of whom one was mildly fond.

What could she do? For the moment she buried her head in her pillow and told Anna that she had no intention of leaving her bed until tomorrow. That ought to settle queries, should a nosy sort come calling. If they learned that the entire house had taken ill, they could scarcely suspect any mischief.

After another round of tea and toast, Sophie dressed in her pale rose robe and made her way to Lady Mary's room to inquire how she fared.

"I suspect I look better than I feel. Dreadful business. I understand it may have been tainted custard. Cook is devastated."

"Anna says Jonathan was here last night." There was a hint of a question in Sophie's words.

"Indeed. I did see him this morning before he left. Poor boy, he was in need of a shave and a change of clothing. I imagine he went home and collapsed in his bed. He looked worn to the bone." Lady Mary studied Sophie as though anticipating an outburst of sorts.

"I believe he took care of me," Sophie continued, walking to the window that overlooked the minuscule garden in the rear of the house. "Is that as shocking as it sounds?"

"Why should it be? He is a relative of yours. Why he came here or how he happened on you when you had need of help, we have yet to learn. Be thankful and do not borrow trouble. I doubt if anyone other than Anna would know and she is not about to tell a soul. Is she?" Lady Mary added as an afterthought.

"I urged her not to speak of this to anyone." Sophie sank down on the cane-back chair near the window. She looked at her hands folded in her lap, then leaned back against the chair. "Goodness, I am as weak as a newborn."

"Perhaps you will feel more the thing by this evening. I sent a note to Mrs. Beauchamp, explaining that the household had been struck down with a dire malady and we would not be able to attend her soiree tonight."

"Good," Sophie said, rising to her feet, determined to return to her room and dress. She feared Jonathan would come to check on them and find her *en déshabillé*.

An hour later found Sophie reclining on the sofa in the drawing room, again sipping tea and nibbling toast. It would be a wonder if she did not fade to nothing if she could eat nothing more than this.

"What are you doing out of bed?" Jonathan demanded from the doorway. "When I left here this morning I believed you would have the sense to stay there for the day."

"I felt better," Sophie replied mildly, truly feeling better just for seeing him. He looked so vital, so alive, and . . . so well fed, she thought wistfully.

He strode across the room to study her face, then sat down on the closest chair. "You had me worried last night," he admitted.

"You weren't here, you know," she advised.

"I certainly was—holding your head, wiping your face, pouring tea in you. Do you not recall anything?"

"Of course I do, although it is a bit hazy. What I mean is that no one must know of your heroism. Think what it might mean!" She gave him an anxious look.

"Ah," he said. He relaxed against the chair, gazing at her through narrowed eyes. "Would it be so grim to marry me, Sophie?" He wondered how much she remembered. Did she know that she had called him her love?

"Not grim, precisely. You are a handsome, pleasant man." Sophie thought wildly. How did one inform the man one simply adored that one would not marry him, even if Society demanded it?

"Well, we shall see what happens. I doubt if there will be any talk. I crept out of here the back way at first light. Unless your neighbors are given to peering out at that hour, I cannot imagine who would learn of what happened. We could say it was a servant. Who would expect the Viscount Lowell to be sneaking out the back gate?"

"Someone with a vile mind and wishing to make trouble, that's who," Sophie retorted. "If anyone knew you had helped me from my dress and petticoat and tucked me under the covers, then stayed by my bed throughout the night it would be farewell to bachelor days for you and good-bye to spinsterhood for me."

"You recall that much, do you?" he said casually, watching her with an intent gaze. "What else do you remember?"

"Did I say something last night?" Sophie cried, trying to hide her alarm. She hoped she hadn't revealed the truth about her fortune, for she'd be in the suds for sure if she had.

"Enough," he said, allowing her to worry.

Chapter Ten

"What am I to do, dear ma'am?" Sophie cried in alarm. "I must have said something untoward. There was that look in his dark eyes that told me I had uttered some words, some phrase that made him vastly curious. I can think of nothing other than the legacy from Uncle Philip. What else could I have said that he might be curious about?" Sophie leaned against one of the pillars at the foot of Lady Mary's lovely canopied bed and gave her ladyship a bewildered look.

"What else, indeed?" Lady Mary echoed, gazing from her comfortable mound of down pillows at her young friend.

"I had hoped he would be gentleman enough to tell me what nonsense I'd revealed, but no! Oh, the vexing creature!" Sophie said, dropping onto the cane-back chair in Lady Mary's room. She was still very weak and had about as much energy as a spent horse.

"You do not look at all the thing, my dear," Lady Mary observed from the luxury of her bed. She settled against the pillows to survey Sophie with some anxiety.

"I am not myself, of that I am convinced. How can I not recall what I said to Jonathan?" Sophie muttered, quite as annoyed with herself as she was with her cousin.

"I believe you must tell your cousin the truth of the matter," Lady Mary counseled after some thought.

"Oh, I should hate to part with the money, I'll confess that," Sophie said. "I know he will demand I give it to him. After all, not only ought it to be his, but I should not have control over all that lovely wealth. I'll also confess that I have become quite accustomed to having nice clothes and things. It would be difficult to give that up." She exchanged an unhappy glance with her ladyship.

"However, I suspect it will out one way or another. Truth has a way of doing precisely that," Lady Mary reminded her. "Best do it now before the situation becomes worse and he learns of the matter from another source."

"How can I at this point?" Sophie asked, utterly miserable with the entire affair. She almost wished she had never been gifted with Uncle Philip's books. Almost.

"Consider it for a time and the words will come to you," Lady Mary said in a comforting way. "When you are feeling better, you will find you are able to cope with what must be done. You know it is the correct thing to do now, do you not? Look at all you owe him. What other man do you know who would have cared for you as he has?"

"I can scarce imagine anyone at all who would care for me as he did," Sophie admitted reluctantly.

"Lord Chessyre, perhaps?" Lady Mary inquired idly.

"I do not know. Oh, now I shall look at every man I meet and wonder if *he* would have taken such care of me," Sophie wailed.

"That is not a bad thing, I believe. At least it provides a certain measuring guide, as it were." Her ladyship closed her eyes, fatigue showing in the lines of her face.

Chagrined that she had tired the dear lady, Sophie rose and tiptoed from the room. Resting on her own bed, her thoughts chased themselves around and around like a puppy after his tail. What had she said in her moment of weakness? How she wished she knew.

She mulled over the matter and by evening she had reached no answer nor any solution. She would simply have to trust to luck that Jonathan would make a slip and reveal what she said—or flat-out demand the money from the books.

The following day she felt sufficiently well to drive out in her curricle. It was a short drive and she didn't pause to chat with anyone, just enjoyed the fresh air after all the rain they'd had. She stopped at Harding and Howell to purchase some wools for her needlework, admired fabric that had just arrived from India, and wistfully gazed at a clock that would look perfect on the drawing room mantel at Lowell Hall.

She'd not buy it. A lady, even a cousin, did not gift a gentleman with such an item, unless it was his birthday or wedding day, or some such event. Jonathan's birthday was in the fall—September, if she remembered rightly. He had always complained that her birthday in June came at a time when they were all at Lowell Hall and she merited an iced cake from the cook and a guinea from her uncle.

Those days seemed like another lifetime now. Rather than a teasing older cousin, Jonathan was an enigma. She still loved him, but he did make it difficult.

"Sophie? Is it you?" Lady Anne joined Sophie by the lovely clock so much admired. "You do not look yourself, my dear."

"Lady Mary and I had the misfortune to partake of tainted food. I truly thought I'd expire," Sophie said with stark simplicity.

"How dreadful. I heard of someone else who ate something off not long ago. Cannot think of who it was. Come, let us go over to Gunter's for an ice and you shall tell me the particulars."

It was difficult to refuse. They had been so close in school days and Sophie longed for a woman her own age in whom she might confide. "Very well, I shall meet you there immediately. I have my curricle. Perhaps you would drive with me?"

"I should like that," Lady Anne said promptly and sent her maid to inform the driver of her carriage to return to their mews, taking the maid with him.

"There, it is so much nicer to have a comfortable coze without another pair of ears to listen," Lady Anne said as the two women settled in the curricle.

Sophie requested the hood be raised to protect them from any sun, so they were now shielded from the groom as well.

It did not take long before Lady Anne had wormed the rest of the story from Sophie.

"How romantic." She sighed over her Gunter's ice when Sophie had concluded her tale.

"I see nothing romantic in having Jonathan hold my head while I was sick to my stomach," Sophie replied with a grimace. As to how she'd felt when she had opened her eyes to discover him holding her hand, well, that had best be left unrevealed.

"But to have that handsome cousin of yours so masterfully take charge and care for you in such a tender manner is of all things wonderful," Lady Anne countered with a smile. She leaned back against the squabs and surveyed Sophie. "You are still not as strong as you might be, dearest. When you feel better no doubt you will see this handsome cousin in a new light."

Something she said niggled at the back of Sophie's mind. That word "handsome." And something else. When she had told Lady Anne about the incident and awakening to find Jonathan holding her hand she recalled something . . . but whatever it was slipped from her elusive memory. Enormously vexed with herself, she listened to Lady Anne's chatter about her baby and how clever he was and how enormously proud Cecil was of his firstborn son, little Edward.

"Just you wait until you and Jonathan have a child and you will see what I mean," she concluded with a mischievous smile.

Sophie gave her a startled look, horrified that she might have revealed the extent of her love for Jonathan.

"Don't be a silly goose, of course I can tell you love him. Any woman of discernment could if they but saw you with him or listened to your voice when you speak of him."

"It does not follow that he will ask me to marry him," Sophie said bitterly. "At the moment I wait for the roof to come tumbling down on my head. Jonathan is the most difficult person—he expects perfection from others and few are the perfectionist that he is, unfortunately. I once charged him with being too reserved and far too demanding. But as you can see, he can be a sensitive and loyal man, caring of those he feels in his charge."

"And are you in his charge, as you call it?"

"He claims he is head of the family now that Uncle Philip has died. He believes it gives him the right to dictate my life." Sophie paused, then added, "In fairness, I must admit that is not completely true. He only wants what is best for me, I feel certain."

Sophie had not revealed the entire story, omitting the part about the money from Uncle Philip and how it had been concealed in the books. It was sufficient that Lady Anne knew about Jonathan caring for Sophie during her illness. Of course it would make it difficult to explain why Sophie feared her cousin, should she attempt such a thing.

"Well," Lady Anne said with a decisive air, "I think he must love you very much. Why else would he behave as he does?"

Sophie didn't reply to this remark. She wished it were so, but strongly suspected it was the opposite. And once Jonathan found out the truth about the money from their uncle, she wouldn't give a pin for the chance of a future with him.

In his comfortable rooms Jonathan looked at the stack of books that he had retained. Actually, few books had found their way to the bookseller. The chap had paid him a handsome sum for those he'd brought, however. The oldest books, the ones of greatest value, were the ones Jonathan had elected to sell for Sophie. He was not a book collector in the true sense of the term. Rather, he enjoyed reading about subjects that interested him and those were the books he had kept. To ease his conscience, he included a sum that he felt fair along with the money from the sold books.

Tomorrow he would return to Lower Brook Street and plow through more boxes. It would be rather nice to see Uncle Philip's books returned to Lowell Hall. Why the fellow had thought to leave them all to Sophie had been a mystery.

Jonathan sighed. She had not remembered what she'd said and so he could never learn whether or not she had meant them. Could he be her love? Unlikely. They so often came to exchange words. She was very stubborn. Indeed!

When it came to that, he supposed he was a trifle reserved as she'd once claimed, maybe a bit too aloof. But dash it all, a man had to keep a certain barrier up or he would be most imposed upon.

Yet she had known who he was. Of that he was certain. She'd not said Chessyre or William, or any other name, she had clearly said *Jonathan*. *"My love,"* she had clearly uttered, although ill and miserable. Wouldn't a person be apt to reveal the truth in a situation like that? he mused. There would be no dissimulation, no attempt to hide real feelings, for one would be too ill to pretend.

Suddenly restless, he rose from his chair to contemplate the limited view from his neat rooms. That view wasn't much, for his rooms were modest. Lowell Hall required a great deal of money to maintain and it would take time for the income from the harvest and rents to augment the sum he'd been left—a sum he'd expected to be far greater than it was. Rather, Jonathan found that for the present he would continue to let out the Garnett town residence and remain where he was. The town house was far too much for a bachelor anyway.

He supposed he ought to marry. But if he could not have Sophie, there was no one else who interested him in the slightest. Society contained a lot of insipid creatures; dull as ditchwater, he'd observed.

A rap on the door brought him from his musings. With a hint of reserve in his manner, he welcomed his caller. "Come in, come in," he said by way of greeting.

"Well, I am glad you do not hold it against me that I have a regard for your cousin. I feared it might cut our friendship, and I'd not wish that." William Chessyre, Earl of Chessyre and the best of good friends, strolled into Jonathan's lodgings with an intent regard for his old friend, coming to the point of his visit immediately. "You'll grant she is a lovely creature."

Jonathan did not want to challenge Chessyre about Sophie at this moment. There was too much on his mind, too much he had to decide first. He scarce knew his own mind, let alone could he cope with the feelings of another. Instead he elected a different tack.

"She has been ill, did you know? Food poisoning near as I can figure. Sick as a cat, poor thing. Lady Mary as well, although not quite as severe." Then Jonathan recalled that Sophie had reminded him not to reveal he had been at Lower Brook Street. "I went there earlier today and learned how they fared. Entire household, from what Jenkens said."

"Food poisoning? Any idea what it might have been?" Chessyre gave Jonathan an alarmed look.

"Custard pie I believe is considered the culprit. Never know for certain, for some are more affected by tainted food than others." Jonathan motioned his friend to join him by the fireplace, where an indifferent blaze sputtered. Jonathan stirred the coal, bringing forth a decent flame.

The men sat their ease in comfortable chairs and went on to other topics, with Lord Chessyre giving Jonathan speculative looks from time to time. His regard was most disconcerting.

The following morning Jonathan decided he would stop at his bank before going to see Sophie. He changed the sum of money into bills of smaller sums that could more easily be spent, pausing to speak with the clerk for a moment, as was not his custom.

The clerk, quite overcome that his lordship was in such a pleasant mood, said, "If you prefer, I could place that money directly into your cousin's account for her. She said she dislikes having large sums of money in the house for any time." He leaned forward in a confiding way and softly added, "Odd, how her uncle left her the money in bills and consols, isn't it? Must have been a trifle eccentric to tuck them into books. I suppose he didn't trust banks," he concluded with a titter. Then fearing he had said too much and had been too familiar, the clerk retreated and became his more distant self once again.

Jonathan nodded politely, not hearing the rest of the clerk's parting remarks. He left the bank in a daze.

Bills! Consols! Uncle Philip had tucked all that money— money that rightfully ought to have been Jonathan's—into his books for Sophie! Jonathan shortly worked himself into a blind rage. Why had that dratted woman hidden this from him? She probably thought he would claim it for himself. And why shouldn't he? Jonathan wondered as, feeling most put upon, he marched down the street, ignoring everyone in his path, even a couple of fellows he knew well. They, poor chaps, fell to wondering what they had done to deserve a cut direct.

By the time he attained the house on Lower Brook Street he had passed the state of a blind rage and reached the condition of proper fury. Oh, he had it under control. No one could ever say that Jonathan Garnett had an unreasonable temper. His was most justified in this instance!

Jenkens opened the door to usher Jonathan into the house, apologizing for having been ill the day before last.

Having no quarrel with the poor man, Jonathan was civil to him, politely informing him he'd come to see his cousin and not to trouble himself. "I shall announce myself," Jonathan said with grim pleasure. He intended to catch Sophie off guard. He'd not give her a chance to fortify herself before his confrontation.

Jonathan paused at the door to the morning room to survey Sophie. She had never looked more beautiful. Although her face was still pale, her blond curls were artfully arranged about her head as in a halo and her dress of pale lilac-spotted muslin was utter simplicity, cut by a master hand. It became her well, as did the soft lace shawl draped over her shoulders. She had been occupied with a piece of needlework and looked most feminine with the flower-bedecked item draped on her lap, her needle poised in midair.

"Jonathan," she cried, jumping up to greet him with a nervous flurry. She tossed the needlework aside and took a step toward him before becoming aware that all was not well. She had taken note of the fury in his eyes, the hostility in his stance.

He guessed what made her nervous. She had concealed the hidden money from him and felt guilty. He suddenly recalled that guilty look she'd worn at Lowell Hall when he'd entered the library to find her packing books. She wasn't sorry to discommode him as she had claimed. She'd worried he might learn about the blasted money.

"Dear Sophie. And how are you this lovely morn? Looking not quite so pulled, I see." His words were full of concern, but it was difficult to keep the mockery from his voice.

She gave him a confused look, then nodded. "I do feel better, thank you. Recovery has been rather slower than I'd wish. Lord Chessyre has invited us to Vauxhall Gardens and I do not wish to postpone it. I have wanted to go for such a long time, you see," she concluded in a rush of artless confidence.

Jonathan studied her. "You could likely afford to go with

Lady Mary if you chose. Precisely how much money did our uncle leave you, Sophie?" His words fell into the pool of silence in the room, obviously shocking his little cousin. She paled and clasped her hands before her, quite at a loss for words for a few moments.

If she had been confused before, she was stymied now. "What do you mean? Uncle Philip left me his library."

"Into which he had placed a goodly sum of notes and consols. How much, Sophie?" Jonathan crossed to stand before her, daring to place a finger under her chin so she might not turn from his gaze. She refused to meet that gaze, looking down instead, her lashes concealing the eyes that would have revealed much to him.

"I refuse to tell you," she declared, deciding it was pointless to deny the truth when he appeared to have found her out.

"I would know," he quietly demanded.

"What is it you wish to know, my lord?" Lady Mary queried as she entered the drawing room, having learned from Jenkens that Miss Sophie's cousin had come to call.

"I suppose you know all about the money in the books," Jonathan replied, turning a cold gaze at her. "That was why Sophie was so stricken when that stray hundred-pound note fell from the book the other day. Missed one, did you?" he asked, looking back at Sophie.

"Do not be nasty, Jonathan. It ill becomes you," Sophie chided while groping for a way to cope with her enraged cousin. Really, she ought to have discussed this aspect with Lady Mary before he confronted her. As it was, she was almost terrified of him in this mood.

"And to think I sold those books for you and hurried to bring you the sum, thinking you might have need for it. That was how I came to be here when you were ill."

"And I thank you again for your care, cousin," Sophie said in a subdued voice.

"I had thought you might speak the truth when so ill. It must have been my imagination," Jonathan said bitterly. "You will not tell me the amount of Uncle's bequest?"

"Why should I?" Sophie countered, her stubborn streak coming forth. "He left those books and all they contained to me, not you. He planned it. He knew full well you would likely refuse to give me so much as a farthing. I know you have never liked me very much—you have made that plain on any number of occasions." She jerked her chin from his clasp and took a step away from him before continuing her defense, glaring at him with hurt eyes.

"I cannot believe you would go so far as to attempt to take away from me that which Uncle Philip wanted me to have. He knew what Father was—an improvident but charming man. It was inevitable that Father would likely come to grief with one of his lunatic investments. It was Uncle's way of caring for me—just as you cared for me in an entirely different way the other evening."

What Jonathan might have replied was never to be known for at that suspenseful and tense moment Jenkens entered to announce Lord Chessyre.

Since his lordship had been much in the habit of calling on the ladies and they seemed fond of the gentleman, Jenkens had allowed him to follow. He entered the morning room totally oblivious to the atmosphere.

"Good morning, Lady Mary, Sophie. You here again, Lowell?" Lord Chessyre commented in jest. "One would think you lived here." Without waiting for an answer to this quip, his lordship turned to Sophie to add, "There is to be a gala program at Vauxhall this coming Saturday and I hoped that if you felt sufficiently well, we could take it in."

"We should like that very much and I believe I am far better today. My cousin offers most stimulating conversation," she said with a sly glance at Jonathan.

"My sister is looking forward to meeting you. I have told her much about you," Lord Chessyre said, continuing to ignore Jonathan. He as much as said that if Jonathan was not going to make headway with his beautiful cousin, he, William Chessyre, was not allowing the grass to grow beneath *his* feet.

Rather than leave, Jonathan retired to stand by the fireplace, refusing to give his friend the field.

Sophie, he admitted reluctantly, looked adorably confused—as well she might. He intended to confuse the chit so much that she would blurt out the truth. He would know what that sum was, the money that ought to have been his by rights. His solicitor would doubtlessly agree with him, Jonathan knew, forgetting that his solicitor rarely ever disagreed with Jonathan.

Jonathan would still like to have known if what Sophie had said the night she was ill was true. No matter what else happened, he longed to know the truth of that endearment.

Mr. Somerset entered on the heels of Jenkens' announcement of him. He carried a bouquet of delicate blooms that he handed to Sophie with a reverence due the Queen.

"I just learned of your illness. I would have brought you flowers before this, Miss Garnett, had I known. I trust you are feeling more the thing by this time?" He glanced at Jonathan, giving him a rather curious look.

Jonathan fumed in silence, wishing those fellows gone that he might continue his challenge with Sophie. However, they stayed. Jonathan stayed as well.

Lady Mary rang for tea, seeming amused about something. She poured and ordered biscuits passed around with the ease of one who could do it in her sleep.

Lord Chessyre mentioned the expedition to Vauxhall again. "I hope you will not be overtired," he said with a glance at Jonathan. "I know your cousin has been much concerned for your health. I'd not wish to have you ill again."

Mr. Somerset took this opportunity to ask Sophie when she thought she might feel up to taking in the panorama at Leiscestor Square.

With a faintly defiant glance at her cousin, Sophie suggested, "I should think that by Monday next both Lady Mary and I ought to be quite our old selves again. Is that not right, my lady?"

"Indeed. I rather long to see that panorama. Cannot think why I have never gone. I suppose it is something one does with friends or relatives and not alone."

"Well, I am very pleased Mr. Somerset will take us, for I long to see it as well." The look she cast at Jonathan was clearly defiant at this point. Let him be angry, let him rant and rave, she would enjoy the company of these very fine gentlemen and ignore his ire.

Jonathan looked as though he might grumble about her jaunting about the city so soon after her malaise, but he didn't say a word. He merely smoldered. He was like a banked fire that would rise to a blaze with the slightest touch.

At last and with great reluctance, Lord Chessyre rose to depart. "Coming, Somerset? I suspect Lowell has some concern that he wishes to discuss with his fair cousin and has been wanting us gone this half hour." He bowed to Lady Mary and paused before Sophie, giving her an earnest smile. "I shall look forward to this coming Saturday with great anticipation."

"As do I, my lord," Sophie said, a genuine smile lighting her remarkable cerulean eyes with vivacity.

"And I will await this coming Monday with equal expectancy," Mr. Somerset said with a courtly bow before Sophie.

"It shall be a marvelous afternoon, I know," she replied with simple directness.

Jonathan decided that she accepted all this homage like a princess. Her utter grace when she rose from her chair to bid the men good-bye was quite enough to make him grind his teeth. How he would like to shake her until *her* teeth rattled in that beautiful head.

Once the three of them were alone Jonathan wondered how best to attack the problem of the legacy from Uncle Philip again. He had not counted upon the interruption from his friends to dilute his anger or allow Sophie a chance to think.

"Really, my lord, I quite forgot to offer you my gratitude for all you did for Sophie while she was ill," Lady Mary said. "I had not realized the extent of your ministrations until Anna told me that she had been felled with the malady and that no one in the house had been able to move a finger to help the one most in need of it. Sophie might have died but for you. How does one adequately thank another for such a gift? Life."

Her ladyship had walked to Jonathan's side and now reached up to bestow a delicate kiss on his cheek, unusual for a woman who was normally a trifle reticent.

Sophie, taking her cue from Lady Mary, also walked to Jonathan and touched his arm. "I know how angry you are with me at the moment. I can only pray that the anger will abate and you will once again become my beloved cousin. I am so very grateful, dearest Jonathan. No matter how exasperated I may become with you, please know that you have my heart . . . that is, my heartfelt appreciation."

Sophie planted a kiss on his cheek as well, taking note of the faint raspiness of his skin, the tang of the lotion he used, the sensation of leashed strength emanating from him. She hoped he didn't catch her slip. She had almost told him he had her heart—which he did, of course, but he must not know it. How foolish if she were to tell him of her love, her long-held passion for him.

Jonathan simply looked down at Sophie, then to where Lady Mary stood close by and shook his head, as though denying all. He pulled the folded wad of notes from his pocket and handed them to Sophie. "Here, you may as well have this money—for the time being, at least. I will consult my solicitor to see what he has to say in all this. I shall return once I know."

Chapter Eleven

"**D**o you realize what I almost did?" Sophie cried once she was certain her cousin was out of hearing. "I almost told that dratted man that he had my heart! Which he does, but I shall *never* let him know it."

"Now, now, dear," Lady Mary said, soothing Sophie by putting her arms around her and patting her back in a most comforting way. "I have often wondered if it might not be a wise thing were a woman more open regarding her feelings for a gentleman. There are ways you might let him know."

"Oh, a silly fan or parasol turned this way and that." Sophie sniffed in dismissal, while resting her head on Lady Mary's shoulder.

"You might try to be a trifle more conciliatory. But I suppose that is why I never married," she reflected.

Sophie pulled back to give Lady Mary a puzzled look. "You were not accommodating? I find that impossible to believe. There is not a kinder, more understanding person in this world."

"I was not always this way. When I was young, I was a stubborn lass—like someone else I know. I wanted my own way once too often and it cost me dearly. So now I let everyone believe I am a spinster by choice. However, I cannot but think every woman—deep in her heart—longs for a gentle companion for her twilight years—some nice gentleman with whom she may share her life."

"Let me know when you attain that great age, dear ma'am. I believe that is some distance off," Sophie said, placing a fond kiss on her ladyship's cheek, which was pleasantly scented with heliotrope and fine French soap.

"My advice is to go to your room and take a lovely nap. I intend to do that very thing. There is nothing like a nap to make the world seem nicer, your problems less harrowing."

"Would that that were true," Sophie said, sighing at the memory of her dear cousin glaring at her after handing her the notes he'd gained from the sale of the books.

She opened her clenched hand to look at the sum. "Small bills," she noted. "A vast number of them. I think I will write him a note of thanks rather than wait to express my appreciation in person. Jonathan can be a bit daunting, especially when he is furious with one." Sophie took leave of Lady Mary, pausing to watch as the other made her way up the stairs to her room.

Acting upon her resolve, Sophie found some elegant hot-pressed paper and composed a stiff little message to her cousin, informing him of her gratitude for his kindness. After sanding it and affixing a wafer to the neatly folded sheet, she gave it to Jenkens.

"Please see that this reaches my cousin as soon as possible, would you?" At his nod, she thanked him politely and also went to her room. She intended to think, but the rigors of her day caught up with her and she fell asleep while considering some genteel way she might let Jonathan know that she loved him with all her silly heart.

Jonathan gazed out his window with unseeing eyes. He had actually gone to his solicitor's office. But upon reaching for the doorknob, he found he could not force himself to open it and go inside. Fool, he chided his cowardly self. He had turned away and walked to his rooms, scolding himself with every step.

But was it really cowardly? Did his initial action not stem from a wish that Sophie had come to him to share the delightful nonsense of their uncle electing to leave her all that lovely money in such a bizarre manner? Had he not known pain that she could not bring herself to confide the slightest thing to him?

His mental meanderings were interrupted by a rap at his door. Fyfield, his valet and butler, answered it and shortly Sir Cecil Radcliffe entered his room.

"This is a surprise," Jonathan said, welcoming the gentleman he knew only casually. He was aware that Sir Cecil's wife, Lady Anne, was a good friend of Sophie's. He offered the gentleman a glass of wine, then gestured him to be seated.

The conversation was general at first—politics, the weather, the state of the economy, the two men finding great accord in their views. Then Sir Cecil got to the point of his visit.

"I had not realized that you were cousin to Miss Sophie Garnett." Sir Cecil shifted in his chair, assessing Jonathan with a steady gaze.

"I have that dubious pleasure," Jonathan assured him while wondering what would come next.

"My wife holds her in high esteem. She's a lovely girl." Sir Cecil's gaze sharpened, his eyes narrowed.

"Exceedingly so," Jonathan agreed grimly.

"What do you intend to do about her? Anne spilled the tale of your taking care of Sophie during her illness and insisted I come to her defense. Egad, man, have you no sense of what is due her?"

"I see that Sophie, in spite of telling me not to relate the specifics to anyone, has elected to share that particular story."

"Speaks well of you, I must say. Anne thinks you a blasted hero. But dash it all, you were alone with the girl in her room for the entire night. What if the maid talks? I assume it was totally innocent, but will Society see it that way? You know how people are."

"I also know life would be hell if I were compelled to marry my stubborn little cousin, who, I may add, hates me with a passion." Jonathan took a gulp of fine wine that deserved better appreciation.

"Are you certain that passion is hatred?" Sir Cecil observed with care.

"I don't doubt it." Jonathan bleakly wished it were otherwise.

"Isn't it possible that your cousin truly does care for you and that the passion is a far better sort?"

"Rubbish," Jonathan said briskly, putting the alluring thought of a passionate Sophie from his mind.

He decided that since Sir Cecil knew of the night spent at

Sophie's bedside, he might as well know the other side of the beautiful girl. So he regaled Sir Cecil—who would be in the nature of an impartial listener—with the tale of Uncle Philip and his legacy to Sophie.

"She gave you no idea as to how much he left her?" an astounded Sir Cecil queried at the conclusion of the story.

"Refused point-blank to say a word."

"Dash it all man, we know that women haven't a head for money. Where has she put it?" an astounded Sir Cecil asked.

"In my bank. A thoughtful clerk chanced to comment on the unusual means of her receiving a bequest—which is how I found out!" Jonathan shared a knowing look with his guest.

"The devil you say!" Sir Cecil said with more than a little amazement.

"All true," Jonathan replied, pouring them each another glass of wine.

"Well, this puts another complexion on the matter altogether. However, Anne said that Sophie is a fine young woman and deserves a better life than being a companion. Her father was a fool—if you don't mind my saying so. Invested in every stupid scheme imaginable. Perhaps your uncle thought her virtue should be rewarded?"

"Virtue rewarded? Nonsense," Jonathan replied, downing his wine. He leaned over to replenish Sir Cecil's glass as well as his own. Sophie had virtues, that much he knew, but he doubted it they were the sort whoever coined that phrase had in mind. He considered the image he carried of her clothed in that lovely wisp of a shift and wished most heartily that conditions were different.

"You do not suspect that she has lost that, er, quality?" a shocked Sir Cecil said, looking askance at Jonathan.

"Nothing of the kind. She is simply a stubborn girl bent on having her way. I suppose that after a life of living with her mother's odd whims and coping with her father's disasters, she rather relishes a bit of money of her own. Her brother has always placed himself first, looking after his own interests," Jonathan added in an aside. Both men knew that sort of chap—there were enough of them about.

"What do you intend to do?" Sir Cecil inquired, far more in charity with Jonathan now that he knew the whole story.

"At first I was inclined to demand she give up the money. After all, those books were in Lowell Hall and once part of the estate." He glanced at his companion, who nodded gravely.

"However, upon reflection, I shall allow her to keep the money. I doubt if it is as much as I first suspected. My uncle was no fool; he'd scarcely give a vast sum to a female to control, now would he?"

"Never," Sir Cecil replied, promptly agreeing with this assessment. "That is quite noble of you, old fellow. Anne has the right of it, you really are a hero. Nice there was enough for Miss Garnett to have that curricle. Anne said it is a delicious little rig-out, to use her expression. Prime cattle, as well," he said.

"I'd forgotten that for a moment," Jonathan said, pouring them each yet another glass of wine.

Behind them, Fyfield replenished the empty wine bottle with a freshly opened one, then discreetly disappeared.

"Gave me three hundred pounds in cash to buy that carriage and cattle," Jonathan said without the faintest slur in his voice. "When I nearly dropped that book another hundred-pound note fell from between pages. I wonder just how many of them there were?" He studied the wine in his glass, holding it up to the light to admire the lovely color.

Sir Cecil was silent, no doubt contemplating hundreds of pound notes falling like a blizzard from between the pages of books. It was clear that he was awed at the prospect.

"Well, I say it is most gentlemanly of you to permit the girl to retain that money," Sir Cecil insisted. "Most noble. Dash it all, Lowell, you are a man among men, a veritable hero, as Anne put it," he observed before rising to leave.

"Well," Jonathan said modestly, feeling extremely in charity with the genial Sir Cecil, "I shall take the books she doesn't want to keep and bring them up to Lowell Hall. The rest I'll sell and give her the money."

"It has been a pleasure to chat with you, Lowell," Sir Cecil said earnestly after setting his empty glass on the side table. "I always knew you to be a fine chap but never realized what an admirable person you are."

"The pleasure was all mine, dear fellow," Jonathan said in reply, sorry to see such an astute gentleman leave. "Give my regards to your lady wife."

Jonathan escorted Sir Cecil to the door, then after closing it, decided he would go over the remaining books to see what they might be. He'd forgotten the contents of his uncle's library. It was not a place in which the youthful Jonathan was wont to linger.

So it was that on the following day he returned to the house on Lower Brook Street to be let in by Jenkens.

"The ladies are out, my lord," the butler kindly informed him.

"Quite all right," Jonathan said, still basking in the approval heaped upon him by Sir Cecil. "I have come to take a look at a few more boxes of my late uncle's books. Could someone bring a few of them upstairs?"

"If I may be so bold, perhaps you would like to look at them yourself first," the butler suggested. "Each box is marked with the contents—history, agriculture, and so forth. It might save you time and bother."

Deciding that it was an excellent notion, Jonathan followed Jenkens along the passage and down the stairs to where he had once hunted for a remedy to give a very ill Sophie. He ignored the cupboards through which he had frantically searched for something that might be of help.

There was a pungency to the beer cellar that gave the search an unusual aspect, he decided a short time later. One could almost become tipsy in such an atmosphere. He selected the boxes he wanted and went upstairs to wait for them. He knew better than to shock Jenkens by offering to carry one up himself. The butler would have been deeply offended.

There were no additional notes fluttering forth from between the pages of a book, to Jonathan's sorrow. After checking the contents of all the boxes, he directed them to be carried to where his carriage awaited him.

"Tell Miss Sophie that I have removed a few more boxes. Once I have disposed of them, I shall return for the remainder.

Perhaps she would be so kind as to make certain that the ones she wishes to retain will be elsewhere?"

Jenkens assured his lordship that he would personally see to the matter.

Once at his home, Jonathan spent the rest of the day examining the books. To his delight his uncle had been an eclectic collector, buying whatever struck his fancy. It was evident that some were books the previous Lords Lowell had bought and kept, for a number of the volumes were exceedingly old, with fine leather bindings not to mention creative spelling.

The following morning Jonathan, with Fyfield assisting him, took those books he decided not to keep to the same bookseller. A generous sum was offered for them which Jonathan accepted with alacrity.

"Well, I feel I am paring down the library to an agreeable number of books that might actually be read, rather than stuffy tomes that will gather dust on the shelves," Jonathan commented to Fyfield, the man who did everything from serving as butler to valet for him.

"Indeed, sir. It will be pleasant to see books in the library shelves at Lowell Hall again, will it not?"

"Dashed odd thing of my uncle to do, Fyfield. Think on it, giving all that cash to a woman!"

The butler-cum-valet was suitably silent in the wake of this statement.

The next day was Saturday and Sophie looked forward to the visit to Vauxhall Gardens with Lord Chessyre, as well as his sister and her husband.

"Do you think this gown and the matching pelisse will be appropriate to wear?" Sophie asked, presenting herself for Lady Mary's inspection.

"I believe that delicate rose well becomes you," her ladyship said after a brief study of the ensemble newly come from Madame Clotilde. The gown was sarcenet with tiny silk roses decorating the sleeves and clustered here and there on the rolled hem. The matching pelisse also had dainty clusters of the silk roses. Through Sophie's curls Anna had threaded a small demiturban, the fine muslin of which was tied in a dainty flat bow.

Sophie pirouetted once again, then sat on the little cane chair near the window of Lady Mary's bedroom. "I vow I am most anxious to see this place of which I have heard so much. My brother related such tales!" Sophie exchanged a twinkling look with her ladyship. "Is it as dangerous as he implied?"

"You must be careful where you go. It won't do to go wandering off down one of those dark side lanes with a gentleman, no matter how fine you think him—or so I have been informed. I would not know about that."

Sophie wished that she could find a gentleman who would be the companion for her ladyship's declining years. She certainly deserved a man who would amuse and cosset her.

"We had best present ourselves in the drawing room, for it is soon time that Lord Chessyre arrives to fetch us. Do you nurture a *tendre* for the gentleman?" she asked Sophie as they made their way down the stairs.

"He is a handsome, considerate man," Sophie replied cautiously. "I like him very much, very much indeed."

Jonathan, who had come to give Sophie the latest sum of money from the book sales, drew in a sharp breath as her words drifted down the stairs to where he waited in the drawing room. There were distinct disadvantages to being a member of the family and being allowed upstairs when others would have been kept in the entry. He quickly walked to the other end of the room and pretended to contemplate the drab view from the windows.

"Jonathan!" Sophie exclaimed when she entered the room.

"I came to give you this money from the sale of the books. You have informed Jenkens which box holds the volumes you wish to keep?" He knew he sounded stiff and formal but the implication of her words had left him reeling.

"I have done so." She crossed to his side, obviously looking to see if he showed signs of having heard her words.

"I see you are prepared for your expedition to Vauxhall. I shall merely give you the money and be on my way. If it is agreeable, I will take the remaining boxes tomorrow. Then her ladyship will have the use of her beer cellar once again." He bowed in the direction of Lady Mary before handing Sophie the packet of money.

"Thank you again, Jonathan," Sophie said, constraint coloring her words and attitude.

"Happy to be of service." He held Sophie's hand briefly, bowing slightly to her before striding from the room.

"Well," Sophie said after looking from the window to see Jonathan taking off in his carriage at a fast clip, "what a mood he was in, to be sure."

"Perhaps he heard your praise—such as it was—for Lord Chessyre?" Lady Mary suggested.

"I doubt it." Sophie checked the amount of money in the packet, showed it to her ladyship, then crossed to tuck the packet well back in the drawer of the writing desk. "I had no idea that those books would bring such a tidy sum. I wonder how many of those books will end up at Lowell Hall? Not many, judging from the money in that packet."

"He did say he would compensate you for the ones he elected to keep," Lady Mary reminded her.

Jenkens announced Lord Chessyre and within a few minutes they had left the house and were on their way to Vauxhall.

Lady Elizabeth Spencer, his sister, and her husband, Mr. Edward Spencer, proved to be utterly charming, if a trifle reserved. Lady Elizabeth had been serving as a lady of the bedchamber to the Duchess of York and seemed vastly pleased to be done with her position, if reluctant to speak of the duchess. She merely murmured that she hoped never to see a dog again as long as she lived.

Sophie, having heard of the Duchess of York's penchant for a vast number of dogs that were allowed to roam as they pleased, could sympathize with her ladyship's feelings.

Vauxhall turned out to be even more enchanting than Sophie had hoped. The infectious combination of throngs of merrymakers, the happy music that floated around them, and bright lanterns casting a glow over all lent a carnival atmosphere to the scene.

She was quite willing to be taken about to see the wonders and charms found within the pleasure gardens.

The puppets delighted her, the rope dancer caused Sophie to

hold her breath in amazement, whereas the statues and busts found in niches along the walks were quietly impressive.

"I suppose this place is not half as pretty by daylight," Sophie mused to Lady Mary as they watched a couple wander off along one of the side lanes her ladyship had cautioned Sophie against. The girl giggled in a manner that revealed she anticipated her walk with eagerness.

"Things that appear magical at night are often tawdry by day," her ladyship replied absently. "Do you know, I thought I saw Lord Lowell over there. I must be mistaken. Surely he might have mentioned it to us were he planning to be here this evening—seeing that he knew we were coming."

"I doubt if my esteemed cousin would be here, of all places. I feel certain you imagined it. I see no one like him at all," Sophie assured her ladyship. Indeed, if Lady Mary thought she saw Jonathan, she was very mistaken. There could be no one who remotely resembled her handsome cousin. He was most definitely one of a kind.

The rack punch was not to her liking, but the shaved ham and delicately cooked chicken were delicious. Lord Chessyre had provided everything he thought might be enjoyable for his guests. His sister praised his efforts and sought Sophie's agreement that William was in all things admirable.

"Elizabeth, you have too long been with the duchess," he said with an uncomfortable laugh. "Do not tease Miss Garnett for her opinion of me, I beg you."

"I think you are a very fine man," Sophie offered, mindful of what Lady Mary had said about allowing a gentleman to know more of what you felt.

He glanced to where Lady Mary sat before exchanging a look with his sister.

"Come, Miss Garnett, I would show you a few of the interesting items that we have missed. We shall return in time for the fireworks." He spoke quietly and since Lady Elizabeth was now chatting with Lady Mary over the price of India muslin, that good lady missed the departure of the couple.

Sophie said not a word when he guided her along one of those side lanes she'd observed. If Lord Chessyre was the fine man she believed, she had nothing to fear from him.

They paused in the shadow of a hedge and his lordship turned so he faced Sophie.

"You are incredibly lovely this evening—in fact every evening. May I, my angelic Sophie?" Without awaiting her reply Lord Chessyre leaned down to kiss her, wrapping her lightly in his arms. It was a gentle salute, not at all like the intense, if brief, kiss from Jonathan.

Sophie had closed her eyes. Now, they fluttered open to gaze at his lordship with speculation. "So refined, my lord," she whispered.

"Refined? Of course. Do you think I would insult you by revealing base passions?" He placed her hand on his arm and resumed their stroll along the lane.

Sophie wondered if she would appreciate being treated like a piece of fragile porcelain. Perhaps his restraint was due to the proximity of others? Surely she was pleased?

Behind them, Jonathan called himself nine different sorts of fool. If he had wanted to punish himself, he had set about it in the right way. But, he reflected, that had been an amazingly passionless kiss. Since he had kissed Sophie more than once, he was well aware that passion simmered under her polite exterior. If she loved Chessyre, she undoubtedly would have responded in a way that would have encouraged him to take greater liberties.

It was a good thing both of them had been so circumspect, otherwise Jonathan might have felt compelled to defend her honor and that would have revealed his presence here tonight. That was a stupidity he would rather keep to himself. Deciding that he had best take himself home before he made a fool of himself, Jonathan disappeared in the throng of people and was gone.

"Look, there is Mr. Montegu," Sophie exclaimed when they had retraced their steps to the Grand Walk. The tulip was approaching them from the Chinese Walk. Behind him could be seen elegant lanterns swaying in the evening breeze.

"My dear Miss Garnett and Lord Chessyre. This is an evening for meeting people one knows. I just observed Lord Lowell in this very area. And I think I saw your friend Somerset around here somewhere." The tulip wore a vague look along with his splendid attire of magnificent coloring, while glancing about himself as though in search of the people he mentioned.

Sophie did not turn to Lord Chessyre lest he see her reaction to the information that Jonathan had been here minutes before them. Could he have seen that kiss? After possibly hearing what she had said of her feelings for Lord Chessyre, what would he think now?

There was little doubt in her mind that *if* he had observed the pleasant and rather proper salute, he would put the worst construction on it. It seemed to her a great failing in men that they never put themselves in the place of those they judged!

"Ah, there's Somerset. I was correct; he is here." Mr. Montegu waved his handsome cane in the air and managed to catch the attention of a soberly garbed Mr. Somerset. When that gentleman joined them the contrast between his subdued attire and the peacocky clothes worn by Mr. Montegu was almost comical.

Fortunately for Sophie, Lady Elizabeth and her husband, along with Lady Mary, joined them at that moment. It saved her from the effort of making any conversation.

"We wish to see the fireworks. Do come along with us," Lady Elizabeth said to those who stood with her brother and Sophie.

Swept along with the others, Sophie kept her worries at bay and enjoyed the fireworks. Catherine wheels and rockets and a myriad of other fireworks soared into the air, exploding with a noise that had Sophie covering her ears. The grand finish was a portrayal of the English flag in full color, as though waving in the breeze.

When they left the viewing area, gay music could be heard. Sophie tried to contain a yawn but was seen by Lady Elizabeth.

"Dear me, Miss Garnett, you yawn. I fear you are not quite as stout as you might wish. My brother told me of your illness. Perhaps it is best if we call it a night. William?"

With obvious reluctance, Lord Chessyre agreed and escorted Sophie and Lady Mary to Lower Brook Street, where he bid them good night with a special smile for Sophie.

The following day Lord Lowell appeared at the house on Lower Brook Street to pick up the remaining boxes of books while Lady Mary and Sophie were away at church.

Sophie was sorry to have missed Jonathan when Jenkens told her his lordship had been there. She had longed to ask him about being at Vauxhall even though she knew it not the thing to do.

It was Lord Chessyre, calling on Monday afternoon, who revealed that Lord Lowell had gone to the country on some matters of importance.

Later Sophie spoke of this to Lady Mary. This good lady observed, "Our heads, my dear child, are influenced by our hearts. A man's heart is influenced by his head. There is no saying what nonsense has become rooted in your cousin's brain."

Nonsense or no, Sophie found she missed Jonathan dreadfully—which was odd, all things considered.

Chapter Twelve

They had not gone to view the panorama on Monday after all, Mr. Somerset being indisposed.

"Poor Mr. Somerset. He was so looking forward to showing us the panorama. He seems to think he will feel more the thing by Wednesday," Lady Mary said. She sat by the window in a new upholstered armchair while working on her embroidery, occasionally pausing to chat.

Sophie poked about in the depths of the new pagoda-roof worktable she had bought for herself. The very latest design, she was pleased with how commodious it was, yet vexed that she couldn't find the color tapestry yarn she wanted. Seated on the pretty scroll-armed settee in the drawing room, she probed and sighed. Her needlework slipped off her lap to fall in a heap on the floor.

"What you need is a dog," her ladyship observed. "You would have something to amuse yourself besides that needlework."

"A cat might do as well," Sophie replied, giving her ladyship an arrested look.

"Cats adore playing with yarns, if you think about it," her ladyship said.

"True," Sophie replied quietly, once more seemingly absorbed in hunting for the elusive shade of blue needed for a morning glory. "I shall think about it."

Jonathan had taken the rest of the books and gone. She had really done it this time. He would most likely never call again. Even the money from that last sale of books had been delivered by a footman. She might as well resign herself to the loss of her dear cousin from her life forever. Dratted man. Why could he not see that he was the only one for her? Never mind that they disagreed on one or two matters.

Jenkens paused at the door to announce Mr. Somerset had come to see them.

"Ladies, how pleasant a scene you make. Indeed, it would make a pretty painting," he said as he advanced into the room, his expression plainly admiring. He bowed first to Lady Mary, then came to where Sophie sat on the lovely settee of striped rose silk. When she gestured to the place at her side, he beamed a smile and sat down.

"I trust you are feeling better now?" Lady Mary inquired politely.

"Indeed, ma'am. It was but a trifling indisposition. I hoped that if you were not otherwise engaged you would do me the honor of visiting the panorama tomorrow afternoon. Your cousin would not object?" he said, turning to Sophie with a questioning look.

"As far as I know, Jonathan has gone off to the country. Something about pressing business at Lowell Hall, I believe. And anyway, regardless of what he says, he has nothing to do with my life." She raised her lovely face, her chin having a slightly stubborn tilt to it.

"You are in first looks this morning, Miss Garnett."

Indeed, Sophie was looking her best, even if her sleep had been restless. Anna had threaded her curls with a rose riband to match the pretty morning gown of rose India muslin that she wore. It fell in graceful folds about her, lace insets peeping out here and there. There was delicate lace on the bodice as well and Lady Mary thought Sophie resembled nothing so much as a confection from Gunter's.

"How kind of you, Mr. Somerset." Sophie regarded him with a benevolent eye, for he was a pleasant-looking man, nicely dressed, with no leanings to dandyism.

He chatted about generalities, enthused on the spectacle to be viewed at the panorama on the morrow, then rose and bid them good day, as was quite proper.

Sophie was about to launch a discussion on what might be seen at the panorama when Jenkens entered, wearing a most pleased expression. "Lord Crewe, my lady."

She set aside her work and rose to greet the gentleman she had met but once. "Lady Mary, perhaps you recall my mentioning Lord Crewe? He was so kind as to chat with me when we were at the Sefton dinner."

If Lord Crewe thought that he had done a favor by chatting with an angelically beautiful woman, he denied it immediately. "My pleasure, completely, Miss Garnett, I assure you."

Again, they began with the usual generalities: weather, friends they shared, and amusements to be found in the city.

"I hope you have not forgotten my promise to obtain tickets for the British Museum, Miss Garnett?" his lordship said at last.

"No, I had not. In fact, I have quite hoped that you remembered." Sophie gave him a questioning and rather hopeful look. The British Museum was one place she quite longed to see.

He explained that the trustee he'd wish to ask, Lord Granville, had been out of town but that he was now returned. Lord Crewe had lost no time in importuning him for several tickets.

"I took the liberty of obtaining them for this coming Friday and can only hope it will be agreeable with you?"

He looked so anxious that Sophie resolved that any matter that might have been pending would have been promptly dismissed.

"We are indebted to you, my lord," Lady Mary said on behalf of both the ladies.

"Indeed, the week is becoming amazingly delightful when we had thought to sink into ennui," Sophie said with an endearing grin at his lordship.

"We go to view the panorama at Leicester Square with Mr. Somerset tomorrow afternoon," Lady Mary explained. She would have said more but Jenkens entered to smugly announce Lord Chessyre.

"My lord," Sophie said with evident partiality, "how lovely to see you again. Of course you know Lord Crewe." She glanced from one gentleman to the other and smiled at their polite hostility, thinly veiled. If she must find a husband—and

it seemed as though it would be a wise thing to do—one of
these men would do admirably.

"You were just leaving?" Lord Chessyre said with excruci-
ating politeness. "I would not wish to keep you from any ap-
pointments."

"As a matter of fact, I must take my leave—but not until we
set the time. If it is agreeable with you, we are to present ourselves at two that afternoon," he said to Sophie. "I have
arranged for us to view the major acquisitions."

Sophie clapped her hands in delight. "I have been so curious
about the Rosetta Stone. Such mystery!"

Lord Crewe made his departure, leaving Chessyre in possession of the place on the settee with the beautiful Miss Sophie.

"It had been such a dreary day and now we have had such
charming callers," Sophie said with enthusiasm, reaching out
to lightly touch Lord Chessyre's arm. "I am pleased to see
you," she dared to say.

That gentleman cleared his throat and seemed at a loss for
words for a moment. "I thought to make sure you were agree-
ably entertained, seeing as how Lowell has left town."

"Yes," Sophie replied, carefully keeping her expression
neutral. "Something about urgent business, I believe."

"He ran out of space in his rooms for all those volumes. He
had to transport them to Lowell Hall. I fancy he wishes to see
those empty shelves at least somewhat full again." Again,
Lord Chessyre studied Sophie with observant eyes. What he
searched for, she could only guess.

"You knew that our uncle had willed me his library?" Sophie watched his face, wondering just how much he knew.

"Lowell mentioned as much. You are very close to your
cousin." It was not precisely a question but Sophie could detect a speculative quality to his words.

"We have known each other since childhood. Of course,
there are nine years between us, but that scarcely counts, does
it?" Sophie waited to hear his reply with more than polite curiosity. If Lord Chessyre was of an age with Jonathan, and if
he agreed that the difference in age was no problem, it meant
that either he or Jonathan—for that matter—would be an excellent candidate for her affections.

"Not in the least. My sister claims a mature man is far more dependable." His gaze was searching again, as though he wondered what might be behind her question.

"Well, I for one think Sophie ought to have a dog," Lady Mary inserted, reminding them she was present. "It is all very well to receive callers and chat about the weather. But she needs to go out and about and not just in that curricle. Had she a dog, she would take nice walks, have time to admire flowers. You cannot admire flowers from a curricle, particularly when you are driving a pair of horses like those chestnuts."

"Are the chestnuts too much for you?" Lord Chessyre asked in alarm.

"Not in the least," Sophie said, not as convincingly as she might have.

"What sort of dog do you favor? Pug, Pekinese, terrier, poodle? No large dog, I should think. You wish to walk, not be dragged through the park at a great clip." He smiled at Sophie and she melted a little at his charm.

"I truly have not given it a great deal of thought. What do you suggest?"

"I know of a small terrier that has been bred up north. A friend of mine obtained one not long ago and is quite pleased with the little fellow. They are small, but long, dogs. His is a pepper color with a large head, long ears, and a funny topknot that hangs over soft brown eyes, with a crisp, shaggy coat. It seems to be a devoted and obedient animal by all accounts."

"I believe I should like such an unusual little dog. Are they difficult to obtain?" Sophie queried.

"I think I could manage to locate one," the earl said with an earnest look into Sophie's blue eyes, one that was returned by her in full measure, revealing some of her liking for this nice gentleman.

Lady Mary cleared her throat after a few moments of that silent exchange. "How kind of you, my lord."

He seemed to inwardly shake himself and permitted a self-deprecating smile to cross his lips. "I will let you know if I have success."

"I have every confidence in you, Lord Chessyre," Lady Mary assured him with a knowing smile.

He then asked if he might take Sophie for a drive in the park that afternoon and both women agreed, Lady Mary adding it would be just the thing to put a bit of color in Sophie's cheeks.

When they were alone once again, Sophie turned to her dear friend. "He is very nice, isn't he?" It was not really a question, but a statement of fact.

"Be careful, my dear girl," Lady Mary cautioned. "If one is at a crossroads, it is wise to know which lane to take."

"You think I might choose the wrong one?" Sophie asked, knowing that the remark had nothing to do with roads.

"It has happened before to others," the good lady replied before resuming her needlework.

Sophie sat, hands idle in her lap, contemplating the gentlemen who had called this afternoon. Mr. Somerset was modest and likeable and would likely make an admirable husband. Lord Crewe was more difficult to place. He wore fashionable clothes, went to the best homes, and knew the very cream of Society. Beyond that she couldn't say. Her instincts told her he was trustworthy, but was that enough?

Lord Chessyre was a different matter entirely. She truly liked him. Next to Jonathan he was the nicest man she had met. Handsome, his blond hair beautifully brushed to one side, and his eyes so gentle and kind, he was every woman's dream. He was thoughtful where Jonathan dictated. Lord Chessyre considered her wishes, whereas Jonathan thought *he* knew what was best for her. Dratted man, why could she not simply put him from her mind? Just because she had loved him from the moment she became aware of her older cousin was no good reason to continue doing so.

"You had best change for your drive with his lordship," Lady Mary gently said, interrupting Sophie's reflections.

"I dislike leaving you alone." Sophie stored her needlework in the pagoda-topped work table and turned to face her ladyship with a concerned air.

"I am expecting callers of my own, dear girl. Maria Sefton is bringing a friend I've not seen in ages."

"It would be more proper for me to stay with you, but I expect you long for a good gossip," Sophie teased.

"Correct," Lady Mary shot back with amusement.

Sophie went to her room, her thoughts returning to a comparison between Lord Chessyre—William, his sister had called him—and her cousin. Anna assisted her in changing into the blue corded-muslin dress, adding a pretty lilac spencer and a jockey hat with a jaunty knot of lilac ribands to one side. The best thing to do, Sophie decided as she made her way to the ground floor of the house, was to know Lord Chessyre as well as possible. The others, too, perhaps. Eventually the right path would make itself known. Life in London had become far more interesting than anticipated.

Lowell Hall was about the dullest place on earth, Jonathan decided as Fyfield assisted him in placing the books on the shelves according to topic.

"There, my lord, I believe that does it," Fyfield said, standing back to view the effect. Since there were fewer books, gaps occurred here and there. But, Jonathan assured himself, that merely allowed for future purchases. He and his descendants would likely want to add a few volumes from time to time. That is, if there were future descendants, he thought gloomily.

What was the matter with him? To leave London at the height of the Season, chancing Sophie to all those other chaps? He had visions of the gentlemen of the *ton* converging upon the house on Lower Brook Street with the intent of carrying off the prize of the Season—Miss Sophie Garnett.

There was no other woman in London with eyes that shade of blue, nor hair quite that color blond—like silver and gold mixed together by a master artist. Her figure was by far the most graceful and shapely—as he had reason to know. Her voice had a pleasing softness and she possessed a better sense of humor than he did, seeing amusement in simple things he tended to overlook. She could make him laugh and he appreciated that quality in her.

"That will be all, Fyfield," he said, crossing to stare off into the distance, toward London.

"Very good, milord. Dinner will be ready shortly."

Jonathan turned his thoughts to London again. Glancing at the clock, he suspected that Sophie would be driving through the park at this hour. He wondered who would be with her. Chessyre? Somerset? Perhaps Crewe decided to make a stab at catching the beauty? He doubted she would entertain Oliver Fane in spite of his distant connection to the wealthy Fanes, of which Lady Jersey was a prime member, and wondered at the man's temerity at seeking Sophie out. Even Reginald Montegu would not dare to ask Sophie to drive with him. But Chessyre would and Sophie had declared that she liked him, liked him very much.

Jonathan poured himself a glass of wine and resumed his blind stare from the window of the library.

The following afternoon brought Mr. Somerset to Lower Brook Street, all eagerness to treat Lady Mary and Sophie to the delights found at the panorama at Leicester Square.

Sophie was quite agog when climbing the stairs to the viewing area. "The Bay of Messina is the first of the paintings, you say?" she demanded of Mr. Somerset. "I believe that is a port in Sicily, is it not?"

"The northeast part, Miss Garnett," he replied while holding open the door for her and Lady Mary.

After the three of them had spent two hours viewing the perfectly splendid painting of the Bay of Messina and the smaller one of The Siege of Flushing, they walked slowly down the stairs, enthusiastically comparing observations.

"Well," Lady Mary said, "I was glad to have my hat tied on, for it was all so real I fully expected a breeze to blow it off. It was like being in the open air!"

"Most astonishing," Sophie agreed. "The perspective was remarkable. At one point I thought I was thirty miles distant from it, while another area was so detailed it seemed I was but a few feet away. Oh, I am so pleased you thought to invite us for a viewing."

"There were a vast number of people in attendance," Lady Mary observed.

"It is enormously popular. I was surprised and most delighted that you had not already been to see it." Mr. Somerset continued in his most congenial manner to chat about the painting's quality and to enthuse on the offerings by the Royal

Academy in the north wing of Somerset House. "Not that I am in any way related to those Somersets," he modestly explained.

Over dinner, dressed for their evening at Almack's, Lady Mary offered her opinion of the young gentleman who had escorted them that day. "A very fine man, I believe."

Sophie noted that the words were kind but not the sort that endorsed, matching her estimation exactly.

Almack's was much as usual, Sophie decided as she danced her way through a cotillion with Mr. Somerset. Now that Jonathan was not around to frown at suitors, she was besieged from all sides. At first it was fun. Later it became wearisome and she almost wished he were there to look down that aristocratic nose of his at some of the presumptuous puppies who dared to ask for her hand in a Scots Reel or a country dance.

"I think not," Sophie murmured to Lady Mary as another of these sprigs approached.

"I must say I miss your cousin. He is so clever at rejecting these creatures without offending them." Lady Mary gave a significant look at Lord Chessyre, who obediently turned up at Sophie's elbow just as the sprig attempted to ask for a dance.

"Sorry, old chap, the lady has accepted my request," his lordship said with great charm.

"You didn't say what that request was," Sophie whispered as the sprig walked away, looking most dejected.

"None of his business, is it?"

"Now you sound like Jonathan," Sophie said with a laugh.

"We peers are like that," Lord Chessyre replied with a mock note of snobbery on his face. "Come with me and select a glass of lemonade and one of those little cakes they set out in hopes that no one will eat them."

"Dreadful man," Sophie said with a playful tap on his arm with her fan.

They strolled along at the perimeter of the room, her hand placed correctly on his proffered arm, their steps matching.

"Heard from your cousin?" Lord Chessyre asked casually.

"Jonathan? Not likely," she said in blunt honesty.

"Had a falling out, did you?"

"Well, let us say he wanted me to tell him about something and I said no," Sophie replied with some evasion.

"I see," his lordship answered. Whatever he saw was not expanded upon. Rather, he informed her that he had stopped by his friend's house to learn the direction of the man who bred those little terriers. The chap happened to be in London for the Season and was said to have several of the little dogs with him. William intended to call upon him on the morrow.

"My," Sophie said in admiration, "you do not let the grass grow under your feet, do you?"

"I believe in taking advantage of every favorable situation, you may be sure. With any luck at all I should be able to offer you the dog by Saturday, if that pleases you?" He handed her a glass of lemonade, studying her all the while, his handsome face lit with interest.

Sophie took a sip, then nodded. "Most agreeable, my lord." She wondered if he intended to court her now that Jonathan was out of the way and she felt a pleasant tingle of anticipation. How many other girls could claim to have such nice and highly eligible gentlemen seek their company?

The following day Mr. Oliver Fane chanced to call while the ladies were quietly at their embroidery. Sophie was not really pleased to see him, but hadn't the heart to depress his attentions. He chatted for a time, then just as he was about to depart he hesitantly put forth his plan.

"Lady Mary, Miss Garnett, I would be pleased if you would attend a performance at Astley's with me this coming week. If you have not been there, it is a most amazing place."

"Well," Lady Mary said, "I suppose I ought to be too old to enjoy such entertainment, but I believe we shall accept your kind offer, sir. I think it promises a good evening. Sophie, do you not agree?"

With such encouragement Sophie could scarcely say no to the gentleman. Puzzled as to why Lady Mary advanced his cause, Sophie politely murmured her agreement, then suggested that he might like to dine with them first, seeing Lady Mary nod her acquiescence.

When they were again alone, Sophie looked at the lady who

had been her employer and had become the best of friends. "I perceive you play a deep game, my lady."

"Perhaps. And then perhaps I simply enjoy stirring the pot, as it were." There was a teasing glance from her ladyship that put Sophie into giggles.

They attended the theater that evening and Sophie looked over the crowd, wondering what Jonathan was doing to keep him occupied for so long. She missed him far more than she ought, given the brangling they indulged in whenever they met. He was the bane and the delight of her life, it seemed.

Even with her usual court clustered about her Sophie thought the theater insipid and was glad when they went home.

Friday brought a much better diversion, for Lord Crewe and his promised excursion to the British Museum was a long-hoped-for treat.

Sophie dressed with great care in a pink muslin gown ornamented with rows of tucks and tiny bows here and there. Her narrow-brimmed bonnet was pink-and-white striped sarcenet with a cluster of pink ribbon to one side and looked most dashing, according to Anna.

Her pains proved to be well received, for Lord Crewe's gaze was most admiring.

"You will vie with the attractions offered at the museum, Miss Garnett. I am certain that more eyes will be directed at you than at the exhibits."

"Oh, I hope not," she said with a smile. "I'd not wish to detract from such noteworthy objects."

He bestowed an approving nod on such modest sentiments, then escorted the ladies off in his elegant carriage to where Montagu House stood in its splendor. Sophie was glad the more stringent restrictions that had prevailed in the past had been relaxed somewhat. Lady Mary's account of her previous visit sounded dreadfully rushed and boring.

The porter had their tickets waiting for them and the three found their way to the room where they were to meet their escort. Rather than wait for a larger group, they were to have a private tour, allowing them to make a more leisurely inspection of items that caught their fancy.

Sophie found herself wishing Jonathan were with her when she viewed a copy of the Magna Carta. Many years ago they had argued about what was in the document, Sophie claiming that there must be more rights for women than revealed. Jonathan, in his superior age, had denied all. From the translation, Sophie gathered he had been right.

The mummies were fascinating, the Rosetta Stone absorbing, and Lord Crewe's company delightful. While a quiet man, he displayed a wonderful sense of humor, quite on the wry side with unexpected depths.

When they left the building after two hours of concentrated viewing, Sophie let out a sigh of pleasure.

"I suggest it might be well for us to repair to Gunter's for one of his famous ices," Lord Crewe said, his hand curved around Sophie's elbow by way of assisting her down the steps. He first handed Lady Mary inside his carriage, then turned to study Sophie's happy face.

"I am pleased that this afternoon gave you pleasure. I trust we may find future outings to be just as agreeable?"

"That would be lovely," Sophie said, wishing she could forget about her dratted cousin once and for all so she might concentrate on these other gentlemen. Why could his dark visage not disappear from her mind to be replaced by another? she wondered glumly.

They were at Gunter's, enjoying their ices—Sophie had pineapple and thought it her favorite—when she saw her cousin. He drove past the confectionery shop at a leisurely pace with an absolutely gorgeous creature at his side. Sophie glanced at Lady Mary to see if she had observed the pair. She had and her eyebrows had risen in astonishment.

"I see my cousin found the country a trifle dull after all. He has come to London to remedy that, and quite nicely, too," Sophie observed thoughtfully.

Lord Crewe had also caught sight of the man he had determined to be his chief rival for the interest of the lovely Sophie Garnett and smiled. The chap had not done his suit the least good by being seen in this area with an opera dancer, of all people. Had he an interest, it would have been better for him were it a lady of reasonable quality, not some dancer.

With a smoothness that came with years of experience in handling delicate matters, Lord Crewe murmured something vaguely about how one never knows about such things and that some gentlemen will have their little peccadilloes. He carefully made it sound as though others might behave in that manner but he would not.

Sophie was glad to leave and once at home she found a great number of things to occupy her time, thus avoiding any conversation with Lady Mary.

All the while she stewed about her cousin. It was as well that they had two parties to attend that evening. Jonathan attended neither one, although Sophie searched for him, trying to appear nonchalant about her inspection of the crowds that thronged the rooms.

"I say," Reginald Montegu said when he chanced to meet her at Lady Beckworth's soireé, "your cousin is back in town. Saw him not minutes ago before I came here. He was headed for his club. Heard his luck is phenomenal since he returned."

Which information plunged Sophie into a blue dismal—that her cousin should be declared to have great luck, most likely because he won that gorgeous creature from another. Bother men, anyway!

"I suppose opera dancers are always on the lookout for a better protector," she said to Lady Mary after Mr. Montegu pranced off into the crowd.

"And what do you know about opera dancers, pray tell?"

"Only what I found in my father's papers. Opera dancers are very expensive."

"Particularly if they are beautiful. Formidable competition, my dear," her ladyship murmured.

"If one were competing in something," Sophie shot back in an equally soft voice.

"You claim you have no interest?"

"I so claim," Sophie stoutly affirmed.

"Silly girl," her ladyship said with a smile as she walked with Sophie to their carriage. "Tomorrow Lord Chessyre will undoubtedly bring that little dog for you. Best think of a name for it. And remember, although you think him a dog, you cannot name the animal Jonathan!"

Chapter Thirteen

The puppy proved impossible to resist. Soft brown eyes gazed up at Sophie and the little tail gave hesitant wags as the pup awaited her attention.

"That mop of hair is so funny," Sophie said with a chuckle as she accepted the puppy onto her lap and cuddled it close, comforting the little dog lest it feel unwanted. "He follows the latest fashion, I believe. That little topknot flopping over his eyes is worthy of the latest dandy!" Her lovely eyes gleamed with amusement as she glanced up at Lord Chessyre.

"I am relieved you like the little fellow."

"Who could resist him?"

"Have you decided upon a name?" Lady Mary inquired, reaching out a tentative hand to stroke the puppy, who bestowed an enthusiastic lick in return.

"Pickles," Sophie said after reflecting a little. "And do not ask me why, the word just popped into my head. But he is a mixture of colors and so are many pickles, if you follow my thinking."

It was clear that the others did not but were far too polite to argue the matter. After all, the puppy belonged to Sophie and he was hers to name.

Jenkens had thought to bring papers and a rug for the floor and so far the puppy had been very well behaved.

"Should we take Pickles for a walk, do you think?" Sophie asked, studying the silly-looking dog with a frown. "I know so little about dogs that I will need your advice as to how to care for him. I'd not wish him to become ill."

"I am at your disposal, Miss Sophie." Lord Chessyre grinned at the prospect of spending time teaching Sophie to care for her pet.

"Perhaps you might walk him in the park, acquaint him with his lead?" Lady Mary suggested. "I would hope that Lord Chessyre might be able to give you a few pointers on training the puppy. All young ones benefit from proper training."

"Indeed, ma'am," his lordship replied, a twinkle in his very kind gray eyes.

"I shall be but a few moments," Sophie declared, rising to place Pickles on the patch of newspapers.

She was as good as her word, promptly returning to the drawing room dressed with a sensible violet spencer over her walking dress of pale violet muslin. She had clapped a small bonnet on her head, tying the violet ribands before hastily catching up her reticule and a parasol on her way out of her room.

Lord Chessyre's admiring gaze did much to restore Sophie's sense of well-being, which had been quite jarred on Friday when she saw Jonathan. Or to be more specific, when she had seen him driving past Gunter's with that *creature* at his side. Of all the ridiculous things to do, that took the prize.

Jonathan gazed into the looking glass that hung above his shaving stand. "You," he informed that reflection, "are a prize idiot. Whatever made you give in to the demands of the fair Kitty to drive past Gunter's yesterday? It was precisely what this farce needed, an idiot to do something outrageously stupid."

He completed his shaving, amazingly enough not cutting himself, then finished dressing and left his rooms to the administrations of the faithful Fyfield.

Sophie had seen him; he was certain she had. He'd had no more than a glimpse of her pale face along with Lady Mary and Crewe inside the confectionery shop. That had been quite enough. How on earth he hoped to redeem himself after this latest fiasco was beyond him at the moment. Perhaps, he thought with hope, he might think of something later. A present? No, Sophie would toss it in his face.

Something would turn up. In the meantime he intended to explore the matter of the money in the books. Why would she not discuss it with him? Did she believe he would try to take the money from her? Could she think him such an ogre?

He had considered it at first, he admitted. Lowell Hall consumed a great deal of money to be properly run. He could have used more to begin the repairs he wished to make to the house and several of the tenant houses. But they could be accomplished at a later date, with money from the estate.

Of course Sophie needed money with which to live. She ought not be required to turn companion to survive, no matter that her first position was with a lady of great charm. The next one could be dreadful.

He strolled along Bond Street until he ran into Lord Crewe, who paused to converse.

"That was quite a charmer you had with you yesterday," he commented eventually.

"Indeed," Jonathan replied, the wry note unmistakable in his voice. "She begged most prettily to take a spin around Berkeley Square. Naturally we had to pass Gunter's tea shop." The rest of his thought was left unsaid.

"Miss Garnett seemed intrigued with your companion," Crewe replied carefully.

"I was afraid of that," Jonathan mused.

"I must say, old fellow, you do make it easy for your rivals," Crewe said jovially before departing.

Jonathan glanced after him, then resolutely hailed a hackney to take him to Lower Brook Street. Here, Jenkens appeared to take great pleasure in telling him that Miss Sophie was off in the park, walking the dog that Lord Chessyre had given her.

It didn't take long to find them. The maid remained in the shadows some distance away. Lord Chessyre stood back, watching Sophie romp with a small puppy that had to be the most ridiculous animal Jonathan had ever seen. How the dog ever managed to see the light of day from beneath that topknot of fluff was beyond him. Yet it was clear that Sophie was enchanted with the pup.

"Well, well, fancy running into you two in the park at this time of day. A bit early for the afternoon promenade." Jonathan sauntered up to the others, keeping a wary eye on the puppy, who appeared to regard him with an impish gleam in his eyes.

"Lord Chessyre has kindly given me this adorable terrier," Sophie said, bending down to scoop the little fellow into her arms. The dog gave her the same sort of look of slavish adoration that most gentlemen seemed to find necessary.

The smile she bestowed on Chessyre was enough to melt armor. Chessyre wasn't wearing any and looked suitably smitten. Jonathan wanted to punch him in the nose.

"It has a name?" Jonathan inquired, seeking to distract everyone.

"Pickles, and do not ask me to explain," Sophie said with a laugh. The pup licked her cheek and she threaded her fingers through that topknot with affection. "Silly pup," she said while both men looked as though they wished the dog to the ends of the earth and themselves in its place.

She put the dog down, fastened its lead on the dainty collar Lord Chessyre had given her, then glanced at him. "I believe I had best take Pickles home before the park becomes crowded with people and horses." She held out a polite hand to Jonathan. "How nice to have seen you again."

Jonathan bowed over that graciously extended hand and barely stifled his exasperation. Her words were each dipped in ice. You could almost see the icicles forming in midair as she spoke. Egad! He had well and truly blotted his copy book this time in more ways than one.

Sophie slowly led Lord Chessyre from the park in an amiable walk to Lower Brook Street. There was a distinctly mischievous twirl to her parasol, he thought. Anna had hung back but kept pace with what looked to be a promising tryst.

Jonathan watched the party go through the park gate, then turn in the direction of Lady Mary's house. He had never quit in a race before and he was not about to now. This simply called for different strategy, that's all.

Sophie longed to burst into laughter. At least, she hoped it was funny. She thought she had seen the last of Jonathan, that she had turned him away from her side forever, and here he was, looking slightly contrite, furious with someone—most likely Lord Chessyre—and more handsome than ever.

"Your cousin did not seem pleased with the puppy," Lord Chessyre observed.

"Jonathan has a rather limited sense of humor," Sophie replied, thinking that was certainly true. Jonathan, so conscious of his position, would not permit himself to escort the silliest-looking dog in the kingdom for a walk in Hyde Park, even if it wasn't the fashionable hour. Yet he had always been good to her, kind to animals, dependable to a fault, and loyal to his family in the past. All of which made his stupid drive around Berkeley Square the more peculiar. Perhaps it was a bet? She wondered if she dared to ask him.

It was Sunday afternoon following divine services before she was able to test her theory. She was sitting with Lady Mary in the drawing room, once again picking through her worktable. Pickles was curled up at her feet, asleep after a hearty meal and a proper walk.

"I told Jenkens not to bestir himself. As a member of the family I scarce need be announced," Jonathan said from the doorway, taking in the domestic scene and noting no other gentleman was with them.

The puppy opened his eyes to give Jonathan an eager look. He struggled to his feet and tottered across the room to plump himself down on Jonathan's polished boots with a hopeful loll of his tongue.

"Pickles! Come here," Sophie said in a convincing way.

Unfortunately, the dog hadn't accepted his rather stupid name and merely sat there, looking from Jonathan to Sophie to Lady Mary in a perfectly pleased way.

Jonathan solved the matter by rather gingerly picking the animal up and depositing him on the rug, where he'd been asleep. "Good fellow. Down," Jonathan said in a firm voice. The pup sat.

"He listened to you," Sophie marveled as the pup settled on the soft rug with a contented sigh.

"Dogs tend to do that for me. Don't know why. I like the creatures well enough, but they do tend to mind me more so than some others." He smiled inwardly as he considered the prospect of Crewe or Somerset trying to make the dog do anything at all.

"If you will excuse me a moment, I want to hunt for a pair of spectacles I think I placed in one of my reticules." Lady Mary rose and walked to the door, a flustered expression on her face.

Jonathan watched her leave with an approving eye, then took the liberty of sitting next to Sophie on the settee. She gave him a glance that was not the slightest encouraging.

"You saw me Friday, I believe."

"I certainly did, as did quite a few other people. My, what a pretty woman you had with you. I can quite see why you would not want to take someone like me for a drive, for instance." Sophie's smile didn't reach her glorious eyes.

Jonathan knew he was in for a difficult time. "It was a damn fool thing to do—pardon the language, Sophie."

"Yes," she agreed, the expression in her eyes softening just a trifle. "I imagine a woman like that could be most, er, persuasive." Sophie's smile became positively catlike. "I thought it might be a wager." Her remark was more in the nature of a question and Jonathan shook his head.

"No, I fear not. You must know that a woman like that is nothing more than a casual acquaintance."

"Really? My father must have had *some* acquaintance, in that case," she murmured, thinking of the pile of bills for expensive presents given to her father's opera dancer that Sophie had found when cleaning out his desk prior to the auction.

Jonathan gave her a quizzical look but did not inquire as to what her words had meant, if, indeed, he had heard them all.

"I want to mend fences, Sophie." He glanced at the door as though expecting Lady Mary to return—which she could at any minute.

"Enough to take me walking with Pickles?" she said, a faint challenge in her voice.

"If that is what you wish, yes," Jonathan said. "I imagine you can get to like the creature after a time."

"Stay for tea and we will take him out after that. Yes?" Her smile reached her eyes this time and Jonathan felt his heart relax.

"Yes." Even if he had to walk the blessed dog, he would do anything to restore himself in Sophie's good graces. He didn't bother to examine why it was so crucial.

Lady Mary entered the room, waving a pair of gold-rimmed spectacles at them. "I found them in the last place I'd expect them to be."

"And where was that?" Jonathan inquired as he assisted her ladyship to her chair after rising when she had entered the room.

"On my bedside table. I forgot that I had read for a brief time last evening. Silly me." She gave Jonathan an innocent smile, then settled in her new chair.

If there was anyone less silly than Lady Mary, Jonathan didn't know who it might be.

Following tea, Jonathan resolutely escorted Sophie and the dog—he hesitated to call the creature Pickles—to the park.

"I do not understand it," Sophie said. She gave the pup a frown, then looked to Jonathan. "I cannot believe how that puppy obeys you. I do believe he would do anything you wished!"

Jonathan gave the silly dog a jaundiced look and shrugged. "I told you, animals like me."

"There is no accounting for taste, I suppose," Sophie murmured as Reginald Montegu approached. The tulipy gentleman minced his way to where they stood while watching the puppy chase a butterfly.

"What a clever little pup," he said, turning to Sophie and totally ignoring Jonathan's presence.

"He is. And so obedient. Lord Lowell can persuade him to do anything." Sophie bestowed one of her seraphic smiles on him and the tulip positively wilted with pleasure.

Montegu was forced to acknowledge Jonathan at this point and gave him a frosty good day. It was evident to Jonathan that the tulip had heard of the escapade in Berkeley Square and did not approve. Jonathan wondered how many other snubs he would have to endure before the ill-advised drive was forgotten.

Once the tulip was gone Sophie turned a speculative gaze on Jonathan. He looked formidably reserved at this point, following the tulip's chilled parting. "He heard." She did not have to say what Montegu had heard, they both knew.

Jonathan ordered the pup to come and Pickles trotted obediently over and sat at Jonathan's feet with a look of slavish adoration on his doggy face.

"It would be nice if others were as obedient," he murmured, half to himself and half to Sophie.

"I believe you are a tyrant at heart," she said, not really joking about the matter.

"Doesn't everyone have a touch of the autocrat in him?" Jonathan asked in surprise.

"No, Lord Chessyre does not, nor does Mr. Somerset," Sophie added upon reflection.

"More pity for them," Jonathan observed as he snapped his fingers and Pickles trotted happily along at his side.

"I do not believe this," Sophie muttered as she tried to woo the pup and he merely gave her his doggy grin and stayed by Jonathan.

By the time they had returned to the house on Lower Brook Street Sophie didn't know if she was ready to forgive her cousin or pommel him. How he had managed to so totally win over her dog while almost ignoring the animal was beyond her, but he had. He gave orders he clearly expected the pup to obey. His voice was firm, as was his manner, and he rewarded the little fellow with a pat on the head.

Sophie reflected that she was probably no better. He expected her to jump when he ordered and all she could do was to ask how high—except in the matter of the money. She refused to reveal the total sum she had discovered and that seemed to irritate Jonathan no end. Well, he would have to remain in that state because she had no intention of telling him the extent of her fortune.

He paused before the house, gazed down at her with a benign look, then said, "If you are troubled about anything, contact me should you wish my help. No bother from the fortune hunters?"

Sophie thought she detected an insinuating note in his voice but his expression was merely polite.

"If I have a problem, I shall be certain to seek your expert help. I feel sure you must have dealt with the predicament of dismissing ladies at some time in the past."

"And some who were not quite ladies," he murmured.

"We go to Astley's on Tuesday with Mr. Fane. I doubt if he truly is sufficiently interested in my modest fortune to actually seek my hand," Sophie said in an attempt to see how Jonathan responded to the news.

He merely smiled in that maddening way he had, and said he hoped to see her again one of these days.

Sophie took the pup into the house, leaving Jonathan to go on his way. He'd made no attempt to come in with her, merely seeing that Jenkens was there to assist if needed. Drat the man, anyway. Why did he have to complicate her life!

By way of contrast there could be no one less complicated than Oliver Fane. He presented himself promptly in time for an early dinner, behaved in an exemplary manner throughout the meal, and escorted them to Astley's Amphitheatre in a most delightful way. He proved to be quietly entertaining and displayed no more than seemly attention to Sophie.

She didn't trust him, however. Jonathan and the others had planted the thought in the back of her mind that Mr. Fane was possibly more interested in her money than in her own self, and that was not the sort of thing that could please anyone. It rather spoiled her enjoyment of the evening's offering.

Lady Mary, on the other hand, seemed not only enchanted by the performances of the horses and their riders, but the other entertainers as well. From the moment the clown entered the circle to cry, "Here we are!" through to the breathtaking feats by the equestrians and on to the grand finale, Lady Mary was like a child. Delighted eyes swept the tableau before her, laughing at the antics of the clowns, admiring the dainty and very lovely female equestrian, and appreciating the commanding manner of the riding master as he strode about the circle with his whip in hand and his air of command, not to mention his quips with the clown.

Somehow, Sophie was not too surprised to catch sight of Jonathan on the other side of the theater. She said nothing to

Lady Mary, not wishing to distract her from her pleasure in any way.

He had a male friend with him, not the lovely charmer from the opera—which, upon reflection, was only logical. The young woman would be performing this evening. Sophie had a spark of satisfaction that Jonathan was here rather than in the green room, awaiting the straw damsel, as her brother called that sort. He had been not pleased when Sophie had shown him the bills for the opera dancer their father had kept, declaring it disgraceful. Whether he had referred to the actual matter or Sophie's discovery of it she had never decided.

"I trust you are enjoying the display of equestrianship, Miss Garnett? You handle your chestnuts with very nice skill," Mr. Fane said with proper courtesy.

"The equestrians are most remarkable," she said. "And I thank you for the kind words on my driving. My cousin would not permit me to drive out unless I could cope with the chestnuts. He made that quite clear."

He glanced across the way to where Jonathan was seated. "Indeed, most commendable."

So she was not alone in spotting her cousin. Interesting.

Sophie said not another word on that regard, but took note of Jonathan's watchful eye from time to time. She suspected his gaze rested on her quite as often as it did on the arena, if not more. She supposed she ought to be annoyed, but actually found it rather comforting that he would go to the trouble of attending Astley's just to check on her safety.

If that was indeed the reason, she considered a moment later when he smiled at an orange seller who leaned up to offer her wares. Surely it was not necessary for him to bend over quite that far or offer that intimately lazy smile to the woman?

Then it came to her why she had accepted so many invitations from the various gentlemen. It was to escape from thinking and possibly brooding about Jonathan. He occupied far too many of her minutes. She had the sense to know that he was not about to offer her anything honorable and he was also too honorable to offer her anything less.

Going out and about with the other men provided acceptable diversions. She only hoped that she could come to care for one of them, perhaps Lord Chessyre. He was the kindest of the lot of her court of gentlemen—a man any woman in her right mind would favor. What a pity that Sophie had begun to wonder if she occupied that state.

"That was delightful, Mr. Fane," Lady Mary said, with a significant glance at Sophie. The three of them strolled from the theater at the end of the performance in perfect amiability.

"Truly charming, far more exciting than I anticipated," Sophie said quite truthfully. "It was most kind of you to invite us this evening." She bestowed a smile on Mr. Fane that appeared to dazzle the chap, for he acquired that muddled expression so often seen on Sophie's admirers when she smiled at them.

Mr. Fane ushered them out with painstaking civility to where his carriage now awaited them. If anything, Sophie decided while they clip-clopped their way through London to Lower Brook Street, Mr. Fane overdid his attentions by being just a wee bit too perfect.

He declined Lady Mary's invitation to have a bite of supper with them.

"I must say I am favorably impressed by your Mr. Fane," her ladyship said as they walked up the stairs to the drawing room.

"He is not *my* Mr. Fane, Lady Mary," Sophie said with an amused laugh.

"Nonsense, you could have him in a bat of an eyelash," her ladyship retorted.

"I certainly hope that my cousin doesn't contemplate an alliance with Mr. Fane," Jonathan said smoothly, stepping forward from the shadows in the drawing room as they entered.

"Jonathan!" Sophie cried, utterly vexed to see her cousin here, now, when she was trying hard to put him from her mind. He'd certainly traversed London at great speed.

He crossed the space between them with remarkable swiftness and took the hand that didn't hold her reticule and fan in his. "I trust you have a share of the family brains, dear cousin."

"Third cousin, to be precise," Sophie snapped, snatching her hand from his grasp.

"I stand corrected. However, we are still family," he reminded. "And I would hope that you are not taken in by that fawning posture Mr. Fane so ably displays. I understand he is a skilled orator in the House of Commons, quite gifted at swaying people to his thinking."

"At least he is doing something constructive," Sophie shot back, yet knowing that Jonathan was bearing the burden of administering Lowell Hall and the area surrounding it.

"Has he so swayed you to his side already?" Jonathan frowned down at Sophie so fiercely that she quailed and wished herself elsewhere.

"What is this?" Lady Mary cried. "Mr. Fane is all that is agreeable."

"Too true, my lady," Jonathan said with a bow. "I do not think him right for my cousin. *Not* for Sophie," he emphasized with a considering look at her.

For some reason beyond her understanding, she found herself blushing and hated it. "Jonathan . . ." she began in a warning voice, only to be cut off by him.

"Just do not do something rash. If you must encourage someone, pick on Chessyre. *He* is a gentleman." With that admonition he made his bows and left the room.

Lady Mary listened to his receding steps until he had gone out the door below. She turned to Sophie and said, "What an unusual thing to happen. I'd not have thought that of your cousin. Personally, I like Mr. Fane. But then, I admire Lord Chessyre as well. I suspect you would do well to take your cousin's advice. It shows a proper concern for you, his cousin."

Sophie murmured her assent, and listlessly wandered up to her room, sinking down on her bed in deepest gloom. Jonathan had actually told her to turn her attentions to Lord Chessyre. It should have pleased her that he approved. Rather, it depressed her to the point that she burst into tears and quite dampened her pillow before Anna entered to assist her into bed.

Sophie was one of those creatures who could cry and never acquire the puffy eyes and reddened nose that so often afflicts a woman in tears. Come morning she went down to breakfast with a calm face and outwardly serene disposition. One would never know that she had sobbed her heart out during the night.

"It looks as though it might rain," Lady Mary observed.

"I promised to go shopping with Lady Anne today so I hope it rains now and is done with it," Sophie replied with more composure than might have been expected. She spread jam on her toast and watched the first of the raindrops slide down the window.

Three hours later the rain had come and gone. Sophie had dressed in a pretty confection of a walking gown that had a matching spencer to go over it. With parasol and reticule in hand she went down the two flights of stairs so to be ready when Lady Anne called for her.

Jenkens assisted her to the carriage a few minutes later and Sophie was subjected to the scrutiny of one whose eyes were far sharper than Lady Mary's.

"We will go to Noah's Ark on High Holborn, for I simply must find the baby a new toy. Edward is dreadfully hard on them. And what, may I ask, has put you to tears, dearest Sophie?"

"It is very complicated," Sophie murmured.

"Is there anything to do with a man that is not?" Lady Anne replied sagely. "Tell Mama," she demanded.

Sophie laughed and proceeded to relate most all her woes.

"To think he encouraged you to flirt with Lord Chessyre," Lady Anne said thoughtfully. "Then, of course you must. It would never do to disappoint him on that score."

Sophie didn't answer right away but thought that her cousin could use a disappointment and that perhaps it was time for her to offer it.

Chapter Fourteen

Sophie faced the following day with heightened anticipation. She would do what she must. There was no other way to go. She might have been proclaimed a diamond of the first water but she knew that her future was as solid as warm oil. It was quite obvious to her that that future did *not* include Jonathan and if she must have a husband, she had better proceed with the business.

Lord Chessyre was welcomed with more than usual charm. He made his bow to Lady Mary, exchanged pleasantries, then turned to Sophie.

"Look, Pickles obeys me much better today," she observed, sharing a smile with his lordship that made him draw nearer to her. She still had not achieved the ability to persuade the pup to mind her as Jonathan could.

Lord Chessyre snapped his fingers at the dog, who simply sat down and stared at him as though he didn't know what was expected.

Sophie nibbled her lower lip in vexation. The terrier had trotted to Jonathan every time he snapped *his* fingers. Why could the rascal not do so for Lord Chessyre?

However, since the dog was but a minor part of her scheme to win Lord Chessyre, Sophie settled on the settee with him, determined to charm the daylights out of the man. She allowed his lordship to amuse Pickles while she set out to entertain.

She thought she was doing quite well with her project when Jenkens paused at the door to announce Mr. Peter Antrobus. Sophie was under the impression that he had never forgiven her for her mix-up with the gig, but apparently at long last he had returned to pay court.

"Miss Garnett, how lovely to see you again. Alas, I was called into the country to see my father. He's been rather ill but is much better now—hence my return to town." The tall, thin, and tastefully garbed Mr. Antrobus turned his scrupulous attentions to Lady Mary, then nodded to Lord Chessyre, giving him a dour look.

Sophie, thinking it might be well for her to entertain as many gentlemen as possible in order to broaden her selection, smiled at the newcomer.

Lord Chessyre watched the exchange and settled back on the settee next to Sophie, encouraging Pickles to play with his watch fob.

Mr. Antrobus stayed the proper time, but didn't leave before inquiring if Miss Garnett would do him the honor of a drive in the park—his carriage had been skillfully repaired and the damage now made invisible.

"I should adore a drive in the park. Let me see, perhaps the day after tomorrow?" Sophie smiled again to lessen the blow that he must wait so long for her company.

The day and time agreed, Mr. Antrobus departed just as Mr. Somerset entered. The two men glared at each other with polite civility.

Sophie shot a glance at Lady Mary, then turned to gather Pickles to her lap. Greetings were exchanged by all and Mr. Somerset perched gingerly on the edge of a chair, darting looks at Lord Chessyre as though wondering when that gentleman might leave. He didn't. Mr. Somerset stayed as long as he dared, begging two dances at Almack's from Sophie before he left.

Lord Chessyre was about to speak when Lord Crewe and Jonathan entered the room together, appearing quite amiable if one didn't look too closely.

Pickles slithered down from Sophie's lap and trotted over to plop himself down by Jonathan, looking at him with doggy devotion.

Jonathan snapped his fingers at the pup and pointed to the small rug where the dog was supposed to stay. Pickles obediently went to the rug, sitting down only to look to Jonathan for approval of his clever behavior.

"Well, I never," Lady Mary said. "My lord, you have a way with animals, make no doubt of it."

"More's the pity," Sophie murmured. Lord Chessyre heard her soft words and grinned.

The most recent additions to the drawing room group made their bows to Lady Mary and Sophie. Crewe moved a chair so he was immediately next to where Sophie reigned on the settee. Jonathan strolled to the far side of the room to prop himself against the fireplace surround that had been so beautifully decorated by Robert Adam.

The entire room bore the evidence of the famed architect's design efforts, but the fireplace mantel and surround were especially fine. They also served as an excellent backdrop for Jonathan's dark hair and his dashing coat of fine navy Bath cloth. Sophie had promptly observed how well that coat became him. Molded to powerful shoulders that had no need for excessive padding, it served as a splendid foil for his white marcella waistcoat that was embroidered discreetly with silver thread. His cravat, tied in a mathematical style, was utter perfection without a single wrinkle to mar its precise correctness. While most gentleman's blue coats had fine brass buttons on them, Jonathan sported large silver buttons of excellent quality. Neat but not gaudy came to her mind before she hastily turned her attention to Lord Crewe.

Each of the men—except for Jonathan—claimed dances that evening at Almack's, asked for walks in the park or drives in their carriages. Precisely why Jonathan was there Sophie couldn't imagine—unless it was to vet her callers, or beaux as Lady Mary referred to them. Sophie tried to ignore him but it was not easy. He was not the sort of man any woman would find possible to disregard.

The afternoon was far advanced by the time the gentlemen left. Not one of them was willing to depart before the others, a detail Lady Mary was quick to point out to a somewhat tired Sophie.

"I had not realized that entertaining gentlemen in the drawing room could be so fatiguing." Sophie paused by the bottom of the stairs to add, "Whatever do you suppose Jonathan was doing here this afternoon? He did not ask for a dance or to take me out or anything. What a vexing creature he is!"

"Perhaps he desires to keep an eye on his charming cousin, my dear girl." Lady Mary took Sophie's arm and walked slowly up the stairs to the chamber level of the house. "Remember, he is the one who cared for you when you were so terribly ill. He is bound to have an interest in your affairs."

"I doubt it. I have this nasty feeling that when I finally decide to accept a gentleman, he will put his nose in and somehow manage to prevent my marriage to anyone I choose. Instead he will put forward his own choice."

"But, my dear," Lady Mary said when they reached the top of the stairs, "he approved Lord Chessyre. All you need to do is bring his lordship up to scratch—it ought not be the least difficult. Providing, of course, that it is truly what you want. It is, is it not?" she gently inquired, looking closely at Sophie.

"Of course it is," a subdued Sophie said.

That evening Sophie wore the silvery tissue gown to the Almack's assembly and found herself under siege.

Lady Jersey had declared herself green with envy while the Princess Esterhazy had bestowed a lofty look of disdain on Sophie's gown. Sophie suspected that if an unusual gown was to be introduced at the assembly, it ought to be worn by the princess. The daughter of a baronet barely qualified for highest Society.

Lord Bolingbroke—a rather staid but wealthy gentleman—insisted upon a quadrille, while the dashing Sir Piers Aubrey—a short but eligible man—demanded a country dance. She had already promised a Scots reel to Mr. Somerset and a waltz to Lord Chessyre, with Lord Crewe claiming a cotillion. The remainder of the dances were quickly sought. For a moment she felt a trifle overwhelmed.

Sophie thought she owed more to Madame Clotilde than her own charms. All this nonsense about her looking like an angel was just that . . . nonsense. As Jonathan had so carefully pointed out, she was scarcely angelic in disposition.

Of course she had no time to take note to see if her cousin was attending the assembly. Glittering lights, lovely gowns, flattering attention from her court of gentlemen prevented that, not to mention dancing every dance.

Lady Anne bustled up with Sir Cecil in tow. "I vow I am surprised that a riot did not ensue once you entered the rooms. I have never seen such a rush. I thought for certain the room would tilt in your direction!"

"Rubbish," Sophie said with a smile. " 'Tis the dress. How is baby Edward?" That might have guaranteed to hold Anne for some minutes, but Mr. Somerset presented himself as her next partner. Sophie promised to hear the latest of Edward's clever doings on the morrow at tea.

She whirled about in a waltz, romped through a Scot's reel, made stately progress in a slow country dance, and all the while searched for Jonathan. She had vowed to ignore him should he come and was disappointed—she told herself—that he had failed her.

Whenever she paused between dances, the crush around her was enough to make her long for a breath of air, almost enough to panic her. But this was what every girl longed for, to become sought after and besieged by eligible gentlemen and she braced herself for her success.

"My dear," Lady Mary said when Sophie chanced to sit at her side for a few moments, "you have received more dagger looks this evening than I could ever count. I should say you are most popular."

"Have you made up your mind as to which one you will accept? They will all propose, you know," Jonathan said from behind her.

"Where did you come from?" she demanded.

"Why do you want to know? Never say you have missed me? I shall not credit that!" Jonathan, arrayed in a splendid black coat and breeches with a plain white marcella waistcoat topped by his simply tied cravat, looked by far the most elegant man at the assembly. With black hose and patent dancing slippers, and his nearly black hair, he was a complete study in black and white and he quite awed Sophie.

"No, you are like a toothache that I hope will go away," she snapped back at him, angry with herself that she had allowed him to think she had searched for him. Which, of course, she had, but she did not wish him to know it.

"I suppose all your dances are claimed?" He stood to one side, studying her with his quizzing glass in a manner that was guaranteed to annoy.

"Yes." She beamed a smile at him, knowing he could not snatch a dance with her here.

He swung his glass from a well-manicured hand while looking about the room. When young Lord Grantly appeared to claim his dance, Jonathan murmured something to the young fellow, who blushed and nodded, looked at Jonathan with awe, and faded away.

"Fine lad, knew I could depend on him," Jonathan said as he led a reluctant Sophie to the center of the dance floor.

"And how did you accomplish this?" she softly demanded.

"I shall give him a driving lesson. He is in need of such," Jonathan replied, looking down that splendidly aristocratic nose at her.

She'd forgotten this was to be a waltz. "You might have had the courtesy to ask me yesterday."

"You would have taken great pleasure in denying me what I wanted. Now, behave and show everyone what an exquisite angel you are—or at least, that you look like one."

Sophie was speechless at that. How he must dislike her to say such nasty little barbs.

However, she had to admit he was a marvelous dancer and had the knack of bringing out the best of her ability—which had not had a lot of practice with the waltz. Her gown floated about her like a mist of silver, clinging, flowing, changing always.

"I must confess," he said into her ear, for he was holding her a trifle too close, "you do waltz charmingly, my dear."

Sophie paid no attention to his words, for she didn't trust a thing he said. She merely closed her eyes to savor his nearness. Tomorrow she would scold herself. Tonight was not a time for common sense.

"What? No snappy retort? No hasty repartee? I am crushed, dear cousin," he murmured, his voice all mockery.

"I wish you were not my cousin," she was stung into saying.

"As do I," he quickly replied.

Sophie was incapable of responding to this. She had asked for it, and now knew his desire that he had no connection to her.

"Tomorrow you will have nearly every eligible male in London at your doorstep. Tell Jenkens to allow in only those of the highest *ton*. He will know who they are; butlers always do. No fortune hunters, no Reginald Montegu, or Mr. Fane."

She leaned back to give him a misty look. "I am touched at your concern, my lord. To have such an elderly gentleman looking after my future cannot but comfort me."

If she had sought to touch a sore spot, she had achieved it. Jonathan gave her a black look and said nothing more.

Lady Mary insisted they remain for the last dance, lest she disappoint any of the pleasant gentlemen who had sought her hand. After the waltz with Jonathan, Sophie found the rest of the evening a blur. She scarcely knew what she did, other than that she spent most of her time dancing with one gentleman or another.

Lord Chessyre claimed the final dance and talked with her whenever the pauses permitted it. He insisted upon escorting them home.

"Your cousin left early this evening," he commented, watching Sophie in the light of the flambeau outside the assembly rooms while they waited for their carriage to arrive.

"Indeed," Sophie replied, wondering if her life would possibly turn out pleasing. The way she felt at the moment she almost wished herself in the Cotswolds again, before she had inherited Uncle Philip's money.

The following morning she sent for her carriage and hurriedly dressed in the simple violet challis carriage dress she had worn with Jonathan so long ago. There was a damp chill in the air, so she added a spencer over the bodice and by the time she made her way down to the ground floor, had a hasty cup of tea, and walked to the front door, the equipage was waiting for her.

"I shall return in good time," she informed Jenkens as she accepted his assistance. She looked to the groom and an-

nounced she did not have need of him this morning. She
wished to be alone—except for Pickles. At the last moment
she scooped him up to take him with her.

"But, miss," the groom protested.

Sophie shook her head and guided her pair from the house
and along to the north and out of the city. She wanted to think
and within the house there was no peace. This entry into Society was exhausting, taxing her patience and her sense of
humor. She needed a breath of country air.

Pickles sat in doggy splendor, tongue lolling to one side as
he relished the wind in his face. He was far too well mannered
to bark at the horses, nor did he seem inclined to chase the cat
that was foolish enough to cross the road about the same time
Sophie sped past.

"Good dog," Sophie murmured, giving him a hasty pat on
his head.

The drive went splendidly. At this hour the road going north
from the city was all but empty of vehicles. Soon Sophie saw a
pretty lane leading off the main road and turned her carriage
and pair in that direction. There was a lovely little river of fast-
flowing water along the side of the lane. Birds darted through
the trees that rose in imposing ranks overhead. Here was the
peace and quiet she had wished for since coming to London.
She might have been in the middle of the countryside instead
of a mile or so outside the city.

All of a sudden Pickles barked and jumped from the carriage seat to the floor of the carriage, then down to the ground,
where he dashed madly along the edge of the river until he
reached the spot where a large branch had fallen into the
water. Brown weeds had piled up against the branch, causing
the water to ripple around it.

Pickles stood at the water's edge, barking fiercely at the
soggy mop of weeds. Sophie slowed the team to a stop.

Then she caught sight of what looked like a thin little face
and she was out of the carriage in a flash, looping the carriage
reins over the nearest branch.

Kneeling at the water's edge, she quickly realized that mop
of brown weeds was actually hair, and it belonged to a small
girl who was tangled in the branch by those very locks.

A glance around her revealed what she should have known—there was not a soul in sight. Since it was unlikely anyone would hear her call, she had better save the child before she died.

Deciding the best way to release the girl was to wade into the river and hold the girl's head above the water while she worked to release the long strands of brown hair, Sophie took action. She tossed her gloves and shoes aside and peeled off her stockings, not bothering to place them in a neat pile as she usually did. Last of all went her small hat, dropped on the same pile of clothing.

"There now, I shall have you out of here in a trice," Sophie said, hoping to assure the girl. She was rewarded with a tired blink of eyelids from a wan face. Poor little tyke, heaven only knew how long she had been struggling to be free of the nasty branches.

Plunging into the chilly water, Sophie ignored her own floating skirts to break off branches, tossing them aside in great haste while supporting the girl's head. One at a time, she freed a strand, then tucked it under the child's head, pinning it with her other hand, so it wouldn't be caught again. It was painstaking work, for the girl had an astonishing amount of hair.

Pickles had trotted off in the direction they had come. Sophie had called him once, then forgot the dog in her efforts to free the child.

The current was strong and the water cold. She could see how easily the girl might have been caught and swept downstream into the clutches of the branch. As well, the stones on the bottom were slippery with moss and weeds. Sophie slipped from time to time, and hoped she would manage to free the girl before she also landed in the chilly depths.

She finished the task of releasing the mop of hair and, carrying the girl with the most gentle care, slogged through the water to the bank of the river. The girl gazed at Sophie with frightened eyes, trying hard not to cry. The little mite was light enough and Sophie had no problem boosting her up to the grassy bank.

"There now, just lie there quietlike in the sun. I shall join you in a moment."

Sophie settled the girl safely, then tried to climb from the river, only to run into trouble. Unless she wrapped her skirt about her waist, there seemed to be no way in which she could get a foothold on the bank to climb out. Sophie dubiously eyed the branch, noting that it was rough and possessed hundreds of little sharp twigs. Considering her bare feet, she'd stab herself to death if she attempted to use that to lever herself from the water.

Then to make matters worse, she slipped on a patch of the slimy weeds and plunged to the bottom of the river. She came up sputtering, dazed, and gasping for air. Paddling to the shore with the hope that she might find a quick way out of her dilemma, she searched for other means of escaping the river. The child needed help and Sophie wasn't doing her much good while in the water. She wasn't doing herself much good, either, for the water was icy cold and she could feel herself turning as blue as the child.

In the distance she could hear Pickles' sharp little bark, one she had learned to identify in the days he had been with her. "Well," she called philosophically to the child, "my little dog can help keep you warm." She hoped. Pickles was so independent about minding her, she really didn't know if he would obey or not.

When the dog came into view, Sophie saw at once that he was perched on the seat of a very familiar carriage! She debated whether to slip under the water and pretend to be gone or face the undoubtedly amused expression her cousin would likely wear.

"Ah, Sophie. Once again I must rescue you from a muddy stream." He drew to a halt, looped his reins about a convenient tree branch, and walked over to survey the situation.

"This is a river and it's not muddy, but it is freezing cold. Do not just stand there. Do something!" Her chattering teeth made the demand less than forceful but it appeared to have the desired effect upon Jonathan.

He pulled off his coat to toss it into the carriage and removed his boots. Then he strode to the riverbank and knelt on the shore. He took her slim hands in his more powerful ones and pulled her not-inconsiderable self from the river to the grassy slope.

Sophie settled herself on the sun-warmed bank, absorbing with appreciation the welcome heat of the sun on her soaking, dripping self. Jonathan put on his boots.

An older woman came running toward them, apron clutched in her hands, calling a name.

The child lifted her head, too weak to respond.

Apparently the mother was too glad to see movement to worry about an answer. She rushed to the girl. "Aye, Betsy, my gel, you would play in the water. Mind, I told you it was cold, did I not?" She wrapped her apron about the child, thanked Sophie profusely, then hurried off to the other end of the lane, where she disappeared from view.

"How did you come here?" Sophie demanded, shivering in the slight breeze that stirred through the trees.

"You recall I promised Lord Grantly a driving lesson in exchange for that waltz last evening? I was keeping my promise to him. Saw Pickles and knew you had to be close by. After all, there cannot be another silly dog like him around, can there?" He reached over to wring out some of the water in Sophie's skirts, mindful of her propriety to a degree.

"What happened to him?" Sophie asked, trying to keep her teeth from chattering and failing. She wanted to tell Jonathan to go away but couldn't find the words. Indeed, she couldn't seem to move. The rescue had taken more from her than would be expected.

"He went to the cluster of houses at the far end of the lane, looking for help. I imagine he was the one who found that frantic mother hunting for her lost girl. You did well, Sophie, my love."

A warmth that had nothing to do with the sun crept through her and she wrapped her arms about herself in an effort to hold it inside.

"You seem to make a practice of saving my life," she said in a small polite voice. "Not only did you pull me from that creek so long ago, but you took care of me that night I was so ill. I can never thank you enough for that. And now, this." She looked up at him, her lashes spiky with water, hair drying in tangled silver-blond curls about her pale face, and cerulean blue eyes full of an emotion Jonathan couldn't determine.

She shivered again, and Jonathan rose and crossed to her carriage to find a small rug she had brought along with her. Right now it was as necessary to conceal the shapely form revealed by the clinging gown as to warm her. "Here," he said, glancing along the lane to see that Lord Grantly was not to be seen.

Sophie welcomed the warmth of the rug, snuggling into it and then smiling at her rescuer. "Thank you, cousin."

He bent over her to study her face, then dropped what was intended to be a hasty kiss on her lips. He'd only meant to warm them. But it didn't work out that way. She had responded as never before and he found himself unable to resist her. It was long moments before he lifted his head, dizzy with the effort of restraining himself from proceeding as he wished.

"Sophie . . ." He wondered what he could say. He'd not apologize for the most delightful kiss he could remember.

"I had best return to Lower Brook Street. Lady Mary might worry about me." She looked at him, very sober and somewhat wary, then slowly sat up, wrapping the rug about her wet shoulders.

There was a tinge of rose in her cheeks, no doubt from the kiss. At least it served some purpose for her, Jonathan thought wryly. She didn't berate him for taking liberties, as well she might.

"You do seem to get yourself in a pickle. That dog is well named."

Sophie bent over to wring more water from her gown. She rose from the bank and sighed in dismay as she caught sight of young Lord Grantly walking toward them. He carried a green bottle and looked anxious.

"Here, I finally found a place to buy some ale. It would be best for you, Miss Garnett, to have a little to take off the chill." He proffered the bottle, politely not staring at the figure wrapped in clinging muslin.

Sophie glanced at Jonathan, who nodded his agreement. She took a swallow, grimaced, for she didn't care for ale, then braced herself for another. She handed the bottle back to Lord

Grantly, and walked to her carriage after gathering her stockings, shoes, gloves, and hat. Pickles danced about her feet, reminding her with a bark that he had done his part in this affair.

While the gentlemen turned their backs and walked toward Jonathan's carriage, Sophie donned the items she had swiftly removed before the rescue. They helped to warm her to an amazing degree. But then, so did the memory of Jonathan's extraordinary kiss.

She plucked the reins from the overhanging branch and prepared to turn her horses so she could make her soggy way to Lady Mary's house. Jonathan came alongside the carriage and leaped inside, forcing her to move over.

"What are you doing, pray tell?"

"Grantly is to follow us to your home. He is in alt at the chance to drive my cattle, so please do not make a fuss, my dearest girl. Just settle back on the seat and mind your manners. I shall have you home in no time at all."

Sophie hugged the rug as well as his words, "dearest girl," to her and said not one word the entire trip.

Fortunately it was still very early and few of the *ton* were out and about. Before long they were at Lower Brook Street and Jenkens ushered the still-dripping Sophie into the house without a change of expression.

Jonathan followed. "You are to take a hot bath, wash those golden curls, then take a nap. I shall see you later."

Sophie hadn't the energy to argue with him. Besides, it might prove interesting to listen to what he had to say. She confided as much to Pickles, who woofed in agreement.

Chapter Fifteen

When Sophie awoke from the nap she had insisted she didn't need, she dressed and made her way down to the drawing room, very much aware that the nap had been most welcome.

Jonathan was there, waiting for her, a small package in hand. He was garbed in fresh attire, biscuit pantaloons under a corbeau coat and his usual white waistcoat—looking elegant and unattainable. "Here," he said, thrusting the neatly wrapped package at her without his usual grace.

She opened the gift wrapped in stiff white paper to find a bottle of scent. "Thank you, cousin." She gave him a wondering look; it was not like Jonathan to give her presents. Was he perhaps preparing the way for something unpleasant? Or could he be interested in her romantically? Or did he think to bribe her to disclose the amount of her modest fortune?

"It is honeysuckle, although goodness knows you have no need of it. The men cluster around you like bees as it is." He tilted his head and gave her a mock leer. It made him look rather absurd, rather than lecherous.

His mockery dissolved any romantic notions she might have nurtured in an instant. She immediately decided he was after the amount of her fortune—although what difference it made to him she couldn't guess.

Sophie sniffed appreciatively and replaced the stopper, then studied his face. She would far rather have him than all the other men in London put together. But, as he had made it most evident she would be the last woman he desired to marry, she had best conceal her own affections.

"After my dip in the river, the scent will help to dispel any lingering effects, I daresay," she said, fluttering her lashes.

"Do not try any tricks on me, I beg you. I was well aware of them before you were out of the nursery." He looked reserved, even a bit angry. "I should like to know precisely why you were in that lane this morning. Alone! No groom along—and I specifically ordered the chap to go everywhere with you. Do you know what might have happened to you had some man happened along with less than honorable intentions? And as for that foolish plunge into the river—well, the less said about that, the better."

"You must know that no woman of sensibilities could allow a child to drown. I did what had to be done." She glared at him, hoping that he might be just a trifle concerned for her, then dismissed that as nonsense.

She placed the bottle of scent on the table and rose to wander restlessly about the room, keeping her distance from Jonathan. "I wanted to be alone—without the groom or anyone else. This visit to London has not been exactly what I anticipated."

He made what sounded suspiciously like a snort.

Ignoring him, she continued. "I had thought to purchase a few nice dresses, see the many places I had longed to view, attend a few plays, enjoy calling on a few friends. I had not expected Almack's, nor the balls, nor the surfeit of gentlemen showering me with attention. It is a trifle overwhelming. I merely wished to go into the country for a bit—away from the pressures."

At last, done with her pacing, she turned to face him, awaiting some caustic remark that would doubtlessly make her excessively blue-deviled.

"Overwhelmed, are you? I shall relieve your mind by telling you that all your suitors must come to me before they can approach you to ask for your hand." He bent his head to study the quizzing glass he toyed with in one hand. "That ought to eliminate all but the determined."

She wished she might see his eyes—they could reveal so much. Obviously he didn't want her to know his thoughts. It must be that he still disliked her and the thought of having to bother with the men who wished to marry her. Pride came to her rescue.

"That is not necessary, truly. I am capable of dismissing a gentleman I do not wish to marry." She clasped her hands before her, standing demurely in the center of the room and wishing she could do something—anything—that might shake that imperturbable calm he wore like a shroud.

"It is more seemly that they approach me first, brat," he said with a snap. He dropped the quizzing glass, allowing it to fall against his immaculate linen, its fine gold chain looking terribly discreet.

"You are an utter beast, Jonathan," she said without heat. "Small wonder I dislike you so."

"And who is it you favor?" he demanded, his face a mask of polite inquiry.

"You once nudged me toward Lord Chessyre and I must say he is very kind."

"Is that the warmest feeling you have toward him?" The question was offered in a mild, offhanded manner, as though Jonathan had little interest in her reply. "No passion, no throbbing heart, no weakness of knees?"

"I daresay affection can grow over the years," she was stung into replying. The only time she had known anything remotely like those feelings was when Jonathan had kissed her and she wasn't about to tell him that!

The look he gave her was unfathomable, certainly beyond her understanding. "You have much to learn, cousin."

She took a few steps back, away from the man who intimidated her more than all the others put together.

"I shall manage," she said quietly.

"I wonder," he said, staring at her with the most assessing gaze she had ever known.

"You are very rude, Jonathan."

"Indeed. It allows me to do outrageous things."

"And what are those?" she dared to ask as he walked toward where she now was backed against the sofa table. "Just what do you consider outrageous?"

How he reached her side so swiftly she never could comprehend. One second he was several steps away, the next he was before her, touching her face, then kissing her with that wickedly delicious expertise she had experienced before.

The kiss was brief. He suddenly drew away from her, leaving her a shaken leaf, trembling as though a strong wind had hit her with enormous force.

"Let me know how Chessyre does. The others, as well. You ought to give them each the same test."

"Measure them against you?" she asked and the voice she'd intended to be strong and scornful came out a breathless whisper. She longed to place a hand against her heart, to still its pounding, and what a blessing it would be if she could just sink down upon a chair, for her knees were as weak as water. It was merely a reaction against the unexpected, she tried to tell herself. Yet she also had to admit that she had tried to provoke him. She had desperately wanted that kiss before agreeing to marry some other man she did not and would never love as she did Jonathan.

"Most of them would never dare kiss a proper young lady. Of course, they do not know you as I do. But—Chessyre might. Perhaps Crewe. They are both gentlemen who know what they want."

"And do you know what you want, cousin?" she softly demanded.

He glared at her and was about to reply—something scathing, no doubt—when Jenkens entered the room.

"Lord Bolingbroke, Miss Garnett."

She flashed a searing glance at Jonathan, then moved forward to greet her caller. "Good day, my lord."

Jonathan crossed to the door, exchanged pleasantries with Bolingbroke, then left, tossing Sophie a mocking look before turning to disappear down the stairs.

His lordship was all flattery and flummery, trotting out the tired imagery of angelic beauty. While it was pleasant, it grew monotonous. As Jonathan had said, she was far from being an angel.

"My dear young lady, I have spoken with your cousin and he has given me permission to ask for your hand."

Sophie was truly startled. She had barely met the man and suspected he was far more interested in acquiring a mother for his children—three, if she recalled correctly—than her as a person. Oh, he might welcome a pretty face at the other end of the table, but she thought his interests were similar to her late father's—opera dancers and the muslin company.

"You do me a great honor, sir, but I must respectfully decline your flattering offer." She could think of no other excuses and apparently he did not require any, for he sighed and chatted a bit before leaving, mumbling something about older women.

"Was that Lord Bolingbroke I saw going down the stairs? Gracious, what a surprise," Lady Mary said as she entered the room, direct from her conference with Cook. She studied Sophie a moment, then added, "Your cousin was here inquiring about you. Did you speak with him?"

"Indeed. He brought me a bottle of scent—honeysuckle. Apparently, like you, he thinks it appropriate for me. I wonder why? Am I so clinging—like some vine, then?" Sophie picked up the pretty bottle and held it close to her chest.

"Of course not. It is a lovely scent for a lovely young woman. What did Bolingbroke want?"

"To marry me," Sophie bluntly replied.

Lady Mary had no chance to ask questions about the surprising offer. Jenkens came up the stairs to announce Mr. Somerset, then ushered him into the room. Apparently the butler had decided that all gentlemen were to be granted time today.

Lady Mary suddenly discovered her needlework and settled in a chair across the room near the window and far from the couple by the door.

"Good day, sir. Lovely weather, is it not?" Sophie began, hoping the burden of conversation would not rest entirely with her.

"My dear Miss Garnett," the worthy Mr. Somerset began, then ran a finger under his too-snug cravat while his face grew tinged with a faint pink. "I would ask you a most important question," he said, plunging into the reason for his call immediately without roundaboutation.

"Would you care to sit down here on the settee?" Sophie said with compassion for the young man. It could not be easy, putting oneself to such a trial.

"I have seen your cousin. He has kindly given me permission to seek your hand in marriage." Tiny beads of perspiration dotted Mr. Somerset's forehead and Sophie knew pity for him. He mopped his brow while considering the object of his desire. "Could you do me the honor of becoming my wife?"

Sophie said all that was proper and tried to make her rejection as kind as possible. She liked him, but the thought of spending the rest of her life with the man was not appealing.

He looked downcast but not surprised, she observed.

"I didn't think you would," he said, dispirited and unhappy. "Your cousin urged me to try, however. And you are most kind, in spite of rejecting my suit. Truly an angel." He rose and took his leave of the ladies.

"Another proposal?" Lady Mary cried softly, lest anyone overhear her amazed query.

"Jonathan has been encouraging these gentlemen," Sophie said in a dangerously quiet voice. She rose from the settee to stride about the room with angry steps. Her cousin must positively hate her to be pushing these men to marry her, so as to remove her from what he perceived as his responsibility.

"Is that so?" Lady Mary inquired pensively. "Well, he is most dutiful, I must say. Fancy him taking all that trouble."

"He said he would interview all my beaux and apparently he has approved every one. I wonder who will be next?"

Several other gentlemen called that afternoon but there was not another proposal of marriage and Sophie knew exquisite relief. Not that she had anticipated any proposal from the likes of Reginald Montegu or Mr. Oliver Fane, but one never knew.

That evening they attended the theater. Sophie relaxed against her chair, knowing she looked good in her gown of cloud white Florence satin. She had worn it before, but that was prior to her becoming known in Society. And besides, she thought it foolish to believe a gown could be worn no more than once.

It was during the first intermission that Lord Crewe entered their box to claim Sophie's attention after first making his bow to Lady Mary. He selected a chair close to Sophie and settled down to converse.

The good lady annoyed Sophie by turning away to chat with Lord Witherspoon, an old friend who deigned to escort them this evening.

"You look as usual this evening—like a heavenly creature who has descended to join us mere mortals." He gazed at her with a hint of a smile in his eyes. She still found him difficult to understand, although pleasant.

"Such fustian," Sophie said quietly with a fond smile.

Apparently her attitude gave him hope, for he leaned forward to take possession of one of her hands. "I am not clever at this sort of thing, for I have avoided even the talk of marriage, but I would like you to be my wife, Sophie."

She had suspected he might propose, but not here, not now. It disconcerted her no end. She found herself faltering.

"I like you, but as a friend, dear sir. I do not think we would suit in the long run," she replied after a few moments of consideration.

He was clearly disappointed and attempted to change her mind—something the first two proposers had not done. The end of the intermission concluded their conversation.

Lady Mary, sensing how things had gone, turned to make some remark about a friend in the audience, with Lord Witherspoon adding acerbic comments. Lord Crewe left.

The following morning Sophie sent for her carriage, hoping a proper drive in the park would clear the megrim from her head. She had awakened with a feeling of impending doom and wished it would go away.

It was inevitable that she would encounter Sir Piers Aubrey in the park, she supposed. That gentleman, seated on a rather showy hack, rode to the side of her carriage with a broad smile affixed to his rather plain face.

Sophie had made up her mind to be kind and pleasant to one and all of the men who had sought her out during her time in London. It was not their fault that Sophie loved another and found it difficult to settle for second best.

"Society's goddess has come to grace the park."

If the gentleman thought he was being original, he was away and off the mark. Sophie was thoroughly tired of being likened to the ethereal. What would it take, she wondered, to rid herself of that image? Something outrageous! But what? While she had been pondering this point, Sir Piers had been making his own.

"Dear lady," he said—still mounted, for he was aware of his lack of height and considered he had an advantage while astride his horse—"I beg of you to marry me."

Sophie longed to laugh. Never in her wildest moments had she expected to have a man propose to her while he was on horseback and in the middle of Hyde Park and she in her carriage, some distance away. The man had no sense of what was proper, that was certain. Did he think to get a jump on her other beaux in this manner?

Remembering her resolve, Sophie rejected him in the nicest way possible. That did no good, for the poor fellow didn't believe her.

"I see it now, Miss Garnett. You want a bit of courting. Dash it all, your beauty has made me too bold. I shall do just as you please." He backed away from where he had detained her in her carriage and called to her as he rode away, "I shall see you later, fair lady."

Sophie gave vent to her exasperation while she guided her pair through the park at a goodly clip. "Of all the nodcocks, he must take the cake," she concluded at the end of a lengthy fulmination.

Before long she caught sight of Jonathan riding along Rotten Row some distance ahead of her. It would be best not to speak to him just now or she would hurl a great many words at him best left unsaid. With a nod at her groom, who, poor fellow, had been forced to endure that ridiculous proposal, Sophie took the first turning and headed toward a less frequented part of the park.

The noise from the carriage and pair no doubt accounted for her not being aware of an approaching rider. It wasn't until he drew alongside with her that Sophie realized that Jonathan sought her attention. She soon brought the carriage to a halt, and was looking at her cousin with undisguised dislike.

"Now what?" she said without any preface.

"Do I detect a hint of umbrage in your dulcet tones, dear cousin? Surely you cannot be angry to be the recipient of so many offers of marriage. A good many girls would be thanking their stars for such."

"You may keep your mockery for someone who appreciates it more than I," she said, furious with the man.

"Do not tell me that you have refused them all! Did they fail the test?"

His face and voice were as innocent as a babe's, but Sophie knew full well to what he referred. Odious creature!

"I do not make a practice of putting gentlemen to a test, but perhaps I ought. I rather think an excellent test would be one of manners and considerate behavior." She gave him a narrow look, intent, and direct.

His horse sidled and pranced a bit, indicating that he sensed his rider was not giving him proper attention.

"Naturally you understand what I mean and no doubt approve my plan," Sophie said in the sweetest way imaginable. "Perhaps you might offer suggestions as to how I could best proceed with my intent? Of course, four of the gentlemen have already approached me. Really, Jonathan, I do wish you would put a flea in their ears that I dislike being called an angel." She gave him a considering look, then added, "Almost as much as I dislike being called 'brat.'"

"But, my dearest of cousins, that is a term of affection. Surely you would not wish to have me call you what I'd prefer?" He gave her a look she could only describe as wicked. It effectively prevented her from asking what it was that he would rather call her, which was a pity, for she really wanted to know.

She flicked the reins and drove off, the sound of Jonathan's nasty little chuckle ringing in her head. Oh, how she longed to box his ears!

The following days saw a number of gentlemen call to pay court to Sophie. She tried to encourage them, knowing that things being what they were, she really ought to find a husband. Unfortunately, her heart wasn't in it. By the following

Wednesday she had almost decided that she would remain as a companion, keeping the rest of her fortune in consols and her money earning interest in the bank as a reserve against her declining years or a bad-tempered employer. However it wasn't what she wished.

The two ladies were gathered in the drawing room, wondering who might call on them this afternoon. Sophie wandered restlessly about the room, fingering porcelain shepherdesses and insipid china dogs. Pickles watched her from his rug.

"Lord Chessyre has sent a note around to request he might have the pleasure of escorting us this evening. Will that be agreeable, Sophie?" Lady Mary asked from her favorite chair by the window.

"Indeed, ma'am. Most agreeable," Sophie said quietly, turning to look at the dear lady, who so ably took the place of her mother.

"You are in first looks today, but I think you are a trifle blue-deviled within," her ladyship ventured to say.

"I am. Nearly all of the gentlemen I have entertained have one way or another either asked for my hand or indicated that they wish to do so. I have forestalled several that I suspected were so inclined. Am I so terribly difficult to please? When it comes to the sticking point, I cannot accept. I am dreadful."

"No, I strongly suspect your heart is not engaged. If worse comes to worse, you could seek your cousin's assistance. I truly feel you ought to marry, dear child. I shan't always need you. Indeed, I am considering a proposal of my own—which is but a seed planted in the gentleman's mind at this point. I should rather see you safely wed than at loose ends on your own."

"I suppose so," Sophie replied listlessly. "May I ask who that gentleman is—the one who interests you?"

"You may not. I'd not jinx the scheme. If one wishes to marry a particular gentleman, it requires careful planning. No general embarking on a battle plan devises more prudent strategy."

"Indeed, ma'am, this interests me greatly. How does one *plan* to encourage a particular gentleman to seek marriage?" Sophie inquired, her lethargy vanished.

"Well, it might be considered a trifle devious. I ought not confide such notions to a young girl."

"I am not that young, ma'am, and I wish to try your stratagems." Sophie abandoned her restless stroll and pulled up a chair next to her ladyship. The woman might be a spinster, but she had most observant eyes and ears. There was no doubt in Sophie's mind that Lady Mary had learned a great deal in this manner and intended to put her theories to work on her own behalf. There was no reason why Sophie could not do the same.

That evening when Lord Chessyre called to escort them to the assembly rooms, Sophie studied him with a highly speculative gaze. Dare she put Lady Mary's conclusions to work? Would it be right? Or ought she plan such trickery?

"The evening is rather fine, I believe," she began. "It is almost mild—for London. It brings to mind descriptions of Italy that I have read. Have you been there, Lord Chessyre?"

"Some years ago with my tutor. Father insisted that I have something of a Grand Tour, even if most of France and the Continent was to be avoided. It was amazing how much we managed to see. You would like to go to Rome?"

"I think it would make a wonderful trip," she said, her voice wistful and full of longing.

Anything he might have said in reply was not to be known, for they arrived at Almack's and Sophie was content to permit his lordship to escort her and Lady Mary up the stairs and into the rooms with his usual courtesy.

It did not seem to make a great deal of difference that she had rejected the proposals of the various gentlemen who had proposed. Although Mr. Somerset did seem to be showing interest in a shy young girl from Dorset and Oliver Fane now paid court to a platter-faced young woman whose father was not only a well-to-do earl but influential within the political realm.

"He ought to have sought her side first," Sophie confided to Lady Mary when that lady observed the pair.

"Indeed. And Miss Fitzroy is a lovely girl, just right for Mr. Somerset."

"Complete with an excellent dowry, so I have heard," Sophie added without rancor.

Sophie danced with all who managed to reach her side and request such a thing. She also kept close track of precisely where Lord Chessyre was and with whom, reserving both waltzes for him as he had requested.

During the first of those, he gave her a puzzled look, then embarked upon undemanding conversation. This soon turned in the direction she desired.

"You mentioned a wish to travel to Italy."

"True. I should enjoy seeing the inspiration for so much of our culture. You must admit that we have shamelessly adopted designs and plans from the Romans."

"They do have a superior culture—one that supports art and music. You enjoy the opera?"

Sophie frowned. This was not the direction she wished to take in the conversation. She shrugged and murmured rather, "I believe the Athertons went there not long ago."

"On their wedding trip, 'tis true."

"Where would you wish to go on a wedding trip were you to be married, sir?" Sophie asked with great daring.

"That depends," he replied, looking so dear and handsome. The black of his coat made a marvelous foil for his good looks and his blond hair gleamed in the light from the chandeliers. He wore a modest waistcoat of embroidered white marcella over his dark gray breeches. His was a most elegant figure among the peacocks like Reginald Montegu, this evening garbed in a sky blue satin coat over green breeches, also in satin. His waistcoat, she observed, was bright yellow embroidered in a bold flower design.

"Yes?" she said, dragging her mind back to the more important element in her evening.

"It depends on who would make the trip with me. If it were a lady I loved and who loved me in return, I should like to go to Rome and watch the sun set on the ruins found along the Appian Way. Or to Athens and sit midst the Parthenon to see the sunrise. We would make an excursion to Delphi to view the ruins set atop the mountains from which one can see the distant sea. Up there you are far removed from the rest of the world, with the tinkle of the goat bells in the olive orchards and the soaring of eagles above to entertain you."

"How very romantic," Sophie said, a twinge of conscience tugging at her. "You must have enjoyed seeing that very much."

"I could see it again," he replied, gazing into Sophie's eyes with intent.

The waltz came to an end at that moment and Sophie silently walked along the side of the room with him until they reached Lady Mary.

Jonathan awaited her and swept her off to a stately country dance with only a minimum of greeting.

"Very intense conversation with Chessyre," he said when they met in the course of the dance.

"I am obeying your instructions, dear cousin," Sophie said, thankful that there would be little contact between them during the dance. Of course she hadn't counted on the warm clasp of his hand as they moved through certain of the parts. She steeled her heart against his effect on her.

"Which ones?" he queried at their next meeting.

"I promised I would make more of an effort and you see, I am."

He said no more to her, merely escorting her properly to Lady Mary afterward and retiring to the card room.

The second waltz with Lord Chessyre gave her hope, for he immediately turned their conversation to the subject of Italy and wedding trips.

"Would you truly enjoy such a trip, Sophie?"

She admired the gentle manner he had, the politeness of his address. There would be no blunt confrontation from him, nor would he be likely to kiss her with harsh fierceness as had Jonathan.

"Yes, I believe I would."

He said nothing more, but Sophie had high hopes that he would come to Lower Brook Street on the morrow.

Indeed, when he escorted them home following the assembly, he requested permission to call the following day.

Sophie said yes.

Chapter Sixteen

"I cannot think of a thing to do—that might be deemed outrageous. I suppose my mind is not sufficiently naughty!" Sophie cried to her pet.

Pickles merely perched atop her bed, looking sympathetic but unable to help in the least.

"Perhaps I am a better person than I had realized?" she asked the pup, then grinned at the very idea.

Rising from her bed, where she had spent considerable time mulling over the matter, Sophie slipped a cloak over her walking dress to protect her against the cool breeze that blew. Snapping her fingers at Pickles, the two went down the stairs to the entry. Here Sophie attached the dog's leash and they headed for the park with Anna trailing silently behind.

Women didn't keep opera dancers so she could not dash madly around Berkeley Square with one in her carriage—and she didn't think she would wish to invite a bit of muslin up for a ride. Women didn't attend blood sports like boxing or bull baiting and she confessed the sight of blood was not pleasing. Women didn't race but Sophie was not about to endanger her nice little carriage by doing something stupid like challenging another to such a thing.

She was simply too practical.

A long walk in the park provided no answers. Having considered herself somewhat improper for so long—because she dared to make her own way in the world instead of dwindling away to nothing in her aunt's attic—it was astonishing to discover just how conventional she was.

Of course, there was that secret she concealed—that her charming and debonair cousin had nursed her through the long night when she was so ill. Had that reached the ears of anyone of the *ton* she would have been disgraced beyond the pale. Never mind that she was out of her head most of the time—he had been in her room and had helped her to bed. He had also removed nearly all her clothing and Sophie grew warm just thinking about it.

"Sophie? My, you are deep in thought." A familiar voice hailed Sophie.

"Lady Anne! I do beg your pardon. I have been trying to think of something outrageous to do so that no one would seek my hand and I would need rescuing, but I cannot."

"That seems a bit drastic. Are you certain it is necessary? Perhaps there is another solution to your dilemma?" Lady Anne smiled, her eyes lighting up at the prospect of some amusement.

Sophie, much struck by this suggestion, walked along with her good friend, her nursemaid, and baby Edward, and began to discuss possibilities.

Across London William Chessyre, Earl of Chessyre, sat with his good friend Jonathan Garnett, Viscount Lowell. The two stared out of Jonathan's window at a most uninspiring view of chimney pots.

"I have decided that the time has come when I ought to settle down, marry, and begin my nursery," Chessyre mused. "We all must do it sooner or later."

"True," Jonathan agreed. "The family line and all that. Although for my part, it would be later rather than sooner."

"Why so against the married state? Surely there is some damsel you favor? You are not growing any younger," Chessyre pointed out rather bluntly.

Jonathan winced at the truth. He had put off thinking of his future without Sophie as long as possible and now that had to be faced.

"There is something," Jonathan admitted in an unguarded moment.

"Someone or something stands in the way? I cannot imagine you allowing that, my friend." Surprise clear on his face,

Chessyre took his gaze from the uninspiring view to stare at Jonathan.

"Ironic, is it not? I want the unobtainable." Then Jonathan realized he was on the verge of confiding his dilemma to his friend and drew back from revealing the entire story. If Sophie favored Chessyre, then she would have him. That was the least Jonathan could do for the girl he had loved for so long.

"Let me understand—the woman you desire cannot be had? Why?" Chessyre devoted his full attention to Jonathan, fixing him with such a commanding look that Jonathan found himself explaining in part.

"You see, there is this young woman I wish to wed, but I overheard her say she favors another. I would hardly want to ask her to marry me under those circumstances. Would you?" Jonathan hoped he had not revealed too much. His reserve was such that it was difficult for him to share his private thoughts.

Lord Chessyre shook his head. "Egad, no." But he considered the matter at some length, trying to think who it might be that his friend wished to marry. The only woman he had spent any time with as of late was his cousin, and they argued more often than not. It could scarcely be her. So who could it be? Mystified, he didn't query Jonathan, knowing it would avail him nothing.

"Well, I intend to try my luck soon," Chessyre said, rising from his chair and taking a step toward the door. He paused, adding, "Is it customary for any gentleman seeking your cousin's hand to discuss it with you first?"

"No," Jonathan said vehemently. Then more reasonably, he added, "She may do as she pleases. It is nothing to me. The brat is nothing but trouble."

Chessyre gave his friend an astounded look. "Nothing but trouble?"

"Remind me to tell you someday," Jonathan said, rising from his chair. He picked up his hat and gloves, found his favorite cane, then joined his friend. "Shall we go? I believe I should enjoy a round at Gentleman Jackson's about now." The misty rain suited him to a tee.

* * *

Late that afternoon found Lord Chessyre walking up the stairs at Number 12 Lower Brook Street. Jenkens ushered him into the drawing room, where Sophie was seated near the window, reading to Lady Mary from the newspaper. She dropped it to the floor when she saw him and abruptly rose from her chair, looking decidedly disconcerted.

"Lord Chessyre, what a pleasant surprise. I am pleased to see you."

He wondered how Lowell could think his cousin nothing but trouble. She looked sweet and defenseless and had never done anything outrageous that he knew about.

"Lady Mary, Miss Garnett. I am pleased to see that I am the only gentleman to brave the rain this afternoon. There are distinct advantages to being hardy, I see." William bowed over the hand of each lady in turn, then took a position close to Sophie.

Lady Mary agreed, then gathered her needlework in her hands. "I just recalled that I must inform Cook of a change in plans. Poor woman becomes so flustered at changes. Excuse me for a few minutes."

William smiled at her obvious ploy to give him some private time with Sophie. That was fine. Not having asked a lady to marry him before, he might be a trifle lacking in polish.

"Lady Mary is most thoughtful," he ventured to say.

"She has been more than kind to me," Sophie replied. "Come, will you not join me on the settee? I should think that standing becomes tiresome after a time."

William sat at her side, studying her all the while. She darted glances at him, but they were not coy or flirtatious. She looked guilty—or perhaps uneasy might be a better choice of words. He wondered why.

"I think perhaps you know why I have come today. Like all the others before me, I am here to place my offer before you."

"Oh," Sophie cried softly, "I did not think that the proposals were known. I have not told a soul."

"Servants are not known for their reticence. I expect all it takes is one who shares a story with a friend."

Sophie thought of that night that Jonathan had remained with her, sitting on her bed at her side. Anna had seen him. Although she was loyal and would not deliberately tattle, what if she inadvertently mentioned it to someone else? If Sophie wanted something outrageous, why, the scandal would be far beyond that!

"Your gentle blushing does you credit. I admire a woman who does not spread stories of her many conquests."

She put her hands on her warm cheeks. If he but knew. Ought she tell him? Did he deserve to know the truth about her? "I am not an angel, so please do not liken me to one. Sainthood would sit uneasily on my head, I assure you."

He reached out to take one of her hands, enfolding it gently in his.

Sophie inhaled sharply at the touch of his ungloved hand over hers. She *did* like him, but was that enough?

"Marry me, Sophie." He said no flowery words, offered no pleading looks. Rather, he leaned over to place a firm, gently reverent kiss on Sophie's lips.

Jonathan had mockingly told her to compare his kiss with the others. William Chessyre was the only one she'd permitted close enough to kiss her. And his kiss was—nice. Pleasant. Warming. But it didn't make her knees turn to water or her heart pound or make her tremble like a leaf in the wind.

"You do me a great honor, sir," she began, only to be stopped by another gentle kiss. He lingered over the kiss, wrapping her in his arms carefully as though she were fragile porcelain.

What would it be like to be treated like this forever? Sophie wondered. Would he, like her father, satisfy his passion with an opera dancer or some bit of muslin? She strongly suspected that she would not like that in the least—if for no other reason than the enormous cost of the arrangement. Opera dancers held their favors quite dear, it seemed.

Once released, she opened her eyes to gaze up at him, confusion swamping her senses. This was what she wanted, to marry Lord Chessyre, was it not?

"I can see that I have put you in a quandary, dear Sophie. I may call you Sophie?"

She nodded, too bewildered at her reaction to his proposal and his kiss to speak.

"Do not give me an answer immediately. I have waited this long, I can wait a bit longer."

"Jonathan . . . you spoke with him first?"

"Indeed," he said with a smile. "He warned me you were nothing but trouble, but he sounded more like an elder brother when he spoke."

"Oh," Sophie cried, half ready to tell Lord Chessyre that she would marry him now. This instant. And banish Jonathan from her life forever.

"There, Cook is quite satisfied," Lady Mary declared as she entered the room, giving Sophie and Lord Chessyre a sharp look while crossing the room.

"And I have stayed my allotted time, I believe." He rose to linger over Sophie's hand, searching her eyes for a clue to the answer she would ultimately give him. He liked her better than any woman he had met to this point in time. He didn't really believe in love. That emotion was a fabrication of poets. But he thought that he and Sophie could rub along together tolerably well.

He took leave of Lady Mary and the room was plunged into a brooding silence.

"Well?" Lady Mary said at long last. "Am I to know what went on here while I bided my time belowstairs doing quite unnecessary things?"

"I am sorry, dear ma'am. He asked me to marry him—quite as I expected." Sophie considered her older and wiser friend, wanting to ask advice, yet loath to reveal all.

"Am I to wish you happy?"

"I do not know. When it came to the sticking point, I could not say yes." Sophie turned to face Lady Mary, her face revealing all her inner torments.

"But you did not say no?"

"He asked me to think the matter over. And indeed, it is an enormous step for me—for any woman. We commit ourselves to another for the rest of our lives. The very thought quite overwhelms me."

"Why do you not consult your cousin? He strikes me as a man of great good sense." Lady Mary darted a knowing look at her young friend, then turned her attention to the needle-work in her lap while looking as bland as milk.

"Perhaps I shall," Sophie murmured, then rose to drift from the room to mull over this unexpected reaction to something she thought she had wanted.

"Well? Am I to give congratulations?" Jonathan asked of his friend, dreading to hear the expected reply, yet perversely wanting to know the worst. At least he was in the privacy of his rooms; there was no witness to his reaction to the news.

"Not yet. She seemed about to deny me, then I asked her to think it over."

"Egad, has the girl no sense then?" Jonathan questioned with a lighter feeling in his heart. "Could she truly think of rejecting you? An earl, no less?"

"I do not believe her heart is engaged. And I confess mine is not. But she is the first girl with whom I felt I might be reasonably content. And I doubt she would cavil at a mistress—did she know of it."

Jonathan longed to punch his friend in the nose. A mistress! He considered such an arrangement when married to his precious Sophie? Jonathan couldn't speak, he'd likely give his anger away—and all else as well.

"At least she does not consider our age difference a barrier. She asked me some weeks ago if I felt nine years to be too great and I said no. Seems she thinks like my sister, that a mature man is more desirable."

"Did she now?" Jonathan quietly replied. He felt as though he had been hit with a bolt of lightning. Chessyre was the same age as himself and that meant that Sophie did *not*—as he had always believed—consider him too old. But what to do about it now? It was too late for him. He had as much as given his best friend permission to marry Sophie and it seemed that she was considering the offer rather than promptly turning him down as she had all the others.

And she *had* turned them all down, from the meek Mr. Somerset to the dashing and wealthy Lord Crewe. Perhaps . . . But no, how could he stand against Chessyre with his gold locks and those gray eyes that the women declared so romantic. Jonathan saw nothing romantic in his own appearance. He was too ordinary.

But, he realized, there was one thing he had to set straight. He owed his friend the truth. What if that maid let the tale slip out some occasion when she was with a confidante? The scandal could make life most unpleasant for Sophie and William Chessyre.

"There is something you ought to know, my good friend," Jonathan began.

"That sounds serious," Chessyre replied, lounging against the fireplace surround to survey Jonathan.

"Do you recall some weeks ago when Sophie had the food poisoning and was so terribly ill?"

Looking confused, Chessyre nodded his recollection.

"I came to the house, thinking to give her the money for the books I'd sold. Found the door unlocked, the house in darkness. To make a long story short, I also found her very, very ill. She was on the bed in her room. I undressed her, put her under the covers, and remained with her that night. She desperately needed someone to care for her—sick as a dog, she was. Everyone in the house was ill as well, so there was no one else to help. However, the maid saw me the next morning. I was sitting on Sophie's bed, sponging off her face when the maid entered the room."

"By Jove!" Chessyre cried, clearly astounded by the implications of the revelation.

"Should that maid open her budget—as far as we know she has not done so to date—the scandal would be frightful." Jonathan sat back to see how his friend would take this information.

"You must understand, this places an entirely different complexion on things," Chessyre said, giving his friend a look that pleaded for understanding. "If I truly loved the girl, I would proceed with no qualms and consider the world well lost for it. However . . ."

"However, you are not passionately in love with Sophie," Jonathan finished for him.

"Somehow passion and such innocence don't seem compatible."

"You've not kissed her?" Jonathan said mildly.

"Honorably, I assure you. She is properly chaste. She is sweet, but untutored," Chessyre said with a smile.

"And you have little patience with teaching the unlearned," Jonathan said with amusement. He vividly recalled his kisses with Sophie. They were fiery, not sweet, and he would be overjoyed to give his darling Sophie all the lessons she needed, even if it took a lifetime.

"But I have asked her to marry me. I cannot with honor tell her I have changed my mind. What a coil. I wish you had spoken about this before."

"I suppose I hoped she would reject you as she had the others," Jonathan said quietly, for the first time giving a hint as to where his affections lay.

"Egad," Chessyre said, for the first time putting together a great number of things.

The following morning Jonathan paused before the front door to Number 12 Lower Brook Street to brace his nerves. He should have had something stronger to drink than coffee. It was provident that Sophie had sent round a note requesting his presence this morning as soon as might be. It seemed she had something she wished to discuss with him. He wondered what it might be. The dog? Her carriage? Or something scandalous?

Jenkens welcomed him to the house and accepted his hat, gloves, and cane with the murmured assurance that Miss Sophie waited for him in the drawing room.

As Jonathan trod the stairs to the first floor, he pondered his own problem. Nothing Sophie could think of could match what was on his mind. How to persuade her to decline an earl and marry a lowly viscount? He must have rocks in his head.

Sophie was standing by the window overlooking the street, so she must have seen him arrive. Her blond curls angelically haloed her head; she wore a simple gown of lilac muslin that enhanced her appearance of delicacy. He crossed the room, feeling as uneasy as though he were facing an enemy, yet he had known Sophie all her life. Doubtless it made things more difficult.

"Good morning," she said, seeming as ill at ease as Jonathan felt. She had heard his footsteps, finally turning to look at him, her eyes most troubled.

"At least it isn't raining," he replied, studying her face. "You sent for me," he reminded her after a long silence during which she simply stared at him.

At these words she turned away, gazing at the house across the street—a singularly uninteresting piece of brickwork and windows. Pickles sat on his rug, looking from one to the other.

"Lord Chessyre asked me to marry him," she said quietly.

"And?" he prompted, wanting to have her thoughts out in the open so he might know the worst.

"I truly thought I could, you see. I thought that because he was kind and good and considerate that it would be enough for me. I do not love the gentleman and I suppose there are a great many marriages where that is the case. But I had hoped to be different."

"That does not seem to be a great problem. As you mentioned the other day, affection can grow."

"Do you think so? I wonder. He treats me like fragile porcelain and I am nothing of the kind. You above all others know that, Jonathan."

"Aye, brat, you were always trouble for me."

"And I still am." She turned to face him squarely, taking a deep breath as though preparing for an ordeal. "We have a problem, you know."

"We?" he echoed, drawing her from the window to join him on the settee. "What is it?" He settled down, still holding her hand, waiting for what was to come.

"When I was ill, you took care of me. Anna knows you must have undressed me and put me to bed. Jonathan, you saw me nearly bare!" She swallowed hard, looking everywhere but at him, then continued. "I know that nothing amiss occurred— you would never take advantage of a helpless woman. Anna knows that as well, she has heard me praise you often enough. But if she were to talk . . ." Sophie finally raised anguished eyes to confront Jonathan.

"I have thought of the same thing. Often."

"I could never agree to marry Lord Chessyre without telling

him about this, and yet I feel it would diminish his regard for me. I should like to have a husband who trusts me, Jonathan." She inched closer to him, a very distraught sprite.

"I agree, most definitely."

"What am I to do? Lady Mary thinks it well for me to marry. Yet if I cannot wed the one I love, I vow I would rather remain alone the days of my life."

"There is someone you love, Sophie?" He stroked her hand in what he hoped was a soothing way. The touch of her skin had no soothing effect on him; it set him afire. He recalled her words, that he had seen her garbed in very little and realized that he could not allow another man that privilege.

"Did I say that? No! That is yes, but I cannot reveal who it is," she wailed, bursting into tears.

Jonathan drew her closer, letting go of her hand and wrapping his arms about her as he so enjoyed doing. She completely ruined his cravat and he cared not the least for it. He would give her anything she wished if things could go his way.

"This man does not return your love?" Jonathan questioned when her sobs had subsided. "The cad. How could anyone not love my Sophie?"

"He does not. You do not, either, Jonathan. You have said so often enough, calling me brat and worse." She looked up at him, her lashes spiked with tears and her cheeks pink with emotion. "Oh, Jonathan," she cried, nestling against his chest again, her sobbing cutting him to the quick. From his rug, Pickles gave Jonathan a reproachful look.

When he thought she had cried her fill, he tipped her face up so he could see her eyes—never mind the delectable mouth—and tried to explain.

"You see, my little love, when you were born, I thought you had been brought by the angels, so perfect were you. You were a good baby, your nanny said. As you grew up, I quickly discovered that you were less angelic under that pretty covering. You toddled after me, getting me into all manner of trouble because you were not supposed to be where I was, doing the things that growing boys did."

"You taught me how to swim," she recalled with a sniff.

"Aye, but I swam in the buff and you in your shift. Your nanny was scandalized. Thank heavens it went no further than that!"

"We were very young," Sophie said with a chuckle.

"You were trouble," he reminded her.

"You were very understanding when I demanded to learn how to ride a horse."

"Your father was less when he found out you had taken Brutus," Jonathan said, running his hands over her curls as he had done when she was little and needed comforting.

"The beast. Brutus, not father. A very nasty horse." She nestled against him, her face almost buried in his cravat.

"It seemed as though it was always one thing after another. And then there was that last summer—when you turned sixteen." He held her firmly in his arms when she would have drawn away.

"The forfeit," she whispered. She looked up to search his eyes, her expression wary. "You kissed me."

"With pleasure and a great deal of shock, I might add."

"Shock? I thought I was the only one who believed the earth had tilted on its axis." She half smiled at him, a tender, loving look, he thought.

"I was afraid to be around you after that, afraid of what I might do, I suppose." He watched her with caution.

"You detested me. You had such a dreadful expression on your face when you left that year. I intentionally never went to Uncle Philip's again if I knew you were to be there. I couldn't endure the thought of your snubbing me. You are terribly good at that, Jonathan."

"But you came for the reading of the will. You did not have to, you know. The will might have been read and your portion communicated to you later. I wanted to see you and thought that the bequest might bring you to me."

"You had wagered whether I would come or not," she recalled.

"I bet you would and you did," he said. "And you got all that lovely money from Uncle. I truly do not care how much—you deserve it," he said fondly, his hands caressing her back.

"You kissed me again. You have kissed me several times," she declared. "One would think you enjoy kissing me. Do you, Jonathan?" She toyed with his ruined cravat, not meeting his gaze.

Jonathan wondered how best to answer that leading remark. Should he confess? Brave men only die once, he remembered reading somewhere. Stupid thought. "Can mere words express my delight in kissing you, my dearest heart?"

"I did rather wonder, you know," she whispered.

"I once read something that I believe applies to you, *mon ange*." He gave her a smoldering look, then continued. " 'And now I see . . . a perfect woman, nobly planned to warm, to comfort, and command. And yet a spirit still, and bright— with something of an angel-light.' " Jonathan kissed her lightly on her forehead, for he knew better than to come near her lips. "When Wordsworth wrote of a phantom of delight I wonder if he had met you, for you were delight from the first moment I saw you. One smile was all it took. I was your humble slave."

"Jonathan Garnett, you have never been humble in your life!" she cried in mock anger. "And assuredly never mine!"

"Ah, but that is where you are wrong. I have been yours for quite some time—devotedly yours. Even if you don't believe it, 'tis true."

This time he found it necessary to convince her with a kiss, and not one on her pretty forehead. He released her slowly, watching her lashes flutter before she gazed up at him in her direct way.

"You are going to tell Chessyre that you are very sorry, but that you believe you would never suit," Jonathan instructed firmly.

"Yes, Jonathan," she said her eyes filling with mischief. "And then I shall prepare to be a spinster?"

"Did I not say you were planned to warm? To comfort? You need someone to do that. You need me, Sophie, my love."

"Oh, I do, dearest Jonathan. I do."

"And I need you, my beloved Sophie. Your warmth and comfort are truly desired. Do you remember that you called me your love that night I cared for you."

"Did I? That was foolish of me, to open my heart to you. I was unconscious." Her gaze remained fixed on him, warming as she felt her love returned.

"I believe you meant it. I wondered about it from then on— if you cared for me more than you would admit. You once said you hated me," he reminded her while holding her close.

"True, for not loving me as I love you, have always loved you. Dearest Jonathan. Tell me again?" she begged.

"I love you, I want you for my wife and I'll never take no for an answer," he replied with a broad smile before he elected to savor another kiss.

"You never would, as I recall." Sophie wrapped her arms about him, prepared to relish this new intimacy with the man she had adored for so long.

When Lady Mary peeped in from the doorway, she drew a satisfied sigh. Life was as it should be.

Pickles settled down on his rug. All was well.

SIGNET REGENCY ROMANCE

ROMANCE FROM THE PAST

☐ **THE SECRET NABOB by Martha Kirkland.** Miss Madeline Wycliff's two sisters were as different as night and day. One was bold and brazen and had wed a rake whose debts now threatened the family estate, but the other was as untouched as she was exquisite. Now Madeline had to turn her back on love and get dangerously close to a nefarious nabob to save her sister's happiness and innocence ... even if it meant sacrificing her own. (187377—$4.50)

☐ **A HEART POSSESSED by Katherine Sutcliffe.** From the moment Ariel Rushdon was reunited with Lord Nicholas Wyndham, the lover who had abandoned her, she could see the torment in his eyes. Now she would learn the secrets of his house. Now she would also learn the truth about his wife's death. And now she would make Nick remember everything—their wild passion, their sacred vows ... their child.... (407059—$5.50)

☐ **THE WICKED GROOM by April Kihlstrom.** It was bad enough when Lady Diana Westcott learned her parents were wedding her to the infamous Duke of Berenford. But it was even worse when she came face to face with him. First he disguised his identity to gain a most improper access to her person. Then he hid the beautiful woman in his life even as that passion of the past staked a new claim to his ardent affection. Now Diana had to deceive this devilish deceiver about how strongly she responded to his kisses and how weak she felt in his arms. (187504—$4.99)

*Prices slightly higher in Canada

Buy them at your local bookstore or use this convenient coupon for ordering.

PENGUIN USA
P.O. Box 999 — Dept. #17109
Bergenfield, New Jersey 07621

Please send me the books I have checked above.
I am enclosing $_____ (please add $2.00 to cover postage and handling). Send check or money order (no cash or C.O.D.'s) or charge by Mastercard or VISA (with a $15.00 minimum). Prices and numbers are subject to change without notice.

Card #_____ Exp. Date _____
Signature_____
Name_____
Address_____
City _____ State _____ Zip Code _____

For faster service when ordering by credit card call **1-800-253-6476**

Allow a minimum of 4-6 weeks for delivery. This offer is subject to change without notice.